SWAN ISLAND

Durham: 1920s. Ella's happy childhood in Swan Island is abruptly ended when her father dies, leaving the family bankrupt. Ella and her mother must go and live with her grandmother, who runs the Silver Street Café, but Ella vows to return to her childhood home one day. After a first, unhappy marriage, she settles into steady domesticity with David Black, but there had been another doomed romance during the early years of the Second World War, and Ella has never forgotten Harry. It has been years since she last saw him, but old memories are stirred when he comes back into her life...

SWAN ISLAND

SWAN ISLAND

by

Elizabeth Gill

Magna Large Print Books
Long Preston, North Yorkshire,
BD23 4ND, England.

British Library Cataloguing in Publication Data.

Gill, Elizabeth
    Swan Island.

    A catalogue record of this book is
    available from the British Library

    ISBN   978-0-7505-2907-5

First published in Great Britain 2007
by Severn House Publishers Ltd.

Published in Large Print 2008 by arrangement with
Severn House Publishers

Magna Large Print is an imprint of Library Magna Books Ltd.

Printed and bound in Great Britain by
T.J. (International) Ltd., Cornwall, PL28 8RW

Prologue

1951
The West Coast of Scotland

It was September, the best time of the year in western Scotland, when the lochs and the sea have had all summer to warm up. The evenings were short, the sun was setting spectacularly in pink, mauve and white from a clear blue sky, and Ella and David Black had arrived at the hotel in time to change before they went downstairs to the dinner of the Steelfounders' Convention.

There was no time to go to the beach, David had said with regret in his voice. Ella had been glad of it. Coming back here had been hard enough, she did not want to disturb the memories which had not surfaced in her mind in many a long day.

The last time she had been here was before the war. She remembered the little bed and breakfast place standing on its own on the headland, the too-short beds, the lemon-coloured room which Mrs McDonald had been so proud of, the way she and her first husband Jack and their friends, Agnes and Harry, had gone out in a rowing

9

boat at night and caught mackerel, you could see them shimmering in the clear aqua-coloured water.

The silver sands of Morar. Even its name was like a whisper. The tiny roads before you got to Mallaig with their passing places had silence, peace and each time you stopped and got out of the car there was nobody about. She could have been prejudiced thinking that the further you got into Scotland the more spectacular the scenery became.

The lowlands were lovely but there was nothing to beat the way the hills scooped down toward the valleys here, how the mountains would soon become covered in snow, and how every time you reached another little gray and white town with its low buildings in the background against the foothills the lochs were deep, still, mysterious.

She stood in front of the mirror in the hotel bedroom and tried to shake off her mood. There was no point in going back over things. The war had long since ended, the sounds and sights which reminded her of things that were finished were all very well but they had nothing to do with why she was here. She must put thoughts of the past from her mind.

It was a lovely room, nothing like Mrs McDonald's guestrooms had been. It had its own balcony which faced the beach. David was out there, looking at the view. He had the door open.

'You're letting all the cold air in,' she said.

'It isn't cold,' he said, 'it's wonderful. Come out and take a look.'

'If it isn't cold then the midges will be out in full force.'

David scoffed at her for being unromantic but she didn't take any notice of him.

'We're going to be late if you don't hurry up,' she told him.

He paused, reluctant to come inside, but then did so, closing the glass doors behind him.

'Pretty dress,' he said.

Ella regarded herself with satisfaction in the long mirror beside the dressing table. The dress was turquoise satin with silver threads running through it, trimmed with dark raspberry velvet, scooped neck and low with a velvet bow to one shoulder. She thought it suited her dark looks, black hair and blue eyes.

'Isn't it? Iris helped me choose it.'

Iris was David's only sister. She and Ella had scoured the Newcastle shops. He looked good too; he was wearing evening dress, the white of his shirt accentuated his beautiful green eyes and the black of his suit contrasted with his straw-coloured hair. He was tall and slender and had more presence than any man she knew. Elegant was how David looked, she thought; she was very

11

proud of him.

They left their room and for a few moments, as they walked down the hall, Ella wanted to stay there, as though she had had a forewarning about how badly the evening would go. That was ridiculous. They were there for business but it was going to be fun too, she was sure of it

As David closed the door, however, she regretted leaving the view of the sea and she thought how nice it would have been if they could have stayed there and had gin and tonic and lingered another half hour or so. She knew though that she would not have been able to dismiss from her mind the little blue, black and white fishing boat which she and Jack and Harry and Agnes had hired so very long ago, just before the war. Before everything went wrong. She recalled how they had seen one of the local men fishing, his tortoiseshell cat standing in the stern of the boat, watching as he hauled in what had undoubtedly been her tea.

They had laughed when the cat cried and purred for the fish, as the man beached the boat and helped her out. He had told the cat that it would not be long before the shining catch was cooked and on her plate. It had no doubt also gone on the plates of his wife and himself because with the cat in his arms he had had a bucket over his arm full of mackerel.

Ella brushed off the memories once again and went down the stairs with David ready to enjoy her evening. She didn't know anybody but it wasn't difficult. All she had to do was hang on to David's arm, smile and be introduced to people.

There was a champagne reception. Some of the women wore dresses which were almost as good as her own. They were all long, many off pretty white shoulders and some women wore diamonds around their necks or in their hair. The men all looked alike and made a contrast with what their wives were wearing.

The dining room was huge and the view from its floor-to-ceiling windows was over vast lawns. The curtains were tartan – blue, white and black – like the boat had been and the carpet was also dark. Ella thought it looked good. It was a shame that it didn't face the sea but then you couldn't have every room facing the same way. Big white cloths covered the round tables and silver cutlery and crystal glasses glistened and sparkled beneath the chandeliers. It seemed very grand, Ella thought.

The main course was salmon. She didn't really like fish but it was done simply with new potatoes and fresh vegetables and the wine was a deep golden colour. She and David didn't have many opportunities for evenings out and she wanted to make the most of it.

There would be dancing later, she had seen the ballroom across the hall and the stage where the band had set up their instruments. Ella loved dancing.

After chocolate pudding and coffee there were speeches. The speeches were boring and they went on and on. She became impatient. Why talk so much when the band was waiting? She could hear, when the speaker stopped talking, the band tuning their instruments, and she thought she could also catch the sound of the waves crashing down on the beach. Or was it just a memory? It was a calm evening, the water was probably just breaking gently on the sand.

Ella longed to escape. By the end of the third speech she smiled at David and got up and walked out as though she was going to the ladies' room but she didn't. The doors to the garden were open and they were tempting. She walked out. The night air was warm on her bare shoulders and face, and she walked a little way. She couldn't go too far in such heels, she wasn't used to them and she hadn't worn heels in weeks. She went slowly across to the rose garden.

She had roses at home in Durham, a great oblong bed, edged with scalloped stone, and she treasured them. Her favourite was a huge cream rose which stood right on the edge of the bed next to the path and the green house. It flowered there, somehow out of the limelight but obviously happy where it was, year after year without being disturbed other than pruning in early spring and some manure dug in. All her roses were wonderful with special scents and delicate mauves and pinks to the brighter bolder reds, so dark they looked blue and yellow with red flecks in the centre. There were white climbing roses around the little cottage on the end of the house.

She had a big back garden which you walked into through a red wooden gate and beyond a high dividing wall. On this side there were raised flowerbeds and also beds which bordered the lawns. There were two greenhouses on the same side; the second one connected to the first by a door in the middle. On the other side of the garden were redcurrants, black and white currants, gooseberries, rhubarb, rows of potatoes, cabbages, cauliflowers and carrots and further down a leek trench. She loved her garden, but she was always interested to see what other people did.

She was just about to venture further to see the rest of the gardens properly when somebody said her name softly behind her. When she turned around she almost fainted. There, behind her, tall, dark and wearing evening dress, was the only man she had ever truly loved. Harry Reid.

She stared. Her senses told her that he was a mirage, a ghost, and that she should run. That would be foolish. It was obviously just a coincidence. She gave herself plenty of time, drinking him in, thinking how good he looked. He hadn't altered at all.

No, that wasn't true, he looked older. He had been so very young the last time she had seen him. Now he must be thirty or more. He looked wonderful, of course, his clothes were obviously very expensive, they fitted him so well.

'Why, Harry,' she said. Her lips had turned to putty and would not make any other sounds and her emotions banged against one another in turmoil.

She had hoped they would never meet again, had known very well that he was long since back from the war, had avoided places she had thought he might be, looked for him in crowded streets, imagined meeting him in a hundred different ways but not like this for some reason. It should have been obvious that he would be here.

'Hello.' He moved closer. His blue eyes were cold on her. 'You weren't expecting me, eh?'

He was smoking a cigarette, one of the Turkish kind that she remembered he had liked so much. The smell of them took her back to the war and all the things that she had tried so hard to forget. She thought that

16

she had succeeded. Now the illusion broke like glass dropped on tiles. How appropriate that they should meet again here, in the place where she had fallen in love with him.

'I am a shipbuilder, after all,' Harry said.

He looked down at the cigarette in his hand for a few seconds and then he said, 'I would say that it was good to see you except that it isn't of course, not really.'

Ella didn't know what to say. She stood, unable to move or to speak. She could not even shift her gaze from him.

'I suppose it was inevitable that we should meet at some point,' he said. 'I thought perhaps we could be polite to one another. Now I'm not quite so sure.'

'It was a long time ago.'

Harry threw down the half-smoked cigarette, put his foot on it, and said, 'You know I hate it when people say things like that, as though ten years was a bloody eternity, as though passing time wiped everything out, as though people stopped longing for one another when a certain number of years had gone. There are some things you never forget and a great many that you never forgive.'

'I didn't say I'd forgotten you.' Ella said quickly, 'and it isn't ten years.'

'Something like that. I should think you haven't forgotten me, especially here.' It was so close to what she had been thinking ever since she got there that she wished she could turn away without being rude or even better run away. 'You were thinking about me?'

Ella wanted to deny it but it would have been dishonest and would have seemed like a betrayal somehow.

'This is where I realized that I couldn't live without you,' he said.

Ella shook her head as though she could shake off his words, but she said nothing.

'And don't think that I've forgiven you,' he said, 'because I haven't, or that I ever will. I won't.'

Ella couldn't look at the direct blue gaze.

'I don't think I want to carry on this conversation,' she said.

'After such a long silence don't you think you ought to give me an explanation?'

'I wrote to you lots of times.'

'Did you? I didn't get anything from you.' He clearly didn't believe her and it made her panic, thinking how much time and sweat she had spent over the letters, especially the one telling him she was going to marry David, how she had almost decided not to send it, how she had agonized. All for nothing. 'That was good of you when I was stuck in the bloody jungle in Burma, my friends being mown down by Japs. The last words you said to me when I left were that you loved me and you would wait for me.'

'I'm sorry.'

'What happened?'

'I met David.'

'That's all? You met David? What altered, what changed, how could you ... give me up when I wasn't there? How could you do that to anybody, most of all somebody you had said you loved, who loved you, somebody you had slept with, somebody?'

'Harry–'

'How could you do that to me after all we'd been through?'

She couldn't even look at him, she tried not to think how in love they had been, of his touch, of his body, of his mouth. He had meant everything to her and she had dismissed him in a letter. It seemed so awful now, such a trivial way of brushing somebody aside. She couldn't remember how she had felt, she didn't want to remember.

'I didn't know what had happened,' he said. 'All through the rest of the war I had to go on without knowing anything. It was torture. Then I came back and I heard that you had married David Black. I couldn't believe it.'

'It was only how things worked out.'

'Worked out? What on earth does that mean? Are you trying to tell me you stopped loving me when I wasn't there? How could you do such a thing?'

She wanted to tell him that she had not stopped loving him but it was now inappropriate. Perhaps not even true any more.

'I wanted to give you everything. I wanted to give you the whole world,' he continued.

'I should go,' Ella said. She would have walked straight past him but he got hold of her and somehow she had known that he would. His fingers closed around her arms and she was shocked at how his touch brought back all her old love for him.

When she looked up he said, 'I have missed you so much,' and he drew her to him.

She had forgotten how good it felt to be in his arms, the caress of his hands on her back through the thin material of her dress. Thoughts of David finding them rushed through her head.

'Let me go.'

He didn't. Ella took a deep breath.

'It's over,' she said. 'It was dead and buried then.'

He held her tighter.

'It was nothing of the sort. You gave me up without a single word from me, without giving me a chance or a reason and I don't believe it was anything but fear because Jack had died and you were afraid the whole thing would happen again. That's not a decent reason for doing anything and it isn't like you. It will never be over between us. You know that as much as I do. For whatever reason you married him, it wasn't because you loved him more than you loved me. I know that. You betrayed me and everything there was between us and for what?'

He kissed her and momentarily Ella gave in because she remembered just how wonderful the kisses had been; they had not changed, despite the years and all they had both been through, and she was afraid now, desperate to get away, to pretend this had not happened. She wanted to run back to the dining room. She struggled, pushed her hands against him. He let her go then. Ella's heart was beating so hard she could hardly breathe.

'You gave me up for some ghastly safe little life and after all I had done,' he said.

'It isn't a ... a "ghastly safe little life",' Ella said, almost crying, 'you know nothing about it. You know nothing about David and me. We have a wonderful life, it's—'

'Liar. He can't even afford a decent dress for you.'

In those seconds the dress which she and Iris had chosen so carefully turned to rags in Ella's mind, became something she wished she could tear off, her face burned with shame.

'It's a ... it's a beautiful dress,' she said, thinking even as she said it how stupid she sounded. What did she care what he thought? What did any of it matter now? The past was gone. She had killed it off in her memory when she could stand no more.

She was not going to have it resurrected because Harry chose.

She wanted to tell him that she hated him, except it would have sounded so shallow, so pathetic and it wasn't true; she could never hate him. She knew that he was only saying such things for something to say, anything to delay her departure, because when you loved somebody so very much every second of their time was valuable. Every moment spent in their presence was the best moment you could ever have.

She couldn't run, her shoes wouldn't allow it, but she hurried back as fast as she could. Suddenly the thought of another speech or two seemed inviting but when she got inside she couldn't see for tears and was obliged to dodge into the ladies' room and repair her face. She needed to recover her emotions before she returned to David.

She sat before the glass and cried. The tears, freed, ran down her face. God knew what it was doing to her carefully applied make-up but she couldn't see. Sobs wrenched at her body. She tried to control herself but she couldn't. How hideous, how awful. Why did he have to turn up and ruin everything? Why did she remember everything she had ever felt for him? Had she really thought she could forget it?

As she sat there a girl came out of one of the cubicles. Ella had thought the place was empty and was horrified that she could be heard, seen, that she could not mop her face convincingly and quieten the sobs before the girl came and sat down beside her.

She turned away, dried her eyes and tried to pretend that nothing had happened. Perhaps the girl was the unfriendly type or so caught up in her own life that she wouldn't notice. She turned back to the mirror and glanced at the other face there.

She couldn't have been more than twenty-two or -three and she was lovely, so beautiful that Ella couldn't help but look. She sat on the stool next to Ella. She was blonde, her skin was milky, she wore a dress so expensive that it made Ella's dress look cheap.

There was nothing to it, it was plain black and contrasted superbly with her looks and she wore pearls about her neck, as only the very young can; real pearls, Ella felt sure. Her long smooth neck and bare shoulders were exquisite. She had slender arms and fingers, and on the left hand she wore a wedding ring and a diamond solitaire which glittered so much under the lights it was hard to look at it.

Ella felt physically sick at the thought of the dress. The girl smiled shyly.

'Are you all right?' she said. To Ella's surprise she had a soft Durham accent.

'Yes, I ... I just had a shock.'

'Summat that made you cry?'

'It's a ... a beautiful dress you're wearing.'

'Me husband chose it.' She turned her eyes up to heaven. 'Do you really think it looks all right? I know nowt about things like that.'

'It's exquisite.'

The girl grinned suddenly.

'If you're crying over a man dinnat bother. None of them's worth it, not even mine.'

'You're married.'

'Oh, aye.' She laughed, showing perfect teeth and there was a rueful twinkling look in her eyes. 'What he married me for nobody will ever know. I married him for his money. At least that's what I tell everybody. Can't have them thinking I fancy him.'

'You're so young,' Ella said.

'He picked me up out the muck. Brave lad,' she said. 'Somebody's not being nasty to you, are they? Because if they are I'll sort them out for you. Here.' The girl took a tiny silver flask of brandy from her evening bag and offered it to Ella. She took it and downed a mouthful of the brandy, which was warm and soft as it hit the back of her throat. 'Is that better, pet?'

'Much better, thank you.'

They repaired their make-up.

'You look a treat, you really do,' the girl said and then they got up together and made their way through the foyer.

The speeches had thankfully finished and

the music had begun. The girl walked in front of Ella, who stopped suddenly. She could see Harry Reid, he was standing just inside the door, near the bar. What was he thinking of, waiting there for her?

As the blonde girl reached him, he smiled at her and she kissed him and then he turned to Ella and said, 'Rosemary, you must meet Ella. She was the girl I left behind me. She married somebody else and broke my heart.' He spoke lightly but Ella did not miss the bitterness behind the words. 'Ella, this is my wife.'

The girl laughed but there was now a reserve to it as though she saw Ella differently. Her eyes had changed and were guarded, perhaps even suspicious.

'It's grand to meet you. And don't worry about things, nowt's worth it.'

Harry led her off to the dance floor and Ella stood, rooted, watching them waltz elegantly about the floor. She felt a kind of jealousy she had never encountered before in her life. It shot through her like a firework. She walked around the edge of the dance floor until she reached her husband. He got to his feet.

'Would you like to dance?' he said.

'I would love to,' Ella said.

One

The Great War was over by the time Ella was born. Unlike many of his friends her father had come through it, come home to the girl he loved. Ella was her parents' only child.

She was born in the tiny city of Durham, in the borderlands between Scotland and England, in Northumbria. They say there are other cities in Britain which are as beautiful as Durham but it isn't true to the people who live there. As Ella had always lived there she was sure there was no place which came anywhere near in any way.

Her ancestors had lived there for hundreds of years. They were border people, Scots and English intermarried over the centuries with all the fine prejudices which you gain when you live in such a place.

The River Wear loops grey around the city, and the castle and the cathedral, which have been there for eight hundred years, make people gasp at the beauty of the buildings. They sit there stark and exquisite in the light from the Wear, above the city and its bridges, the old houses, the twisting cobbled narrow streets and the little shops. And there is always the warm sound of Durham accents of the people in the town.

Durham voices are as warm as winter soup and the people are kind and hospitable and see to one another, even when they have nothing. Pit people and farm folk and those who run small businesses within the city. People know Durham as the city, Newcastle is always called 'the town', and in between there are tiny villages dotted across the landscape, and the Wear runs its winding way through the dales and down the narrow valleys before it hits Durham City.

Ella lived in a particular part of the tiny city, the part they called Swan Island. It was a very long time since the name had been used, most of the area was now known as Elvet, but it lived on in her childhood home.

To her delight home was not called 'house' or 'manor' or 'hall', though it had always been one of the most important houses in the area. It was always just 'Swan Island' as though it needed no other explanation. From her house Ella could see the river going in both directions. Up where the road splits in two and becomes Old Elvet and New Elvet, she could see the castle and the cathedral and the people scurrying about the town to work and school, and those pleasure-bound for walks or lovers' meetings or the local pubs.

Her parents had been born there, had met

there, and had been very much in love, but did she remember that they were or was it just that her mother had said so often enough that Ella believed it? She believed in the laughter of Swan Island and the presence of the man that she and her mother had loved, the dark-haired blue-eyed man she knew she resembled so much.

The house in her memories was a great sprawling building of red brick, with high chimneys and huge windows, and from the top of it you could see most of the middle of the city; the narrow streets, the silver rooftops, the castle, the cathedral and the green, and the riverbanks where in the summer people took boats out and there was the regatta and picnics.

She could see the hills which made up the city and several of the roads out, winding their way up to the tops and then to the little pit villages and towns beyond which went to Sunderland, to Newcastle, to the south or to the Durham dales where small farms made up the communities and sheep were dotted across the landscape and way above were the moors where it was harsh in winter and gorse provided a yellow snow upon the land most of the year round.

The house was famous because you could only reach it over a bridge; like the entrance to an old fortified castle there was but one way in and the river surrounded it on three sides. A house had been there for hundreds of years and to Ella's pride the Armstrongs had lived there all that time. She planned to stay there for ever and ever, to raise her children, should she have any, and to bring her lover when she had one. When Flo, who looked after her, read her stories she thought of the fictional house as Swan Island and the characters as its inhabitants.

The house was always full of flowers, her mother loved them so much; the gardens were great floods of colour and scent and they twisted and turned in crazy paving paths away from the house so that they were secret and mysterious. Here and there high walls shrouded the intricacy, and bushes and shrubs allowed their delicate flowers to fall and strew the path, a carpet for the feet that should walk upon them.

At the end of the gardens lay the ruined church which at one time had been the parish church for that area until another church was built nearer to the main part of the town and people moved on. Ella thought of it and of the time when people would come across the bridge to the little church on Sunday mornings. She could almost hear the tramp of their feet when she was lying in her bed.

She didn't remember it as anything other than ruined. Inside flowers and bushes took charge and all around it were the graves of local people long dead, the names of the border people, Nevilles and Armstrongs and Elliotts, and dozens of others who were buried there. Her mother was given to seeing that the churchyard there was not overgrown; everything was tended, the gardens, the house, her husband, her daughter.

Ella was very happy with the security and all-absorbing love which an only child can know. She knew her parents adored her. She had a fire in the bedroom, a big room all to herself, she had beautiful clothes and lots of toys and went to a small private school in the city and had friends to tea. She had Flo, who was younger than her parents and had been there all of Ella's life as far back as she could remember, almost like one of the family except that she went home to her mother each night, but she was always there to look after Ella when her mother was not about.

There was a cook and Mr Frobisher, who did the garden and looked after the car. He would cut and bring in flowers for her mother's delight all the year round.

The cook was Mrs Robson – another good border name. Ella cared for them all. They were so kind to her. Mrs Robson made coffee cake with chocolate icing for tea. Flo would play games with Ella when she had free time and they would go for walks on the towpath at the riverside, name the flowers and trees and stop and have ice-cream or tea and cake.

The house at Swan Island was everything that a house should be. No other house was ever like that again, even though from time to time through her life Ella tried to make other houses so. It held her heart.

It sounded silly to say such things but it did. It held within it all the dreams of her life, all the sweet memories of her childhood, her father's love, her mother's devotion, the songs that her mother would sing, though she had no voice. She used to joke about how she could not hold a tune but all the old songs which her mother sang to her were precious to Ella.

All the silly jokes that her father told her and the way that his face would crease while he told them meant more to her than anything in the world.

Her parents would go to dinner dances and he would wear evening dress, tails and white gloves and black patent leather shoes and her mother would wear a green satin dress with green sequins and a fox fur cape around her shoulders.

They would be gone all night and Ella would sleep in Flo's room because Flo would stay when her parents went to dinner dances or when they stayed away overnight for any reason.

In the morning they always brought back treasures for her, conical shaped hats with an elastic to go under her chin, paper streamers, little trumpets which made strange noises. They had loved each other then, Ella knew. And they had loved her.

The first ten years of Ella's life went on in this blissful way and then quite suddenly it ended.

Flo always woke her. She heard the thick velvet curtains being pushed back to let in the daylight. It was raining, it was a dark November morning and she sat up in bed expecting Flo's voice but her mother came to the bed and sat down.

She pushed back the unruly dark curls from Ella's face and she looked to Ella as though she had been crying. She couldn't remember having seen her mother cry before.

'Ella, there isn't a good way to tell you this so you'll have to forgive me for saying it but I want you to know. Other people have told me that I should pretend, that I should say Daddy has gone away, but then you would look for him coming back and he isn't coming back. Daddy has died and we must now do the best we can.'

Ella didn't remember what was said after that. There seemed to be a good many people in the house, she could hear the sound of their voices from the open door of her bedroom.

Flo was sent to help her though Ella had

not had anybody do such things for years. Ella thought that Flo was trying to hold back the tears, she kept turning away and using a very sensible voice and after Ella was washed and dressed, they put on their coats. She remembered that they did not go downstairs and when they went out for the day they went down the back stairs.

It was not a day for going anywhere, the rain lashed down with a wind behind it. Flo was very kind, talking about the ducks on the river and the big birds which they didn't know the names of, trying to catch fish. The rain fell down and was lost in the water which flowed under Elvet Bridge.

'Can we go home yet?' Ella said and heard herself saying it for at least the third time. 'I'm bored.'

'Not yet.'

'Can we go somewhere else then? Can we go to your house?'

'We can go to the teashop and have cake.'

'I would rather go to your house.'

Ella persisted and in the end Flo walked her up North Road, under the viaduct where the trains ran over, and up what seemed to Ella like a steep bank towards Nevilles Cross. Then through a dark alley which came out into a little yard and there she hammered on the door and a big fat untidy looking woman came to the door.

'Our Flo,' she said, 'what are you doing

here at this time of day?'

'I brought Mrs Armstrong's lass,' Flo said.

The woman surveyed Ella with sharp eyes.

'Howay in, flower, you look frozen.'

It was not freezing inside the house, a great fire blazed across the room. There was only one room. Ella had not imagined that people lived in such small houses and the fireplace was a big kitchen range with brasses at either side which shone in the fire's reflection. At the far side of the room there was also a big chest of drawers and in the middle a table and chairs and a sofa under the window.

Flo's mother, for Ella assumed it was even though nobody said so, made tea for them and gave them big pieces of custard pie. At one point Flo and her mother went into the pantry, to look for cake, and talked in low voices. Ella was surprised that they thought that she could not hear.

'Gone, is he?'

'Aye,' Flo said.

'And not before time,' her mother said.

Ella tried not to listen. She didn't want to be rude but she could tell the conversation was not complimentary.

Flo shushed her mother but her mother went on.

'Mrs La-di-da won't be able to stop on there then.'

'I don't suppose she will, no, but there's

no reason to crow, she's a nice enough woman.'

'Nowt was ever enough for her, Flo. Now she'll get to know what it feels to be like the rest of us. It'll be like being back to where she came from. Death is a great leveller.'

Ella pretended she was deaf and ate her custard pie and the egg and ham pie which Flo's mother produced. There was also a cake with big cherries in it.

While they were sitting there a young lad came in. Ella didn't hear him knock, he just walked straight in as though he belonged. Maybe Flo had a brother, but then he took off his cap and as he did so said, 'Hello, Mrs Stewart,' and Ella realized he couldn't have been.

'Walter, come and sit with Ella and have some cake,' Flo's mother said.

'I was wondering like,' the tall, skinny youth said to Flo, 'if you could get tonight off and we might go to the pictures.'

'I can't,' Flo said, 'things are bad at the house. What about tomorrow?'

'That would be grand,' he said. 'Is it right what I heard then?'

Flo pulled a face at him. He glanced at Ella but she was ignoring them all. She didn't want to know what people were talking about and since she was sure it was about her family she had decided the best thing to do was ignore it and get on with eating her cake.

They were nice to her though. Flo and Walter played Lotto with her after tea and she began to wish she did not have to go home because everything was going wrong there and since her mother had assured her that her father would not be coming back she was reluctant to face the changes.

Her mother never told lies so Ella thought it would be much better if she could stay here longer, maybe even to sleep, though the narrow stairs were dark and did not look enticing. She had a feeling that there was not a room for each person as there was at home, and she did not want to share a room or a bed with anybody else.

Eventually Flo decided they should go back, as Mrs Armstrong would worry. Ella tried to pretend that nothing had happened as she watched the people struggling up towards the bus station and the railway station.

If she craned her neck back over as they walked home she could see the viaduct for quite a long time and from time to time see and hear the trains which went on their way up to Newcastle and Edinburgh or down to York and London. It was the kind of day which blew people's umbrellas inside out. It looked so normal, Ella could not believe that disaster had struck in such a way.

Two

That evening her mother walked her through the darkness, through the rain, past the black shop windows, up and down the tiny, twisting streets, through the Market Place, past St Nicholas Church which nestled in the corner next to the pubs and shops with its long spire that stretched up into the night sky, and then Ella and her mother walked down Silver Street. They didn't go to Framwellgate Bridge at the bottom, they stopped halfway down, where her grandmother lived. Her grandmother was their only relative, as far as Ella knew.

Her mother walked her up the steep stairs – there was a shop on the ground floor and the steps went up to one side with a separate entrance and door – and there was the café which her grandmother ran.

Ella sat in the café, a big room with lots of tables and chairs and a linoleumed floor, and her mother told her to stay there for a few minutes, she wouldn't be long. Ella was inclined to say could she go up too but she didn't, and then her mother went up the next flight of stairs to the living quarters to talk to her grandmother.

Ella wished she could go, she loved her grandmother's house. It was tiny, like a dolls' house almost, with two small bedrooms, a sitting room and a tiny kitchen where she would go on Sundays when the café was closed.

She loved the attic rooms best, though they were very cold in winter, but it was dark up there and had old trunks and boxes full of things which her grandmother had not quite discarded. It was musty and hot in summer but from the tiny windows you could see across some of the rooftops.

They would have tea sitting around the fire or on fine days her grandmother would take them out and they would have picnics on the riverbank. Her father had never gone on these outings, her mother always said he was too busy. Grandma was a baker and she made the lightest sponge cakes with jam; cheese scones which she covered in thick farm butter; and little fairy cakes, each covered with pink icing.

They would feed the ducks and waterhens at the water's edge and walk from Framwellgate Bridge around the loop to Elvet Bridge. There was garlic white on the riverbanks and in the spring there would be hyacinths.

'I knew it would come to this, somehow I knew.'

It wasn't that her mother was glad for what had happened, even though she had begged Verena not to marry him. My head was turned, she thought. He was somebody, he was so far above me, like the stars are above the ground. I was so proud that he wanted me, that he asked me to marry him, that he talked so fine and his family were so well known and they had the wonderful house.

'Is there nothing left?'

'Only bills.' Verena got up as she spoke. She was embarrassed that, having apparently done so well, she had come to this, having to ask her mother if she could move back in when she had thought she was done with this place for ever. She had been so glad to escape. Her father had died, her mother kept on the café and she had spent her young life there. How happy she had been at Swan Island. It was over now. She could barely afford to pay the staff what she owed them. Her mother, however, seeming to sense what she was about to say, forestalled her.

'You and Ella must come and live here.'

'I don't want to put on you, it isn't fair.'

'Things aren't fair,' her mother said, smiling at her with sympathy in her expression, 'surely you know that by now.'

'I thought it was going to be different for us.'

Her mother came over and put a pudgy

hand to her face in caress.

'It isn't that different for anybody, my petal. You collect your things and come here and we'll sort everything out.'

'I have to stay there for a certain length of time. There's so much to do,' Verena said, reluctant even to think of leaving the house she loved so much. She couldn't come and live back here, yet what else was there for her to do? On the other hand she wanted the comfort of having her mother there, she had always been there, so reliable, never complaining. How had her mother managed to be such a selfless person? The only time Verena could remember her mother disagreeing with her was when she wanted to get married and even then she had let Verena get on with it since it was so clearly what she wanted.

'Come here to sleep then. Get rid of the help, sell what you can from the house – I daresay the auction rooms would take most of it, you've got quite a lot of good stuff there–'

'Most of it's already been sold,' Verena said. 'We needed the money.'

'Well, do what you can and try not to worry.'

The sympathy was too much to bear. It made Verena cry.

'You'd better go down to that little lass. She's had too long a day. Take her home while you still have one,' her mother advised.

Her mother was gone a long time and Ella grew impatient. She could hear the rise and fall of their voices but nothing more. When her mother came back her grandma was not with her and Ella was sorry because next to her parents she loved her grandma best.

She couldn't understand why her mother had taken her if it was only to sit alone and grow impatient in the silence but perhaps, she thought later, it was like holding a shield or a blanket and her mother had needed her there. She was only relieved to see her mother come back down the stairs. She stood up.

'Aren't I going up to see Grandma?'

'Not tonight.'

'She'll think I'm rude staying down here.'

'She doesn't think that at all,' her mother said, taking a firm hold of her hand and walking her down the steep stairs and out into the night.

When they got home they sat in front of the fire. Though sandwiches and cakes were put in front of them they couldn't eat anything.

Her mother said to her, 'We shall be leaving Swan Island. We will go and live with Grandma.'

'Why do we have to go?'

'Because we can't stay here any longer. We

won't have any money, you see. The house will have to be sold. Do you understand?'

'I think so,' Ella said, 'but it's our house. Our family has lived here always.'

'Not any longer,' her mother said.

Ella thought there was a grim note in her voice.

'What about Flo?' Ella couldn't even consider that she would be losing Flo as well as her father.

'She'll find something else and she'll come and see us.'

'But I don't want her to come and see us. That'll mean her living in another house. Couldn't she come and help in the café?'

'I suppose she could if she wanted to, but she might not want to, Ella. You can't run other people's lives for them.'

Ella managed to get Flo to herself after her mother had told her they would be moving.

'Will you come with us and help?' she asked.

Flo looked serious.

'The thing is, Ella, I'm courting.'

'Courting?' It was Ella's mother who spoke as she came into the kitchen.

Flo lifted her chin.

It seemed like the final desertion somehow, some man taking Flo away, the young man who had arrived in Flo's kitchen at their house seemed an unlikely husband to Ella.

'Walter and me, we've been courting for nearly two years and he's asked me to marry him and, although I like you, I don't think I would want to help out at the café instead of looking after you, do you see? I have to look after my man now.'

Verena said, 'How lovely for you, Flo. Will you come and see us?'

'If we stay here I will but we might be moving away to Darlington. Walter is up for a job there.'

'I do hope you'll be very happy with your new husband,' Verena said.

Ella couldn't say anything. She ran away and cried at the bottom of the garden, where she was hidden from view among the tall trees.

It was very late when Flo got back to the tiny house in the back street which had always been her home. Her mother looked up from pulling coal forward on to the fire. Flo sighed.

'I told them Walter and I were going to be wed and I couldn't stay on.'

'About time,' her mother said, but when Flo said nothing her mother came to her. 'I know you're fond of the little lass, but you and Walter will have bairns of your own and you'll feel more for them than you ever felt for somebody else's. You take my word for it. Stop worrying about them. They wouldn't worry about you. There's you and Walter to think of now, that's what's important.'

'Can we live here with you until Walter starts his new job? We could go to his mam's but–'

'Of course you can. It'll be nice having a man around the house again. Will Walter not mind?'

'I haven't asked him. I think he took it for granted that we would live with his mam, but to be honest she doesn't seem to want me there and she has already got their Fred and Bessie living there.'

That evening when she told Walter she had told Verena Armstrong she was leaving and getting married Walter seemed pleased.

'And I'd like us to live with my mam,' Flo said firmly.

'There's not a lot of room at your house,' Walter said.

'More than at yours with your brother and sister both at home. Do you mind, Walter?'

'I suppose not. Your mam is all right, but once I get my new job everything will change. We'll have a house of our own and that'll be grand.'

Ella was the only child at the funeral. She didn't understand why other children weren't there but she overheard people talking afterwards and lots of people came to the house and stood about in groups, looking out of the windows, holding cups and saucers and saying how sad everything was.

'That bairn should never have been at the funeral,' she heard one old lady in black say to another. 'It isn't the place for little ones.'

Her friend, seeing Ella nearby, nudged her and shook her head.

Flo was there and Ella knew it was the last time she would see her. She kept following her around as she handed out cakes and she noticed that Flo went into the kitchen and cried. Darlington was not a long way but it was far enough that Ella knew she might never see Flo again.

'Walter is going for a job at the rolling mills and then we'll have our own house.'

'That'll be lovely for you.'

'I know but I don't want to leave my mam,' Flo said, smiling through her tears at her own daft ways.

Ella half thought that Flo might ask them to the wedding but it didn't happen. When the funeral guests had gone, the kitchen was tidy and the cook had given Flo a bagful of food to take back with her, she put on her coat and left. Ella accompanied her all the way down the drive and had to put up with Flo kissing her and crying some more and then watching her as Flo walked away down the road towards the bus station and out of her life.

Three

The days that followed were dreary. Men came with a big van and took the furniture away. Mrs Robson went off with barely a word. Mr Frobisher came for his money to the study and then he disappeared too. The rooms seemed so much bigger as they were emptied and things which Ella had thought she did not care for, such as the pretty pink-and-white dressing table in her bedroom, were taken away.

Many of her toys went too. Her mother explained that they could not take them. Ella clung to her special teddy bear and story books and tried not to think about all she was losing.

She missed her father so much that the rest was nothing but detail. She kept waiting for him to walk in and say it had all been a mistake, or to wake up and discover it was a bright morning outside and it had been nothing but a nasty dream.

Her mother looked so pale and thin that Ella was worried something might happen to her too. Also her mother sat down and explained to her that she could no longer go to her school.

'It costs money,' she said, 'and we don't have any now. We'll find another school for you to go to.'

'I don't want to go to another school,' Ella said, suddenly afraid that there was going to be nothing familiar left in her life.

Her mother didn't argue. Finally the day came when they had to leave the house. It wasn't like their house any longer. None of their possessions were left. A car came to take them to Silver Street and she knew that it was for ever, that the happiness she had known then was over.

Swan Island was nothing but a dream after that, something she could picture so well in her mind in the darkness. She always dreamed that she and her mother went back and her father was there, and she was running down the path to the front door over and over. He was opening the door and she was flinging herself at him and saying, 'I knew that it wasn't true. I knew you were here waiting for me,' and then she would awaken in the cold grey light of the new day and she would be in the tiny bedroom which she shared with her mother in her grandma's house in Silver Street, where the light never fell because the cobbled street was narrow and the road twisted away towards Framwellgate Bridge.

If the weather was fine, the windows were open and she could hear the river and the sound of the gulls making their way in from the coast in bad weather but it was winter then and the weather set in to be cold.

The snowflakes went horizontally past her window, which looked out over the backs of the houses, and it was dark when she awoke. It was long before teatime and people did not linger in the café or the shops or streets, they hurried home to their firesides. Ella would sit upstairs and watch them and long to go home to Swan Island, where she was convinced her father was waiting.

From early morning she would hear the clattering of the crockery and the moving of tables and chairs because her grandma kept the café which opened at half past nine and people would come in, knowing that she opened early. Her grandma was famous for her ginger cake, her scones, her stotties, her sweet tea. The smell of baking was always the over-riding smell there.

The smells at Swan Island had been different, Ella thought; the honeysuckle which entwined its way around the bridge, the plums which fell and split in the autumn in the long grass in the orchard, the warm spaniels as they slept beside the sitting-room fire, the milk which was fresh and sweet, the eggs which were newly laid and golden-yolked, the cigarettes and gin on her parents' breath as they kissed her good-night, her mother's perfume, like wild exotic flowers, her father's neck, like limes.

Even the dogs could not come to the café. People didn't approve of dogs in cafés apparently. They had gone to Yorkshire to live with a gamekeeper. Ella tried to convince herself that they would be happy there, she missed them almost as much as she missed her father.

He would carry her to bed and her parents would sit down there together and one of them would read her a story. Often if her mother read it, her father would fall asleep on the bed but her strongest memory was of them both there, of them laughing together, of their voices floating by as she went to sleep.

Their voices would haunt her always and the way that the house at Swan Island would never change in her memory. It was always the same. Somewhere beyond time and place she and her father and mother were at Swan Island and nothing could spoil that, nothing could alter it. It was the most precious thing that she had ever had.

Four

There was a hardware shop on the ground floor. Mr Wilson ran it. He was an old man and it was a very interesting shop. He had pots and pans and crockery and tools for mending things and spanners and screw-drivers.

The stairs to the café led from beside a gunnel – the narrow passage which led to the back of the buildings and along down to the riverbanks. The stairs were steep and they led on further past the café and up to the second and third storeys. On the first floor was the café itself, it was a big single room and there was a long counter and beyond it a kitchen. On the second floor was their living accommodation, two bedrooms, both small, and another tiny kitchen, a sitting room and the attics above and that was all.

Ella could understand, when she saw the size of the bedroom she and her mother would share, why her grandmother had not wanted furniture or belongings. There was a double bed in it which they would both sleep in, a wardrobe and a little table under the window which doubled as a dressing table

and her mother put on it things like hairbrushes and clips. The silver hairbrushes
which had sat on her mother's dressing table
at home had gone along with her beautiful
clothes, shoes and coats. There was no room
for anything else, and Ella thought with
regret of the lovely big bedroom with the
view over the garden which she had had all
to herself.

When her mother saw the bedroom for the
first time and put their suitcases down on
the floor, she had said dismally, 'This is
where I used to sleep. Strange to come full
circle.' She went and gazed out of the dirty
window at the rooftops. 'I loved it then and
I missed my mother when I married and
moved out. I missed this place. People told
me it wasn't far to go, but your whole life
changes when you marry and in the beginning there were lots of times when I wanted
to come back here. Now it's the very last
place I want to be.'

Ella had wanted to ask why they had to
come here, why they could not have a house
of their own but she'd known the answer to
that. Money. Money was the most important thing in their lives, no doubt in everybody's lives. She had not understood until
then.

At the first playtime at her new school,
which was across the street and up the steep
hill out of the Market Place to an area called

Claypath and beyond into Gilesgate and then down a side street, she stood by herself on the edge of the yard and watched the girls playing with skipping ropes. The boys were in a separate yard all of their own so she didn't know what they were doing, she could just hear them.

She knew nothing of boys, her previous school was just for girls. She hadn't dared address anyone and nobody spoke to her. She was dreading dinnertime. Where would she sit? Her mother had told her that she must stay there until tea time; there was to be no break from her new surroundings, no respite.

Just before dinnertime on that first day, as the children were streaming out of their classrooms through the main corridor, one big boy got hold of her arm and he said to her, 'You are the Armstrong lass, aren't you? Your dad done himself in.'

Ella stared after him as he ran down the corridor and then she followed and when she reached the doors which led into the playground and to the main gates she opened them and went outside. She heard one of the teachers shouting after her so as soon as she got beyond them she began to run.

Her mother had taken her to school so she was not quite sure of her direction. She had been so afraid of yet something else new to be faced, that she had not taken anything in.

She ran blindly down the hill and across the Market Place and down the steep bank towards her grandmother's café, and then she ran up the stairs even faster and burst into the café.

Her mother was waiting on tables. Ella was shocked. Her mother had never done such things, she had had people to do all that for her, yet here she was in an apron and one of those daft little hats which waitresses wore, and she was carrying a tray holding pink-and-white cakes and a pot of tea. She was smiling and talking, though Ella knew it was the very last thing she wanted to do.

Then her mother saw her and Ella ran out again and up the stairs and into their bedroom. She slammed the door and sat down on the bed. She was breathing very hard so that she could not cry efficiently and she gasped and retched as her body shook.

It was not long before she heard footsteps and her mother, still complete with uniform, followed her inside. She sat down on the bed.

'What is it, Ella? What's happened?'

'I hate that school. I want to go back to my own school where all my friends are. I hate it here. I want to go home. And what are you doing dressed up like that? You look really silly.'

'You've only been there half a day,' her

mother pointed out. 'You have to give it a chance.'

'I'm not going,' Ella said.

'You have to go.'

Ella had caught her breath by now and was sorry she had called her mother silly. She sat up and looked at her mother because she needed the vital question answering.

'A boy, older than me, in the top class, he told me my dad had ... he said–' she didn't look at her mother – 'he said, "Your dad done himself in".'

Her mother didn't comment but Ella heard the change in her breathing.

'What an awful thing to say,' she said.

'Is it true?'

'No, of course it isn't. It was an accident.'

'An accident?'

'Yes. He was taking pills because we were having a lot of money worries and he just took too many, that's all. It can happen to anybody when they're worried. It was a mistake. He went to sleep and didn't wake up. He didn't mean to do it.'

'How do you know?'

'How could he ever have chosen to leave you and me like this? He would never have done it.'

Her mother's voice shook as though she was being brave because she had to.

'Then why do people think it?'

'Because they lead such boring lives that

they enjoy other people's problems. There were a lot of folk around here that were very jealous when I married your dad. He could have chosen a rich lass like himself but he didn't, he chose me and I was proud of it. I'm still proud of it, still glad I did it in spite of what's happened, so don't listen to anybody, Ella. He was a very silly boy to say such things and you would be a very silly girl if you listened to him and believed him.'

'Are you sure?'

'Quite sure,' her mother said.

'I don't want to go back.'

Her mother took off her apron and the awful little white cap and put on her coat and she led Ella by the hand back to school and into the classroom, The teacher was kind to her and that afternoon they did painting. Ella liked painting and the teacher praised the pretty yellow flower she had painted and she was much happier when she went home at tea time. Her mother was waiting by the gates. Ella hugged her.

But when she was in bed that night she remembered how her mother's voice had shaken and how her eyes had shifted, and she realized that her mother only hoped the truth was that it was an accident. She didn't know it and couldn't know it for certain.

Five

When she was eleven Ella went to the girls' grammar school, down by the river. She liked it much better than the primary school. For a start there were no boys and during the first couple of years that was good because she decided she had never liked boys and never would.

There were no men in her life. It was mainly women who came to the café, with their sisters, mothers, daughters and friends. They brought their children but boys only came to the café when they were very small. Then, Ella thought with distaste, they quickly moved on to sports, football, cricket and the like, boring things.

Her mother and grandmother were very busy. There was the baking to do. Her mother was particularly good at cakes and her grandmother at bread and pies. They made apple-and-blackberry tarts in the autumn, thick fruit cakes in the winter, strawberry and raspberry jam to put on the scones when the days were warm and so that was how Ella came to think of the seasons; they just went on, round and round, and she got used to that.

She got home one hot July afternoon and ran up into the kitchen and there was her grandma.

'Where's my mam?'

'She went upstairs to lie down. She wasn't feeling well.'

This, Ella thought, was unheard of. Her mam never lay down during the day. She was about to dash upstairs when her grandmother stopped her and laid a hand on her arm.

'I think she's asleep. Let her sleep on, it'll do her good. She's had a lot on her plate, you know, she gets tired.'

'Don't you get tired, Grandma?'

Her grandmother kissed her.

'Why don't I give you a piece of raspberry tart which I've just made and a nice cup of tea?'

'That would be lovely, Grandma,' Ella replied.

Shortly afterwards her mother came back downstairs and Ella thought no more about it until a week later when her mother went missing again.

That evening Ella found her grandmother alone in the café, washing the floor when it was late and all the chairs were on the tables and she thought her grandmother looked tired as well as her mother.

She said, 'I'll do that, Grandma.'

Her grandmother protested but Ella

insisted and every day after that, when it was late and the café was closed, her job was to wash the floor. She hated doing it but she hated even more how tired her mother looked and how her old grandma was trying to do everything.

Within the week she had gone to her grandma and said, 'Don't you think my mam should see a doctor?'

Her grandma looked clearly at her, turned away for a second or two and then she said, 'She has done.'

'Why didn't anybody tell me?'

'It's nothing to worry about.'

Ella did worry because it seemed to her she was always coming in from school and her mother was upstairs and on Saturdays, when the café was very busy, her mam could only work for a short period and then she had to stop and go and lie on the sofa up-stairs. Ella found herself waiting on and helping her grandmother in the kitchen and her grandmother began to teach her how to bake. She was good at it, her grandma said, her scones were the lightest she had ever tasted and Ella was happy to be good at something which was so useful when her mother wasn't well.

They took on a waitress in the restaurant, a woman called Winnie who was slight and skinny but smiled a lot and was nice. When Ella came home she had to help because there was always so much to do at that time of day. She discovered that she liked working in the café and talking to the customers. She liked the sound of their conversation, their laughter, the way that they enjoyed the meals she brought them and sometimes they would leave tips for her so that she had a little bit of pocket money.

In spite of visits to the doctor her mother did not get better. On Sundays she did not want to go on walks by the river or to the shops when they could spare a few pennies for treats of some kind. She would lie on the day-bed by the fire and when the weather was warm she would sit by the window and watch the activity in the street below.

Ella was resentful that her mother was ill and Sundays were so dull but she kept her feelings to herself. It was not her mother's fault that she felt so bad. Her grandma would sometimes go out with her, but as time went by she seemed reluctant to leave her mother at home by herself. Soon, although friends from school would come round and ask her to go out, Ella began to refuse to leave the café, even though her grandmother urged her to get some fresh air.

Her mother was cheerful and Ella remained so but when she went to bed at night the old fears haunted her and she thought of her father's death and what life would be like without her mother. She tried to imagine it because somehow if you could imagine things they would never happen, it was the old spell.

You imagined the worst to keep it from you, but her mother went through the whole of the summer season without making any kind of jam, without baking at all.

Ella began to take days off school to help. Not that her grandmother asked her to. Her grandmother seemed increasingly aware that she needed to spend time with her mother and that she had no time to herself and would try to encourage her to go out when the weather was fine, but Ella had no inclination to go anywhere. She was too afraid that if she went out she would come back and her mother would not be lying on the sofa.

Ella was thirteen in the September and that autumn her mother began to stay in bed all day. It was the hardest time of Ella's life. She could not sit with her mother all day, in any case her mother did not want her to, and she could not watch her grandmother struggle with the work and not help because the café was their whole life, it was their living.

When she thought back to that autumn, she pictured herself running downstairs to help and then running upstairs to sit on the bed and read or talk or try to keep her mother cheerful. Her mother was cheerful, it was Ella who was not. She went to bed exhausted each night from pretending to be happy, and she went on working hard at school because her mother always asked how she was getting on and Ella wanted to please her.

'Your education is very important for your future. You might do all kinds of things. You stick in at school, do well,' she said.

It was a cold November day that she came back from school and there was, for the first time that she could remember except on Sundays, no sound at all from the café. She had run up the stairs and already she was realizing that it was different.

She opened the door and it was not like it was when it was closed up every night, the floor washed, the surfaces scrubbed, everything put away in the kitchen, the chairs upended on to the table, everything had been done but haphazardly and it was only mid afternoon. Winnie, who helped in the café, was nowhere to be seen. Neither was her grandmother. It was deserted.

She ran out of there and was about to take the next set of stairs when her grandmother came to the top of them and she was crying.

'Oh, Ella,' she said, 'you're all I've got left now.' She seemed so old and so defeated.

Six

Ella went straight back to school after her mother's funeral as she knew her mother would have wanted her to, but at the end of the first day she came home to find the smell of burning from the kitchen and her grandmother crying upstairs as she had never done before. She rescued the scones from the oven and thankfully they were brown rather than black. Winnie was at the counter where a woman was complaining about the wrong change. Ella went across.

'Can I help?' she said, and Winnie let her give the woman her change without any fuss. Then she put on an apron and went over to where three different sets of people were waiting to be served. 'I'm so sorry,' she said, 'we won't be a moment.'

Her grandmother came slowly downstairs and into the kitchen and put the scones on to a wire rack. She was not crying any more.

'I'm all right, Ella, really. You go and do your homework.'

Ella didn't argue but she didn't go upstairs to do her homework. She helped to serve in the café and she got on with the washing up. She determined from then that she would not go to school. She would put in the odd day to begin with because school was where she was meant to be but gradually over the next few weeks she just didn't go any more. Her grandmother was too upset to be left and because they were all the other had they were afraid to let the other person out of sight. She panicked, thinking that when her grandmother died she would have no one or she would die and then her grandmother would have no one.

She didn't like to tell people what to do but from the beginning she had to tell Winnie because if she was left alone she was apt to make mistakes in the change she gave, in the orders she took, so Ella took to giving her easy things to do while she did the difficult ones herself.

Winnie was consigned to collecting the dirty dishes, wiping the tables and doing the washing up. Ella did almost all the baking. She had the touch, her grandmother said.

It was the highest compliment a baker could pay and she soon realized that making scones and bread and cakes might be difficult for other people but it was second nature to her. She soon became very proud that she could do these things so well without apparent effort and it didn't bore her.

No matter how many times she did these things she loved the glistening sugar and the smell of scones coming from the oven.

People queued to get into the café because word soon got round that it was the best place for morning coffee and afternoon tea in the whole of the small city.

Her grandmother was good on the till and at being nice to people. Ella kept busy so that she would not think about her mother dying and being laid beside her father in the churchyard, and how the stone which had been for him had her mother's name newly etched.

The café flourished. She put so much effort into everything, she did not sleep and would be up hours before everybody else, baking bread and buns so that she was able to open early for breakfast, something nobody else seemed to have thought of so that people came to the café because they had nowhere else to go and because the smells coming from the kitchen were so enticing.

She cooked bacon and left the door to the street open and the smell was too much for people to go past the door without stopping. They would come inside and have bacon and eggs, or bacon sandwiches, and very often toast and butter and marmalade to follow.

Ella liked making marmalade. She and her grandmother spent hours in the evening after the café was shut, at that early part of the year when the marmalade oranges came in and they would cut up the peel and boil the sugar and it was so satisfying pouring it into jars and having it cool and set.

One day, the winter after her mother died, she heard people talking in the café that Mr Wilson was thinking of retiring so when she had time she went downstairs to the hardware store and found Mr Wilson talking to a customer.

'Won't be here much longer now,' he said, 'I'm getting too old and my wife isn't well.'

Ella waited until the customer had gone and the shop was empty and then she said, 'Did you mean what you said about retiring?'

He looked sharply at her.

'Now, young Ella, what has it to do with you?'

'It might have a lot to do with me if the place is vacant. Did you mean it, Mr Wilson, or is it just an idea for the future?'

'Are you thinking you might expand the café?'

'I thought we might, yes.'

He smiled.

'You'll make a fair businesswoman yet, you will. No, it's the truth. I've had enough and I've got some put by. I can't stand on these poor feet all day any longer and if I never see another screwdriver, pot or pan for sale I'll end my days happy.'

Ella ran upstairs. Her grandmother was in the office, poring over the accounts, at the top of the house.

'Don't bother with those, Grandma, I'll do them later.'

'I can't see as well as I could,' her grandmother said.

Ella told her about what Mr Wilson said.

'We could do with the space.'

'We'd be running up and downstairs all day.'

'Not you, Grandma, the waitresses. We'll employ another one. There's no reason at all why we shouldn't have the café on two levels.'

'People won't like it.'

'They will like it because we'll be able to pack lots more people in. At the moment we've got queues and in the cold weather or when it's too hot people don't want to wait. We could rent Mr Wilson's place. We could get a dumb waiter fitted. I think we should do something about it now before somebody else wants the shop.'

Mr Wilson retired, they took on the downstairs and another waitress, Gloria, to help and they began to make money. The Silver Street Café became one of the places where people wanted to be.

The university wives would come to the café for coffee and cake. Ella made chocolate cake with coffee icing and coffee cake with chocolate icing and date and walnut, carrot cake, and ginger cake in loaf tins.

Young men would bring their fiancées and those who were courting would come for lunch, for the egg and ham pies and home-made soup. Ella made soup with whatever was in season and she knew it was a novelty. Usually women only made broth. Ella made carrot soup, leek and potato, and onion, dark and caramel coloured from brown sugar.

The older women would come in groups and the young mothers would bring their children in for afternoon tea. Ella made gingerbread men for the children and teacakes for their mothers. She only wished she had sufficient energy to open in the evenings, she felt certain there was another kind of trade just waiting for her to turn her hand to it.

After the café was closed she and her grandmother would eat. They never ate pies or cakes, they always ate meat and vege-tables. Her grandmother was very good at dinners and she loved cooking, she made stew in the cold autumn and winter days and even in the summer if it was wet, and it was the only thing they had to look forward to because they went to bed early; her grandmother because she was always worn out by the labour and Ella because she needed to get up before five to start the next day.

The only free time she had was on Sundays

and then she would go to the cathedral, to Matins for morning prayer, and to light candles for her mother and father. She liked the walk through the Market Place and up Saddler Street and on to Palace Green and it was always beautiful no matter what the weather.

She loved the way that the cathedral was so welcoming, always open for people, providing refuge over the years. Inside it was so cool and dark and the stained glass windows threw coloured sunbeams on to the stone floor. In the dark winter days she liked going in because the candles flickered and burned in the sweet gloom at the front, and the people who ran the cathedral were friendly and got to know her well and would smile and acknowledge her. The cathedral, Ella thought, was just as much her home as the café.

It didn't cost anything to go in and you could light a candle and sit there and talk to God if you wanted to or if you didn't want to that was all right as well. Nobody bothered you. You didn't have to be quiet and there was always something happening there as though God was busy and had lots of things going on around him.

She didn't always pay much attention; she would sit there and remember what life had been like at Swan Island, her happy childhood, life with her parents. She would remember them, think of them, hope they were happy in heaven. Sometimes she talked to her mother, apologizing for not having stayed at school longer, for not reading more, for not being the kind of person they would have admired.

She thought her father would have appreciated her business sense and the way that she had made the café so successful and in time, she thought, I might meet a man and fall in love and have children and my mother would surely have wanted that for me, that was what she had when she was so very happy herself.

Even though it didn't last, it was only eleven or twelve years out of her life, her mother had had that and Ella promised herself that she would too. She wouldn't go on working at the café her whole life. Somebody would come along and she would fall in love and they would be married and everything would be all right again.

In the meanwhile, on Saturday nights when she was getting ready to go to bed she was aware of the noise beneath the windows of the café in Silver Street; young people going out in couples, laughing and talking and walking hand in hand from somewhere close by. She would hear music and knew they were going dancing.

She tried not to torture herself with the idea that they went back to their families later. She knew that many people did nothing of the sort and that many young women were in a worse state than she was. Some plied their trade of a Saturday night in the shadows of Elvet Bridge, so people said, and she'd heard of others who were too poor to eat well or have any of the comforts that she and her grandmother managed.

But it did not feel like that on the loneliness of Saturday nights, when the young men walked down the winding road towards Framwellgate with their sweethearts or when they were married in the cathedral or St Nicholas Church in the Market Place where she sometimes went to evensong. She envied them so much and even though she knew it was wrong to do so she could not help the feelings.

Sometimes girls she had gone to school with called in at the café with their friends and she could see how they had gone on at school. Some of them were going to become teachers and a small number were going to university. She envied those girls most of all.

They spoke excitedly of their plans and their studies and Ella would go back into the kitchen and want to never ever bake another scone, she was so tired of the repetition.

She tried introducing new ideas but people wanted to stick to the old ones and her life went on and on, over and over, until she did not think she could stand the monotony of it any longer. And then the feelings would pass and she would find again the joy in her work and be glad that she was in charge of her own business, at least that was how it felt and that was good.

And then in the late afternoon one summer a young man came into the café with his mother. He was taking her out for tea. Ella had never seen them before but the moment she saw him she knew she would want to see him again. The woman she did not pay much attention to except to note – and Ella was an expert by then – that she was probably a university wife, she spoke in a refined voice and was very confident.

He was lovely with dancing brown eyes and thick brown hair. He smiled at her straight away and when she asked him what they would like he said, 'Everything. Twice,' which made her smile and his mother told him not to talk nonsense but that everything was good and they would have sandwiches and cakes and some tea.

He kept glancing across at her. It was lucky in a way that she was there. She had two trained waitresses and she rarely got out of the kitchen as there was so much baking to do. However Winnie hadn't turned up because her mother wasn't well (and Ella knew how that felt) and the other girl, Gloria, was even now putting on her coat because she thought she had a cold coming on and cafés were no place for people with colds. So Ella had come out of the kitchen and put on an apron and was enjoying waiting on people because she did it so little these days.

She had, in any case, finished baking for the day and even though she would have to start with the accounts when the place was shut and rise even earlier in case neither woman was able to come in the following day, she was happy to be there with her customers.

She liked the contented sounds that people made and took pleasure in the fact that she had contributed towards it. She liked to see them tucking into their cakes and pies and their cups of tea. She liked the clatter of the cutlery, the sound of cups, saucers and plates being used and how they talked and smiled and enjoyed being in her café.

She paid no more attention to the young man and his mother because her grandmother appeared and gave them their bill, but the following day he was back again and since she was still short-staffed Ella was serving again. He was by himself and he lingered.

Eventually she had to go over to him and say, 'We're closing now. Perhaps you would like to come back tomorrow.'

'I would like to come back every day if

you're going to be here.'

Ella didn't know what to say.

'I'm Jack Welsh. What are you called?'

'Ella Armstrong.'

'How do you do?' he said, as though they were meeting for the first time. 'You wouldn't like to go to the pictures with me, I suppose?'

'I have a lot to do.'

'I could come back later.'

'Even then.'

'What about Saturday?'

'Saturday,' Ella said, trembling at the very idea, 'would be wonderful.'

Seven

Then he had gone she did all the things she still had to and was very tired by the time she finally tramped upstairs for her evening meal. She could hardly eat it and she wondered whether she would manage Saturday evening and she was not sure how to broach it with her grandmother. However, when she mentioned it to her grandmother, she seemed pleased.

'You spend far too much time working. You never go anywhere,' she said. 'Get yourself out for an hour or two and have a good time. He must be a very nice young man.'

'How do you know that?'

'I think his father is some kind of professor at the university. I know his mother slightly. She's been coming here for tea for years.'

'Grandma, you noticed.'

'I have to keep an eye on you,' her grandma said, but her eyes twinkled.

Ella could not help being impressed. To think that his father was so important and clever and he occupied one of those wonderful places that she could never aspire to. Perhaps Jack would become a professor of some kind and they would be invited to wonderfully clever parties where people would talk about books and paintings and music, all the things she knew nothing about and had rarely encountered. His family might live in a lovely house in the town and they would know lots of like-minded people.

By bedtime she had herself married to him and she had to laugh because it was all so ridiculous. She hardly knew him, she might never know him well.

She thought Saturday would never arrive. When it did she felt like running upstairs and hiding but she had not been out for so long she was excited too. She went outside when she heard him knocking on the door and he had a car, a low slung red sports car. Ella stared hard.

'Isn't she beautiful?' he said. 'Get in.'

It was a warm night and the hood was down. They drove across the bridge and up North Road and out into the country.

'It's too nice an evening to be inside,' he said. 'Let's go for a drive.'

Ella was happy to do that. The car picked up speed and they drove away from Durham and into the country, down the banks from the high ground into the dale, where the views were of the trees which followed the river and the small farms and the high hills in the far distance which led to the moors. They stopped at a little pub in Wolsingham, the first village of the dale; the Bay Horse was at the bottom of the last big bank, and they sat outside, drinking and talking.

People passing by stopped to admire the car and Jack chatted about the car, and about his friends, and Ella was content with her half of beer and the novelty of being away from the town and her work and even, she thought guiltily, her grandmother.

On the way back they stopped.

'What are we doing?' she said.

They were sitting on top of the hill looking down into the dale and the lights were beginning to come on in the houses. He leaned over and kissed her. Ella hadn't been kissed before but she hoped it was going to happen many times in the future. Jack's kisses were wonderful.

They drove back and all the lights were on in the houses by then and when she got out of the car and unlocked the door and went up the stairs her grandmother was standing at the top.

'Oh, I was worried. You're so late. I thought something had happened to you.'

Ella ran up the stairs and kissed her.

'I'm fine, Grandma, nothing to worry about at all. I had a wonderful time.'

She could not sleep for thinking about Jack: the car, the kisses, her freedom. She had a long lie-in the next day and had plenty of time to think about him because he didn't get in touch. Every day that week she thought he would come to the café but there was no sign of him. By Friday she was disappointed and beginning to wonder what she had done wrong.

Saturday was a very long day. Both women were back to work by then so Ella had only the usual amount to do and for once it was not enough to keep her mind away from Jack. She was closing up when she heard somebody running up the stairs. He arrived, breathless, at the top.

'Ella,' he said, 'are we going out tonight?'

Somehow she felt as though she ought to have said no, but she couldn't remember the word and the idea of sitting around with her grandmother for the evening was not something she thought she could have managed.

Her grandmother declared that she was going up Claypath to see some friends and she had been going to ask Ella to come with her, but she hadn't liked to as she knew how Ella was obviously so keen to go out with the young man.

Ella kissed her, flew upstairs to change, and when Jack came for her in an hour she was ready and waiting.

This time it was not a fair night, it was raining so they couldn't have the hood down and she was rather inclined to say that she would like to go to the pictures but he wanted to drive to another little pub and they did so. On the way back they stopped and he kissed Ella until she couldn't think, and then he wanted to put his hands on her body and she wouldn't let him. She couldn't even contemplate such a thing.

'What's wrong with you?' he asked.

'Nothing, I just ... nothing.'

He took her home and this time Ella wasn't as excited as she had been the first time. She felt as though the whole thing was going beyond her control and she could not respond when her grandmother asked her whether she had had a good time. Her grandma said nothing other than that she had had two glasses of port and was ready to go to bed.

It turned into a pattern that week when he

arrived even later on the Saturday evening and Ella very stiffly told him that she could not go out with him. Jack seemed surprised.

'Are you doing something else?'

'Yes.' She concentrated on putting the chairs on to the tables. To her consternation he started to help her. 'I can do it.'

'Ella, look. I'm sorry if I'm not getting this right but I like you a lot and ... I really want to see you. Please come out with me.'

'You aren't happy unless you're ... getting hold of me.'

He grinned.

'That's what men do, or try to do. Sorry. I will behave like an angel if you will come out with me. Tell me what you would like to do?'

'I would like to go to the pictures.'

'All right then, we will. And we won't even sit at the back. We'll sit in the front row and eat sweets like the children do.'

Charm, that was the word for it, Ella thought, Jack had charm, lots and lots of it. And he was sincere, she could see. They sat in the front row and he bought her chocolates and didn't even try to hold her hand.

Afterwards they walked to the nearest pub and he bought her gin and tonic. Ella had never tasted anything like that but she remembered her mother drinking it.

'It isn't what I asked for,' she said.

'Just try it. I think you'll like it,' Jack said, smiling and sitting down.

The smell was enough to transport her back to her childhood, her mother leaning over her and kissing her goodnight. The taste was wonderful. Jack offered her a cigarette. She had never smoked either and she felt wicked and self-indulgent. He walked her back to the outside door of the café and kissed her neatly and carefully and then she was disappointed.

You stupid person, she told herself as she wafted up the stairs, do you know what you want or are you just the kind of girl for whom nothing is sufficient?

That week she didn't worry about him coming in to see her, she just expected she would have to wait until early Saturday evening, and then on Thursday at lunch-time, when they were very busy and she was in the kitchen, she heard Gloria shouting through.

'There's a lad for you,' Gloria called.

When she looked up Jack appeared at the kitchen door with an armful of flowers, dahlias, spiky, red and yellow.

'I pinched them from my ma's garden,' he said. 'Are we going out Saturday then?'

It seemed strange to her that a professor's son should talk like Jack, so freely, so casually, as though he seemed to want to be disassociated from whatever his parents were but perhaps that was what some people wanted. She would have given anything in the world to have her parents, to be their daughter, to be like them, to be able to claim them as hers.

Her grandmother, however, was impressed and took the flowers from her and put them in a huge cut-glass vase.

'What a nice young man,' she said.

He took her to meet some of his friends. He seemed to have so many. Every pub they went into somebody called his name or came over to clap him on the back and say hello. Ella liked that he was so popular but she began to wish very much that she could have him to herself and would suggest that they go to other places so that he would not know anybody or to the cinema.

They began to go out more often. She could not take up too much time in this way or her work would suffer but it was difficult to say no when she had spent so many months at the café without a break.

Her grandmother encouraged her, saying that they would manage, but she did not want her grandmother to have to do too much, she was getting too old for that. So Ella sometimes had to turn him down and she had a feeling that when she wouldn't go he went out anyway and she began to resent the time they spent apart.

'Do you see other girls when you aren't with me?' she asked, and he laughed and said that he did nothing of the kind but she wasn't sure she believed him. Jack wasn't the sort of lad to sit around waiting for anybody.

He saw her grandmother at the café and often now he would drop in about half an hour before they closed and her grandmother would insist on giving him tea and he was always hungry. He did not suggest she met his parents and when she mentioned it he brushed it aside

'Why don't you want me to meet your parents?' she asked, one Saturday night when it was late and they had come home and were drinking coffee. Her grandmother had gone to bed.

'You'd have nothing in common with them.'

'Do you mean you think they wouldn't like me?'

He assured her he meant nothing of the kind.

'Your mother seemed very nice.' Thinking about it Ella thought Mrs Welsh had not been back since the first time she had seen Jack at the café but perhaps she came when Ella was in the kitchen.

There would be no reason for her to stop coming unless she regretted having taken her son there because of what had happened since. Maybe he hadn't told his parents about her at all in which case there was no reason for his mother not to come there.

She questioned Winnie and Gloria and they seemed to think Mrs Welsh had not been in lately.

'Funny,' Gloria said, 'she used to come in at least once a week.'

None of that brought Ella any comfort.

If it was serious, if they were thinking about getting married, she would need to meet them but they were not thinking of such things so it didn't matter. That was what she told herself anyway.

Soon it was nearly Christmas.

'What's Jack buying you for Christmas then?' Gloria asked, one Monday afternoon when the rush was over and they were closing up for the day.

'I don't know.'

'Something nice, eh, seeing as how his family has money.'

'I don't know that they have.'

Gloria looked knowingly at her.

'His mam came from a wealthy family so they do have even though his dad only works at the university.'

This was the very opposite view that Ella had taken of the situation and it made her smile.

'Well, you must have known they did have,' Gloria said. 'Seeing as how he has that sports car and everything. A lass who lives near me, Molly, she used to go out with him. Gave him up.'

'Why was that?' Ella asked.

'She didn't say,' Gloria said and Ella was very inclined to make further enquiries but thought it better not to. She and Gloria no doubt had very different ideas about what made a couple. It could be that he had given up Molly but Molly did not care to admit to having been let down by a young man.

She did however mention this to Jack and was rather satisfied when instead of saying loftily that he had grown tired of her he said, 'Oh, yes, I remember Molly. Very pretty. She got bored with me, I think.'

Ella laughed to think that anybody could become bored when they were in Jack's company, but it was such a relief that Molly had given him up for something simple like that.

She thought a great deal about what Jack would buy her for Christmas but tried not to depend on anything. Why should he buy her anything at all? Maybe something very inexpensive. She didn't know what to get him. If she spent a lot of money that might be embarrassing but if she didn't buy him much it would look silly if he had gone to a lot of trouble.

She consulted her grandmother who suggested she might buy him a pair of driving gloves because Jack loved his car and anything to do with it would be a good idea, so that was what Ella did. They were expensive but she imagined it was a thoughtful present and he would be pleased.

The café would be closing down over Christmas and she was looking forward to the time off. She was even hoping that he might invite her to his home if they were having people over. She and her grandmother were always on their own at Christmas, and, while it was very pleasant not to have to work, it would be fun to meet new people and see what Jack's family were like.

Enquiries brought her no help. What were they doing?

Jack's brow furrowed. Nothing as far as he could remember.

'But what do you do on Christmas Day?' she asked.

They were sitting by the upstairs fire, it was late, her grandmother was in bed. She liked being in the living room with him, drinking coffee and hearing the noises beyond in the streets. She thought it would be like this if they were married. She must stop thinking like that.

'We invite all our boring relatives. If I had somewhere to go I would.'

'You could come here.'

He shook his head.

'No, I can't. My mother insists on my being there and it's the only thing I do all year. Besides, my uncle and aunt will be there.'

Jack worked for his uncle. His uncle had some kind of business in Newcastle but whenever she mentioned it he confused her by using a lot of words she didn't understand so she didn't like to enquire further. He made some kind of components for machinery, that was all she knew and it did well; his uncle was pleased with him.

'So when will I see you?' she asked.

'Oh, when things get back to normal. The day after Boxing Day I should think.'

On Christmas Eve, however, when she had closed the café and was thinking how nice it would be to finish he appeared in the doorway.

'I've got your Christmas present,' he said.

'I've got yours as well. It's upstairs. Have you time to come up?'

He did. Her grandmother brought them tea and a piece of fruit cake and then tactfully disappeared. Ella gave him the parcel and he unwrapped it very quickly and seemed pleased.

'That's exactly what I wanted,' he said.

Then he handed her a tiny square box. Ella stared. It wasn't wrapped and when he turned it around he flipped open the lid and inside was the kind of ring which any girl in her right mind would have given years of her life for. In the middle was a sapphire. To call it large was going too far but it was big enough to glint and shine. On either side of it was a smaller diamond. Ella wanted to cry. She began to shake.

He laughed. He took the ring from the box and put it on to the third finger of her left hand. It fitted perfectly.

'Will you marry me, Ella?' he asked.

'Oh, yes, I will,' she said and she got up and called for her grandma, who must have been hovering very close because she appeared in an instant.

She cuddled them both and said how pleased she was and how lovely for Ella to have found somebody like him. Jack said no, it was the other way round, he was lucky to have found Ella. It was only when she was seeing him to the door an hour later that Ella said, as they reached the cold night air, 'You haven't told your parents, have you?'

He paused.

'No, not yet.'

'Did they have other plans for you?'

He looked at her and smiled.

'I don't think so. They would probably think we're too young and besides, I was sure you would turn me down.'

'You couldn't have thought anything of the kind,' Ella said, laughing.

'Don't worry, I'll tell them tomorrow and you'll have to come over in the next day or two and meet them.'

'That would be lovely,' Ella said.

After that she had a very nice Christmas

even though she didn't see him. It even snowed on Christmas Day and she and her grandmother sat over the fire, watched the snow falling and made lots of plans for the wedding.

'And when the children come along you won't be able to run the café any more,' her grandma said.

Ella panicked both at the idea of children and of changing her life so drastically.

'I'm not going to give it up ever. We'll manage.'

'You and Jack may want to go and live somewhere else.'

Ella got up and flung her arms around her grandmother.

'I'll never leave you, Grandma. Don't think such things. Jack may be important to me but I will always want you with me.'

Her grandmother cried a little, aided by too much sherry, and then they sat back down by the fire again and contemplated Ella's future happiness.

Gloria and Winnie both stared at the ring on Ella's finger. Not that she said anything and she did not wear it during the day but her grandmother had secretly told them both and they insisted on seeing it when they had a lull. It was the first day back after the Christmas holiday and it had been busy until almost half past five when it turned dark and cold and every sensible person had gone home. Then Ella put the ring on and they both looked.

'It's beautiful,' Winnie said, with a sigh.

'It must have cost him a fortune,' Gloria said, with an even bigger sigh. 'You are lucky.'

That was it, Ella thought, she was lucky. No girl in the world had a young man as nice as Jack. She was very much looking forward to seeing him. He would probably call in later. But Jack did not call in and although she waited all evening nothing happened until she wondered very much whether there was something wrong.

She waited all the next day but he did not turn up then either.

Two days later Jack had not appeared and Ella was not really very surprised when his mother turned up at the end of the afternoon.

Ella hadn't looked so closely at her the first time they met but she did now. She didn't look old enough to be Jack's mother was Ella's first thought. She looked almost like a little girl. She wore her hair longer than mothers generally did and she wore very young looking clothes, not fashionable clothes, rather clothes that she might have worn when she was ten. Ella chided herself, she did not know what mothers were like any more, all she had was her grandmother.

She didn't look anything like him except

that she was very slim, almost skinny and Jack was also slight. She wore big glasses which Ella decided didn't suit her, they made her look like an owl or as though she was trying to look clever and not quite managing it. She had bows in her hair and flat shoes on her feet and a flowered frock and dark stockings, and really Ella was astonished to think that somebody like Jack had a mother who would go out looking like that.

'I take it you are Ella Armstrong.'

'Yes, that's right,' Ella said.

'I am Professor Welsh's wife.'

What an odd way to think of yourself, Ella thought, as somebody's wife, like an appendage of them rather than a person as though her marital status was all she had. Perhaps it was all many women had. Winnie and Gloria were still there so Ella asked her whether she would like to come through into the kitchen.

'I want you to leave my son alone.'

Ella didn't know where to look or what to say.

'He is far too young to enter into an engagement and even if he weren't I wouldn't want him involved with someone like you.'

Winnie and Gloria were studiedly getting on with the clearing up.

'Please don't speak to me like that,' Ella said, becoming annoyed first that the woman had said such things and secondly that she had done so in public.

'I have spoken to Jack on this matter and told him that it is not acceptable to his father or to me. We want nothing to do with someone like you.'

'Someone like me? Are you upset that I run a business?'

'You have bad blood in you, the Armstrongs have always had bad blood. Your father was a disgrace to this city, to his family and his friends–'

'Get out,' Ella said.

'Men like that don't deserve–'

'I said "get out".' Ella made a move towards her and Mrs Welsh left abruptly.

Ella listened to the woman's footsteps and then she went into the kitchen and tried to still her trembling hands. She did not come back out and after a little while her grandmother put her head around the door.

'Ella? Gloria said there was a problem.'

'Mrs Welsh was here.'

'Yes, she said.'

'I didn't know people had talked about Daddy.'

'People always talk. Don't pay any mind to it,' her grandmother said. 'Why don't you come upstairs and I'll make you some tea? Gloria and Winnie have finished and gone and everything is done.'

'I've still got things to do here.'

'No, you haven't. Come along.'

With lagging steps she followed her grandmother upstairs and sat over the fire with tea and lemon drizzle cake which was their favourite. Her grandmother cut her a slice and made her eat it and insisted on her drinking a full cup of tea.

'She said he was a disgrace,' Ella said. 'He always seemed so wonderful to me but other people see him differently.'

'You saw him as a child would.'

Ella looked at her but for once her grandmother was avoiding her eyes.

'What do you mean? Didn't you want Mother to marry him?'

'No. No, I didn't.'

'Was he a bad man?'

'He wasn't bad, he was just ... careless.'

'With money?'

'Well–' her grandmother smiled in relief at the idea and then shook her head – 'that wasn't exactly what I had in mind. He was careless with your mother. He didn't look after her as I had hoped he would but I had thought he would not. She wouldn't be told, you see, she loved him.'

'So he got rid of our money and then killed himself?'

'It sounds so bald but yes, that's what he did. Your mother was heartbroken.'

'How did he...?'

'He took an overdose. He was on tablets from the doctor and he swallowed a bottle

91

of whisky and then the whole lot. She had done her best to keep them from him but when people are inclined that way there isn't much you can do. It was very difficult for her.'

'So she lost everything?'

'She lost him and Swan Island, but she didn't lose you. Children are the saving of us all.'

Except my father, Ella thought, but she didn't say anything. She didn't want to burden her grandmother any further.

She wondered what to do about Jack. Should she somehow send the ring back to his address? She waited for another two days, and then in the morning when they were busy he turned up among the crowd of people, and when she saw him he smiled and came over and took her aside.

'We're not going to let them stop us, Ella. I'm twenty-one. I can marry whoever I like.'

'What about your family?'

'You mean a lot more to me than anybody else in the world,' he said and kissed her. 'I'll sort the legalities out and you sort the church.'

Ella hesitated.

'Jack–'

'Everything will be fine,' he said, 'you'll see.'

Eight

Ella and Jack were married at St Nicholas Church in the Market Place on a cold wet day in January. There was a reception back at the café and all his friends came to the meal which Ella, Winnie and Gloria had prepared. Her grandmother had said stoutly that Jack must come and live with them. Ella had not said that Jack appeared to have no money; his parents had not come to the service and there was no question of even seeing them. Her small room suddenly became a lot smaller, thinking of Jack sharing it.

Her grandmother and Ella paid for everything. This seemed right. Traditionally the bride's parents paid. The reception became rather raucous, people sang and everybody was good humoured. All his friends had brought presents and Ella enjoyed herself very much.

She did not even wish his parents had been there, she did not care any more. She would make the best wife Jack could have, and then they would forgive her for anything her family might have done. Ella and Jack would be invited to tea at the pretty house in the Bailey where they lived, and there would be a party for them and everything would be fine, she was sure of it.

It was very late indeed when the last of the partygoers thanked her and left and she and Jack wended their way up the stairs. He was very drunk by then but she forgave him. Her grandmother had gone to bed. Ella locked up and followed Jack into the bedroom. She could have laughed. Instead of the scary, exciting night she had envisaged the groom was snoring on the bed.

'Jack...' she said, 'you're taking up all the space.'

He helpfully rolled over against the wall and Ella thought the best thing to do was just to leave him there so she put on her warmest nightdress, not very flattering, and got into bed.

He didn't stir. Ella found it difficult to sleep with someone else there but Jack soon stopped snoring, much to her relief, and continued to breathe evenly and deeply all night.

Finally, when she had heard the nearest clock strike four, Ella went to sleep and she was awoken by him saying close into her ear, 'Sorry, Ella. Not much of a wedding night.'

'There'll be lots more times.' She moved away because he smelled strongly of beer. She even wished she had the excuse that she needed to open the café but it was Sunday so she didn't.

She washed and dressed and went down to the kitchen. Her grandmother was already up and about. It was late.

Her grandmother made breakfast and Jack, also washed and dressed and looking rather sheepish, appeared to the smell of bacon and eggs, sat down at the table and wolfed down the whole lot plus three slices of bread and three cups of tea. Then he suggested they should go for a walk.

It was bitterly cold but fine by then. They didn't talk much, Ella put her hand through his arm and they went down the lane to the towpath, down the steps and along past the castle and cathedral walls, with the buildings high above and the windows of the castle glinting in the sunshine, past the old fulling mill and all the way around to Elvet Bridge. Snow began to fall on the towpath and into the river and on the roofs of the little houses making it look like it belonged in a fairytale.

They walked back and mid afternoon her grandmother made Sunday dinner and in the evening they sat over the fire until it was a respectable time to go to bed and this time Jack was sober and Ella was not tired or worried.

Her grandmother had put on the fire in the bedroom and as they lay in one another's arms by the light of it, Ella thought she was the luckiest person in the world.

Jack came back early from work one day in February. Ella was surprised. Usually he did not get in before six. He went straight upstairs without speaking so that when she followed him there she said, 'Is something wrong?'

'They got rid of me,' he said. 'I was apparently only filling in until my cousin came home and now he's home they don't want me any more. I was stupid enough to think that I mattered but after he's learned everything he can about my job...'

'You'll get another job,' she said.

He agreed. He went out looking for work, he said he was seeing contacts and friends who might be able to help him but they were always meeting in pubs and very often over the first couple of weeks he came back very much the worse for drink, and he spent the rest of the day in bed.

She told herself it wouldn't last, it was just until he was taken on by some new company and she looked in the newspapers for the kind of position Jack might be eligible for, but when she showed him the various jobs he laughed and said they were beneath him or they were not suitable.

A month went by and she said to him that perhaps he should make do with what he could get. They were in the bedroom, it was late at night, and he had once again spent most of the day in one of the pubs in the town and had no money so was obliged to ask her for some.

'What do you mean, take what I can get? I'm skilled, I can't just take anything. And it's not as though we're in need of the money, is it? This place is a goldmine.'

'That's not the point.'

Jack seemed on the verge of losing his temper. Blood came rushing to his face, she drew back slightly and then smiled and she thought it was one of the things she loved best about him, Jack always controlled his temper, unlike many men from what she had heard other women say.

'So what is the point, Little Miss Bossy?'

'You aren't doing anything.'

'No, and do you know what? It makes me want to do things.' He got hold of her and pulled her nightdress off, and kissed her and said silly things and put his hands on her until Ella could not even remember what the conversation had been about.

He could talk and kiss her out of her bad mood any time he wanted.

After another fortnight however she was inclined to say that if he couldn't find any-thing better to do he could help in the café.

'Doing what?' Jack said, lighting a cigarette 'I'd like some coffee and a piece of fruit cake if you're not doing anything.'

'Well, I don't mean sitting about drinking coffee all day.'

'I don't sit about and drink coffee all day. I'm going to the pub in a minute or two.'

Ella went upstairs. She knew that he didn't have any money, that in a little while he would come and ask her for some and that she would have to give it to him because he would kiss and tease her until she did. Jack bounded up the stairs.

'Let me have a few quid, Ella.'

'I haven't got any on me.'

'You must have.'

'I banked everything from yesterday this morning and it's early yet.'

'You must have known I would need some. I have no petrol in the car.'

'Walk then.'

'I promised to meet a very influential friend in Newcastle. He's my best friend. He's called Harry Reid. He's been working in the south and his father is a shipbuilder and they have a lot of pull.'

'That's what you say about everybody.'

'It's true, honestly it is.'

Ella said nothing.

'If you don't give me some money I'll have to sell the car. I can't use it if I have no petrol.'

'Then go ahead and sell it,' she said and walked out.

She didn't think he meant it. She didn't

see him again that day and it was very late when he came back. She was on the verge of going to bed. She heard the noise as he came in and that noise meant he was drunk again. She stood at the top of the stairs and as she went down she could see that there was somebody with him.

In the lamplight a tall slender young man looked up at her.

'Hello, Mrs Welsh. I'm Harry Reid,' he said.

She couldn't see him properly, all she could see were the shadows on the stairs but she could hear his voice and, oddly, it seemed to her that she had waited all her life to hear it. He did not sound like a southerner yet there was an intonation somewhere and yes, a touch of Tyneside, the beautiful lilt of the borders. He had, she thought, the most beautiful voice that she had ever heard.

She reached the ground floor and he was holding Jack up.

'Sorry to bring him back like this. He has had rather a lot to drink.'

'Can we get him up the stairs, do you suppose?' she said and Harry agreed and together they managed to get Jack as far as the sitting room where they let him down on to the sofa.

In the better light she could see Harry's face and there was almost something familiar about him, as though she understood his secrets and passions, had been aware of him as a child and would remember him as an old man and yet would always be fascinated.

It was nothing like she had ever felt for anybody before and it astonished her. He was dark haired with blue eyes and a pale skin. There was something in his face which Ella could not define, a vulnerability which she had never seen in Jack's face.

'He wanted my father to give him a job. I'm afraid I told him it wasn't very likely. My father is not the easiest of men and every time they meet Jack is drunk.'

'I'm sure it doesn't help,' she said.

'I think my father has forgotten what it's like to be young. Perhaps he never was.' He paused there and then he said, 'Jack's parents expected a good deal of him, you know. Maybe too much.'

'Did they?'

'His father is an important man in the academic world. He doesn't seem to comprehend that there are other worlds. Jack was very clever, you know, he won a scholarship, but they just wouldn't leave him alone so in the end he left.'

'Did you go to school together?'

'We did. That was where we met because I'm a Sunderland boy.'

'You don't sound it.'

'I have a granny who came from Shields

and I spent a lot of time there when I was a child. My granny was lovely.'

'My granny's like that.'

'You still have her? That's nice. The car is gone, I'm afraid. He sold it to a man in a pub so I had to bring him home. He'll be round for the paperwork in the morning. I should go. It was good to meet you, Mrs Welsh.'

'It was good to meet you too,' Ella said.

When he had gone, and he moved quietly for a man, down the steep stairs and out of the front door into the street, Ella left Jack lying on the sofa and she went to bed.

As she reached her bedroom and closed the door she thought, so that's what a really nice man is like and to think I never knew.

She told herself overnight that Harry Reid could not be as she saw him, it was just that she was angry with Jack and wished he would behave differently. She must be more understanding because Jack was very young, and if he had had such a difficult childhood and had failed to meet the high standards set by his parents it was not very surprising that he was kicking over the traces now.

The new owner of the car did indeed come around the following morning just before midday and Ella left Jack to deal with him.

When he came back up the stairs he called in at the kitchen and said, 'At least I won't have to ask you for any money now. It's not right when a man has to ask a woman.'

It was on the tip of Ella's tongue to tell him that he wouldn't have to ask for anything if he found some work and then she remembered what Harry Reid had said and stopped herself in time. She could not control Jack and doing so would mean that they would start to fight and that was not something she could endure, so she got on with her work and let it go.

That evening however when Jack came home she thought she heard a female voice outside and the day after a girl came into the café, a blonde young woman asking for him, so Gloria said.

'Asking for Jack?' Ella enquired.

'It isn't the first time,' Gloria said darkly and went back out of the kitchen.

There was a lot of talk about the possibility of a war that year. Ella tried not to think about it. They had already fought the war to end all wars but it appeared that a great many mistakes had been made and the rise of Hitler in Germany was not something anybody might feel comfortable about.

He seemed to want to take over the whole world or at least the whole of Europe and nobody was doing anything about it. When anybody suggested this they were told they were warmongering so Ella didn't say anything, but she began to sense a huge uneasiness everywhere.

She worked hard at the café. She gave up thinking that Jack would get a job and since he did not, she went on keeping them and doling out money to him. Her grandmother did not say anything, but Ella thought that she did not approve of the way Jack was behaving.

She lost the soft way that she had spoken to him when he and Ella had first met. Ella gave him as little as possible, just enough to keep his mood sunny and sufficient to get him enough beer to see him through the week.

He said he was bored at the café and she was glad when he did go to the pub. If not he would sit around the place complaining and if she asked for his help he was always going to give it but somehow never did.

She would think about him when she was clearing up in the evenings, or sitting down to have a cup of tea with her grandmother, and she envied him the lack of responsibility which enabled him to behave like this. It must be wonderful to care so little that you could happily go out night after night and have a good time and never give a thought to other people working.

He came back drunk and fell into bed and sometimes she thought she could smell perfume on him, but when she mentioned it he only said wearily, 'I've been to a pub, Ella, what do you expect?'

'With somebody?'

'With the lads of course.'

They went out together when Ella could spare the time and often on Saturday nights they met Harry and Agnes, Harry's girl-friend and other friends in the local dancehalls and pubs and Ella liked being there.

'Let's go on holiday,' Harry suggested in late summer when he had been away for many weeks, working in the south. 'We may not have another chance, the way things are going.'

Ella looked across the room in the pub to where Jack was standing with Agnes and half a dozen others. He was drunk. She knew the signs by now. Jack was a merry drunk, no-body objected. He had an arm around Agnes and she was nuzzling into his neck.

'How can we do that, you and Agnes aren't married,' Ella said.

'Jack and I could have one room and you and Agnes could have the other, that is if you wouldn't mind.'

'If he's going to drink like this I won't mind at all,' Ella said.

'We could go to the west coast of Scot-land. Have you ever been there?'

'I've never been to Scotland.'

Harry looked shocked.

'And it's so close,' he said. 'The border is only an hour away by car. We could call in at Gretna and Agnes and I could be married.'

He was joking she could see but she said, 'Don't you have to stay there three weeks?' suddenly alarmed at the idea that they might be thinking of it.

'I don't know. Three weeks could be a long time at Gretna. It isn't a big town,' he said.

Jack agreed to the idea of the holiday when he finally came back to her at closing time but then Jack always agreed to everything. It was one of the nicest things about him. Agnes when she came over had had far too much to drink. She thought it was a wonderful idea but she wanted to sleep in the same room as Harry who pointed out to her that she couldn't.

'Does he want to marry her?' Ella asked when it was late and Jack was face down in the pillows and almost asleep.

'Shouldn't think so. He has to be careful.'

'Why?'

Jack turned over and squinted at her.

'Because he's absolutely rolling in money and she knows it,' Jack said and went to sleep.

Nine

It was September when they drove to Scotland. Harry took his car. Ella sat in the front because she was car sick if she didn't and she liked sitting there with Harry. He pointed out various landmarks and it was such a pretty route into Scotland, the high hills around straight roads. They went through Glasgow – it had so many poor streets Ella couldn't help but look – and beyond it the hills and lochs.

It was a long way but they stopped for coffee and then for lunch and finally for tea and it was lovely for Ella because she was able to go to other restaurants and cafés and compare them with her own and find them wanting.

Agnes fell asleep on Jack's shoulder and Jack, having consumed half a bottle of whisky as they drove, was snoring. It was late evening, the roads were narrow with passing places and beyond was the bluest, clearest sea that Ella had ever seen.

Harry stopped the car and Ella saw for the first time the silver sands of Morar and she was enchanted. The shadows were falling fast, there was a slight breeze and the cool sand was light, fine, even under her feet. The waves were barely breaking halfway down the beach.

'Oh, Harry, it's beautiful,' she said.

'Isn't it? When I'm away, when I'm having a bad time I always think of it.'

'Have you been having a bad time?' she ventured.

He hesitated so that she thought she had been rude and then he said, 'My father has business concerns in Coventry. Coventry is fine but the business is in difficulty and I'm not very experienced at trying to get it back out of the problems so I make lots of mistakes and my father isn't interested in mistakes. I wanted to be a teacher but he wouldn't hear of it. I wasn't even allowed to go to university though all my friends went.' He smiled. 'You see Jack and I are the very opposite of one another. Together we make one decent man.'

'I think you make a very decent man all by yourself,' Ella said and then had to look away in case he misunderstood. The trouble was she had discovered that she would do almost anything to be in his presence and it was making everything very embarrassing and also wonderful.

The little bed and breakfast they found had short beds, tiny rooms which were meant to be doubles, and big breakfasts. Jack and Agnes did not want breakfast. After trying to persuade Agnes to come down to breakfast the first two days Ella gave up on her and went down herself. Jack had always drunk too much the previous night so she and Harry breakfasted together by the window on bacon and eggs and then went for long walks on the sands. He was easy to be with, didn't talk too much or too little and she liked his conversation.

By lunchtime the others would have emerged and they usually hired a boat and went fishing. Harry even managed to persuade them to go fishing at night, though Jack protested they were wasting good drinking time. They hired fishing rods for the evening and she could see the mackerel in the clear water and she enjoyed the night and the moon and the warmth.

Most evenings they went to the local pub where Jack drank all different kinds of whisky and they played darts and dominoes. There was even a dance one night and sometimes there was music from local musicians. Ella hadn't had a holiday since her early childhood and wished she did not have to go back to running the café, though she worried in case her grandmother, Winnie and Gloria weren't managing. Her grandmother had practically needed to push her out of the door, saying, 'The place won't fall down if you go away for a week. Get yourself to Scotland and have a good time.'

They were away ten days. On the very last day she and Harry went walking on the sands as usual and came back in time for lunch and she ran up the stairs and straight into her bedroom to find her husband in bed with Agnes. She didn't wait to hear any details. As far as she could judge they were asleep.

She ran back downstairs, didn't stop in case Harry was about and would request an explanation. She went outside and on to the beach and there she cried.

It was some time later when Jack came down on the sands, dressed, his hair all over the place, a cigarette in his hand. He ran a hand through his hair and stupidly she thought how romantic he looked, his clothes creased and his eyes still full of sleep. She didn't say anything, she didn't even acknowledge him.

'We weren't doing anything,' he said.

'Of course not.'

'It's not of course not, Ella. You left that room like you were being chased by wasps.'

It was almost a funny image but Ella didn't think anything was funny and was obliged to push the tears away before they reached her cheeks.

'I suppose you've been doing that every morning while I've been out.'

'What, sleeping?'

'Don't be obtuse.'

'What do I know?' he said, finishing the cigarette and throwing it down into the sand. 'Maybe you and Harry have been having it off on the beach. You seem to like him more than you like me anyway.'

'That's not true.'

'Isn't it?' He looked shrewdly at her. 'Let's be honest, you wish you hadn't married me now.'

'I just wish you would be different.'

'How many hundreds of women have married men and then tried to change them?'

'You aren't going to make me take the blame for this,' she said, trying to leave and he stopped her.

'You don't like me. You don't like me in bed and you don't like me out of it. I wasn't doing anything. After all that whisky I'd be pushed to climb on to a horse, never mind a woman—'

'Don't be vulgar.'

'I am vulgar. As I recall it was what you liked about me to begin with.'

'It wasn't.'

'No? What did you like about me, Ella, the fact that I was a professor's son? Did you think we were going to live that ghastly prissy life where people go around asking one another whether they prefer Dickens to Henry James and telling their friends how much they despise Hardy? It isn't much of a life, believe me, I know, I've lived it. I'd rather be drunk and vulgar than a pseudo-intellectual like them.'

'Do you know something, Jack, that's the first intelligent remark I think I've ever heard you make. You are very clever, but you hide it because you can't be one of the lads if you let people know what you're really like. Why don't you grow up?'

'I am,' he said, 'that's the trouble. There are other worlds than Durham. There are better places to be and better people to be with. I will go out and get a job as you are so obviously desperate for me to do, but you needn't think I'm going to hang around here for ever because I am extremely tired of fighting against my parents and the other people who want me to take life so seriously that I'm in danger of suffocating.' With that he walked away.

It wasn't long before Agnes arrived.

'Ella, we weren't doing anything. I went in there to see if you were there and we talked and I'd had too much to drink the night before and I went to sleep.'

'I really don't care.'

'Yes, you do. I'm sorry if you think I want your husband. If you want to cast aspersions anywhere do it to that bastard Harry Reid because he won't marry me. We've been going around forever and I've seen other girls with rings on their fingers and we've been to lots of weddings. I thought he loved me. He keeps me hanging on and I hate it.' She burst into tears. 'If you want the truth your husband is very keen on lots of other women, it isn't just me he makes up to.'

It was a good thing that it was their last day. Ella didn't want ruined memories of their holiday and so she obliterated that last day from her mind and kept the good memories of being there set like stone in her memory, to be stored up with all the other precious memories, the ones she could bear.

Ten

'Where's Agnes?'

It was the following week and they were at home. She had been glad to get there, though she and Jack had scarcely spoken since. It had seemed a good idea to go out with him when he offered to take her but they were in the dance hall and as usual he was across the room talking to other people as if he preferred their company which no doubt he did. She wondered why he had asked her if he didn't want her there. Harry had come across when she came in.

'It isn't because of Scotland, is it? I mean I honestly don't think anything happened between them,' she went on when he didn't reply. He still didn't say anything.

'She isn't poorly, is she?'

'Agnes has given me up,' he said, looking beyond her.

'I'm not really surprised, to be honest,' Ella said. 'You've been going together for a long time.'

'She always saw other people as well as me,' he said, 'and then I met someone else.'

'Then why don't you have whoever it is here with you now?'

'That's difficult,' he said.

'Why?'

He looked past her and dragged hard on the cigarette he was smoking.

'She's married.'

'Married? Oh, how awful.' Her heart beat hard.

'Yes, isn't it?' he said, taking the cigarette and pushing it down and down into the glass ashtray on the bar so hard that several other cigarette stubs were pushed over the top and spilled grey ash on to the wooden surface of the bar top.

'Does she feel the same way about you?'

'No.'

'Harry—'

He smiled and said, 'Why don't you dance with me?'

The music was soft and slow. Close in his arms Ella shut her eyes, afraid that she would cry. Nobody spoke. She wished the music would go on and on and yet she felt as though she was betraying her husband even though she tried not to think of Harry at all. They danced twice and then went back to the bar and he ordered another gin and tonic for her.

He gave her a cigarette and then he said, 'And even if she did her husband is my best friend, has been since I was seven and crying into my pillow at prep school. I feel that we shall always be friends.'

Ella didn't feel anything of the kind. She felt frustrated, angry at fate for dealing her such a hand. She gazed across to where Jack was talking and laughing and drinking with his friends. She smiled blithely at Harry and then she went over to her husband and he put his arm around her, kissed her absently on the cheek and carried on talking as before.

When they got home he said, 'Agnes wasn't there. Do you think she's still upset about Scotland?'

'Why should she be? You said yourself there was nothing in it,' Ella said, turning away before she undressed.

'Why are you doing that?' Jack said.

'Call it natural modesty.'

'I'll call it nothing of the sort,' he said and grabbed her and pulled her down on to the bed and said, in an almost sober voice,

'There was nothing to it, Ella. There'll never be anybody for me but you. I love you very much, much more, I'm afraid than you love me. And I'm going to go out and get a job.'

'I wish you would,' Ella said.

Ella was glad that they had had a holiday in Scotland because things altered so quickly. She had known that it was inevitable they would become involved in the war, and in some ways she was relieved because it seemed so awful to stand about and do nothing while other people were suffering so much, but she did not take the common view that it wouldn't last long.

She was busy so that most of the time she could not believe what was happening and for long hours at once she didn't think about it, she just got on with the work. So she was not prepared for the afternoon when Jack ran up the stairs, into the kitchen with Harry and announced, 'We've joined up. The army.'

Ella didn't know what to say. Jack kissed her and ran up the second flight of stairs to tell her grandma. Harry looked at her.

'Don't tell me. He was drunk and you thought you had to go with him,' she said.

'Something like that. But then it is the right thing to do, Ella. If people our age don't offer they'll have nobody to fight, will they?'

'I suppose not.' Ella suddenly felt faint

and had to sit down. When she had told Jack to go out and get a job she had not expected this.

'He's so excited,' Harry said.

'Yes, I can see.' At least, she thought, it will stop him from drinking so much.

They went off to Brancepeth, only a few miles away, to train and Ella was left to think about the café and try to do all the right things as the hot summer took over and then early autumn. To begin with there were a great many mushrooms in the fields round about. She made wonderful mushroom soup for the café and also found ways of bottling them and drying them so that they would last through the winter.

The early autumn fruits were plentiful and when they had time off she and her grandmother went out and gathered hawthorn and elderflowers for wine and blackberries and then elderberries to make jam.

She and her grandmother looked at the scrubby patch of garden beyond the bottom of the yard, which belonged to the café, and her grandmother bought a rabbit hutch, a small hen cree and even talked about getting a goat for milk and cheese.

Ella managed to talk her out of that, it wasn't practical she said and her grandmother said that in wartime people must learn to be practical, and they began digging over the ground because when the frost came it would break it up and they would be able to plant all kinds of vegetables.

Friends who lived in the country or had big gardens bottled plums or made jam and stored apples and pears in sand or newspaper. Everything which could be preserved was.

During the training at Brancepeth Jack had time off and he would come home. Ella thought he probably had more time off than he told her, that he did not always come home when he was free. She began to think about those nights when he had come home smelling of perfume and she had suspected that he was with other women. She had told herself at the time that she was stupid and needlessly suspected him, but now she could not be sure whether he had slept with Agnes in Scotland. Her memories were thankfully blurred.

She was clearing up in the café late one Friday evening when she heard someone knocking on the outside door so she left the table she had been wiping and went down the steep stairs and opened the door.

Harry stood outside and there was a man behind him, both in uniform. She had still not grown used to the idea of the men like that and she hesitated. She could not see Jack, she found herself scanning the dark street and it was black in the hall behind her, as it should have been but even so she could not see him.

'Ella, may we come in?'

She let them go past her and closed the door.

'Is something wrong?'

'Yes,' he said gently, 'maybe we should go upstairs.'

The light at the top was showing now and in it she could see her grandmother's silhouette. Her grandmother worried about the dark and about answering the door to people they didn't know.

'It's ... it's Harry, Grandma.'

They went upstairs and into the little sitting room and there Harry introduced the other man. Afterwards Ella could never remember his name or what he looked like. Her heart was like the moon on a frosty night, she felt as though it had an icy ring around it. Her hands would not keep still and she wanted to sit down and then didn't as though her legs would not carry her but she knew she would feel sick if she sat.

'There has been an accident, Mrs Welsh,' the man said.

'An accident?'

'Yes. I'm so sorry to have to tell you this but your husband is dead.'

Ella thought it was a terrible joke, Jack could not have died, not when he was so difficult and had so many faults and was so young and merry and...

Harry came over and took hold of her hands.

'It was another young man, a friend. He didn't mean to, the gun went off and ... they weren't very experienced, some of them and ... he shot Jack without meaning to.'

Who had said, Ella thought in wild dismay, that there was no such thing as an accident. It must have been some stupid blundering misguided fool.

'And he's dead?'

'Yes.'

'It wasn't a mistake?'

'No.'

'Are you sure?'

'Quite sure.'

Her grandmother was standing in the doorway. She sat down now with a thump which made the sofa move.

'Oh, my dear,' was all she said.

There was more. Ella could see from the look in Harry's white, shocked face that there was something else.

'The young man who...' It was the officer who spoke and stopped and then started up again and failed.

'Victor Nolan,' Harry said, 'when he realized what he had done he killed himself.'

Ella stared into Harry's blue eyes.

'But if he didn't mean to do it ... why did they let him have a gun after that?'

'He hanged himself, Mrs Welsh,' the

officer said.

Ella put both hands over her face.

'No, no,' she said.

After Jack died it seemed to Ella that if it had not been for Harry she would have gone insane. Could it be that she had died? She was convinced that death felt this way, numb nothingness but Harry was there, he seemed to spend his entire time at her elbow so that she did not have to turn to see him.

They were not even parted at night. She thought she would never sleep again, it was a place where other people went. She and Harry sat over the fire that first night with her grandma and drank Scotch which he had brought with him.

She felt as though the war was no longer anything to do with them which was strange because it had intruded upon and devastated their lives for the first time. It didn't matter any more, she didn't care.

The café stayed open. Gloria and Winnie were there, her grandma supervised. Harry organized the funeral. Only one question bothered Ella.

'Did you tell Jack's parents?'

'Yes.'

'Before you told me?' she guessed.

'I didn't want to leave you alone after I told you and it wasn't fair to them to have a stranger tell them. It's going to be just as hard on them. You always think there'll be another day when you can forgive one another and get together. They have to live the rest of their lives knowing what they did.'

'With a bit of luck they'll blame me: That should make it easier for them,' she said.

'Are you blaming them?'

'No, I'm blaming the war. It knows how to fight back.'

The vicar arrived, saying the right things. He seemed a particularly nice man. That made things easier. He didn't say anything stupid, he had the extraordinary gift of hitting at the middle ground somehow and her grandma chose the hymns because she knew such things and Ella was grateful.

When she mentioned the vicar's tact over a cup of tea, her grandma said, 'I expect he's had lots of practice.'

'I'm sure it doesn't make the difference with some people,' Ella said.

'My father used to say "you get two types of clergymen, church fillers and church emptiers", I think the vicar is most definitely a church filler, don't you?'

Over whisky, two nights later, when her grandmother had gone to bed she said to Harry, 'Do you think I should go and see his parents?'

'No.'

'Don't you think it would make things better?'

Harry fidgeted for a few moments and then he said, 'No.'

'They've already said they don't want to see me, haven't they?' Ella guessed.

Harry shifted slightly in his seat.

'Yes, they have. I heard from my CO that they aren't coming to the funeral.'

The tears slipped down Ella's face.

'Why not? Jack would have wanted them there.'

'He isn't here to want anything, Ella,' Harry said gently, 'and there is no reason why you should get upset about them. They're adults, they have to face the consequences of their actions.'

'He was their only child.'

'You've lost your husband,' Harry said.

'How could they love him so little that they gave up on him like that?' Ella said, getting to her feet because she could bear to sit still no longer. 'I would have given anything to have had my parents while I grew up. When I met Jack I thought they would ask me to their house and be kind to me. They didn't like me. His mother came to the café and told me I had bad blood and I should leave Jack alone. I was in love for the first time. I so much wanted it to be right.'

'You got it right,' Harry said. 'You cannot control what anybody else does.'

'I wanted that stuffy life so much,' Ella said with a touch of humour. 'The insular life of the university. His mother referred to herself as Professor Welsh's wife. I think I envied her.'

'Oh, hell. How ghastly. You can't have done,' Harry said, coming to her and putting an arm around her shoulders.

Ella looked bravely into his eyes.

'I want to go and see Mrs Nolan.'

'Do you think you should?'

'Yes. Can you set it up?'

'If you like,' he said.

The Nolans lived in a tiny pit village just beyond the town. Harry got his hands on a car and drove her there. There wasn't much to it, pit heaps, the pit itself, several grimy rows of colliery houses. The car bumped itself up the unmade back lane. Ella wasn't sure she wanted to go to the front door.

'Do you want me to come in with you?' Harry said as he stopped the car.

'No.'

The gate wasn't fastened. Ella walked up the bare, narrow yard and knocked firmly on the door. It was opened by a fat, middle-aged woman.

'I'm Ella Welsh. I'd like to see Mrs Nolan, Victor Nolan's wife.'

'She won't see nobody.'

'Can you tell her please that I'm here?'

The woman hesitated, recognition dawning in her face, followed by horror.

'Please,' Ella said.

'I'll see,' she said.

The door closed. Ella waited. For several minutes she thought it would not open again and then it did.

'You can come through,' the woman said.

Ella stepped inside and then down another step into the kitchen and through there. A young woman with a baby in her arms was standing by the fire. She could have been no more than eighteen: tiny, dark, white-faced, scared.

'Mrs Nolan? I'm Ella Welsh. I just wanted to come.'

'What for?' The girl's eyes showed her dismay.

'To say that I'm sorry.'

'It was an accident,' the girl said quickly.

'Yes, I know.'

'It was just an accident,' she said again, as though Ella had hardly spoken. 'He couldn't live with it. They were friends, you see.'

'Yes, I see.'

'I couldn't have lived with it either, could you?' The tears began to pour down her face.

'How old is the baby?'

'Six months.'

'She's beautiful.'

'Mrs Welsh, I'm ever so sorry.'

'May I hold her?'

Reluctantly the girl gave the baby to Ella. This girl was luckier than she had been, Ella thought, she had something left of her husband.

'Does she look like him?'

The girl nodded.

'She does. Would you – would you like some tea?'

Ella thought it was the kindest thing anybody had ever said to her.

'Thank you, I'd better not. I have a car waiting outside. Please don't worry about what happened and don't let there be any bad feeling between us. We've lost our husbands to the war and many other people will follow, I'm sure they will. I have the café in Silver Street. I would like it if, when we get over things a bit, you would come there. Bring the baby. What is she called?'

'Susan.'

'Do come.'

Harry was allowed some leave and stayed close-by in a small hotel just across the river for a day or two. It was called the North Star and reminded Ella of the bed and breakfast where they had stayed in Scotland. It seemed such a long time ago now.

After the funeral, when the mourners had gone and her grandmother had retreated wearily to bed, Ella wanted to get out so she and Harry walked through the dark wet night with the shadow of the river and the buildings beyond Framwellgate Bridge and they sat over the fire in the bar and drank whisky. The rain poured down beyond the windows. Ella was only glad to be somewhere that she cared for. It was as though the city held her in its arms.

'This reminds me of Mallaig,' she said.

'How so?'

'I don't know exactly.' She smiled. 'It's the wrong time, the wrong place, Jack isn't here getting drunk or sleeping with Agnes–'

'Ella–'

'Oh please don't pretend. He slept with other women right from the beginning, I could smell their perfume on him when he came home. It was the reason you gave her up, be honest.'

'She didn't think there was anything wrong in it. Would you like some more whisky?' The way that he said it made her look at him.

'You sound as though I'm going to need it.'

'You already need it,' he said, getting up and going to the bar.

When he came back, their glasses replenished, she said, 'And?'

Harry looked down into the golden liquid and said nothing.

'You're leaving,' she guessed.

'Yes.'

'Oh God. Jack is dead and now I'm going to lose you too.'

'You're not going to lose me.' He was looking directly at her now. 'You'll never lose me.'

'That's foolish,' Ella said, starting to cry. 'This is a war. And I know people say it won't last long but I'm a pessimist, I think the bloody thing will last for ever.'

Luckily there was nobody else in the cramped ill-lit room. Why on earth would they want to sit in such a Godforsaken place? Ella thought. The fire was small and black and smoky, the walls were orange brown from years of people exhaling cigarette fumes, the tiny round wooden tables were precariously heavy-topped and the seats were stuffed with horse hair or something equally disgusting and were lumpy.

She and Harry were seated on a wooden settle by the blaze, if that was what you could call such a pathetic attempt at a fire, so it was quite private and it was there that Harry took her into his arms for the first time.

There was nothing lustful about it. He didn't try to kiss her, he just held her there against him until she could bear to think back over the funeral. Could there ever be anything worse than to put the body of a boy into the ground, because Jack had been no more than that, just a foolish boy playing at soldiers, and she thought of Nolan, his widow and his child.

What a harsh beginning to the war for all of them. And now Harry was going away. She did not ask him where he was going, he would not know, could not tell her. She would be left. It was the leaving of Swan Island all over again, funerals and loss and the long looking back.

It seemed to her that she was for ever a child, looking out of the rear window of the big black car, watching all the dreams of her life fade into the distance behind her until she could no longer see the people she had loved so much: her father, her mother and now Jack.

She wanted to run up the hill and make sure that her grandmother was still alive. Harry let her go, she drank her whisky and then they left, walked slowly back up the steep winding street and he left her there outside the front door.

Ella went inside and up the stairs. The light burned small beyond the door of her grandmother's room, she could see it faintly through the space between the door and its frame. Softly she knocked, thought she heard her grandmother's voice and opened the door.

The room was cool, the old lady had a shawl around her shoulders. She put down the book she had been reading.

'Has Harry gone?' she said.

'Yes.' Ella went over and sat down on the bed.

'He's a good lad,' her grandma said.

'Yes.'

'It will get easier.'

Ella tried to smile.

'It already has. At least we don't have to go through the funeral again tomorrow.'

'That's it, Ella,' her grandmother said. 'There's my brave lass.'

Eleven

The war was not obvious in Durham, Ella was aware. They were luckier than a lot of places. There was the blackout from September and the street lights were extinguished, and she had not realized how much she would miss the reassurance of the lighting when the evenings grew dark that autumn.

It seemed darker than usual but she thought that was maybe just her mood and the mood of a great many people. Some were afraid to go out after dusk and the streets became quiet for a while, before people seemed to take heart and, in the city at least, a kind of social life prevailed.

There were a lot of uniformed men about, there was a lot of hearty laughter and people drinking in pubs. The music from the dancing wafted in through her windows on the nights when it was warm enough to open the windows in the spring.

She soon began to long for Jack, to have back the innocence of her first love when she had been happy to go out with him. Now she had no one to go out with, though plenty of men came into the café with their wives, mothers or sweethearts and she was sometimes asked out but never went. She told herself there was too much to do but it was not that. It was that she could not recapture the way that things were. Everything had changed too much.

The first Christmas of the war had long since come and gone and people tried to be as jolly as they could, considering the men who had left and were leaving home, the hardships, the shortages. She was determined and encouraged to keep the café open, it provided a haven for people, a refuge, and many a girl sat in tears over her tea as words of farewell were spoken there.

Gloria would come into the kitchen with gossip so that Ella had to tell her not to talk so much, that she must keep her mind on her work. Winnie had never been a woman who said much and she soon had two sons away fighting so she spoke even less. Often

Ella would let her go early if she was worried about her elderly mother at home because her mother was in poor health and tended to be forgetful. Winnie was convinced she would go home to find that her mother had set the house on fire because she had left the fireguard off and lumps of coal had fallen on to the hearthrug or she would wander into the streets.

Gloria was the only one of them who had a social life because she was not married and sometimes Ella would listen to the talk when they had a break and wish that she could go dancing and forget about what had happened.

After Christmas it was very cold indeed. That spring the Allies mined Norwegian waters. Hitler marched into Denmark and Norway, and British troops set sail.

In May, Gloria and Winnie hurried into the café with the news that Middlesbrough had been attacked. It was the first industrial town to have been targeted and it brought the war so close to Durham that for the first time it somehow seemed real.

German bombers bombed central London in August and after that things got much worse. That September several hundred people were killed and thousands of homes destroyed as for seventy-six nights the Luftwaffe besieged the English cities.

Sometimes Ella would go and stand outside and she could see the aeroplanes in the sky and she knew that they could see the landmark that the cathedral made and that they were trying to find and bomb Consett Ironworks.

Perhaps because of its almost hidden situation they did not find it but she would worry about the people she loved and the people she knew and everyone else. She especially worried about Harry and wondered whether he would ever come home and if and when he did whether he would bother to come to the little café in Silver Street.

By the summer she had given up thinking she would see him again. Every moment was taken up with the café. It was now considered a restaurant and was open from early until late which Ella thought her duty because people gathered there at all hours.

She provided newspapers, books, sofas, small tables and more and more people would come there, often just to listen to the wireless and smoke and drink coffee. No matter how long they were there she did not ask them to leave and they did not seem to object when she pushed in more and more seating and tables, some of them low just for tea and cake.

Ella specialized in apple turnovers, vegetable pasties, honey cake, welsh rarebit. She enjoyed the challenge of trying to make new recipes with few ingredients as rationing of bacon, sugar, butter, meat, cheese, jam and eggs made things more difficult for restaurants. Rhubarb snow made with golden syrup was a favourite as was summer pudding, and for dinner she made potato salad, onions with sage and cheese, and stuffed marrow. Sometimes in the evenings, when it was very busy and every seat was taken, people would even sit on the stairs and talk and drink tea.

There was a wonderful atmosphere in the place which Ella and her grandma and the waitresses personified. They always greeted people as though they really wanted them there – Ella specifically told them that they must. Everybody was welcome.

Ella kept chickens and learned to wring their necks when they had stopped laying as some did because there was no good corn to feed them on. It was hard to begin with but she steeled herself and she became very good at chicken stew and rabbit pie.

One of her neighbours kept goats, British Alpines, lovely animals with long black and white ears, so there was always a supply of warm milk and there was goat's cheese which was a luxury and so white and wonderful that their customers could not get enough of it.

The male goats were slaughtered when they were young, being of little use, and there was many a casserole which everyone called lamb. Ella came to think goat tasted just as good if not better than lamb but perhaps it was just the circumstances.

In the dusk Mr Miller, the goat keeper, would walk his nanny goats down the back lane and away out of sight. It made Ella merry to watch their black and white coats in the dusk as they disappeared out of sight around the bend in the road, following Tom Miller who sang as he walked.

In the November of that year as she was closing up after a particularly hard day Ella heard somebody come into the café.

'I'm sorry, we're closed,' she called, then she turned around as a tall dark man appeared in the shadows. She gave a little scream of joy and surprise. It was Harry.

She ran into his arms and he swung her round off her feet, his embrace was so fierce.

'What on earth are you doing here? Isn't there a war on?'

He smiled.

'No, really, Harry,' she said as he released her, 'what are you doing back here?'

'My father was taken ill.'

'Oh, no.'

'They thought he was dying so I had to come back. I think it was just a ruse to get me to stay here and build the blessed ships. I don't want to do that and he's perfectly capable by himself, at least he will be in a day or two.'

'A day or two? Is that all you have?'

'I have to go back tomorrow and now that he's out of hospital and at home with my mother I thought I would come and visit my favourite café. And I've heard how you've done great things here to keep morale going.'

'You look tired,' she said.

'I am.'

'Come and sit down.'

'No, I want to take you out.'

They did. She washed and changed very quickly while Harry smoked and talked to her grandmother, and then they went dancing and she had not realized quite how much she wanted to dance.

They drank gin and smoked cigarette after cigarette. She wanted to stay out all night just in case they never got the chance to do so again and so the night had almost greyed into morning when they found themselves standing in the middle of Framwellgate Bridge. It was there that he turned her to him and kissed her for the first time and Ella heard the birds of the morning singing and then she remembered that it was Sunday.

'Do you have to get back?' he said.

'No.'

'Shall we go to my hotel?'

They did. They sat by the smoky fire for a

while as they had done once before and then he said, 'Do you want to go home?'

'I should.'

'Because of your grandmother?'

'No.'

'Because of the memories of Jack?'

'Something like that.'

He nodded and threw his cigarette into the fire and was about to get up when Ella moved. She didn't know she had been about to touch him, about to kiss him. Her dreams at night were all of Jack and it was strange how everything was just as it had been.

She had awoken in the night and expected to find him lying beside her, the dream had been so real and she had cried, remembering the love between them and then she had known that it was over, there was no way back, there never would be. The truth of the matter was that she loved Harry much more than she had ever loved Jack.

'Is your room nice?'

'It's as bad as the rooms at Mrs McDonald's were. The bed was built for midgets and the view looks out over the backyard.'

'That's perfect,' she said.

There was a small fire in the room, so small that it was nearly dead in the grate but within moments of him getting down to attend to it the new sticks broke into flames which licked around the coal. There was nothing but one tiny light which showed very little of the shadowed furniture.

'What time are you going back?' she asked.

'Let's not talk about it. I know you don't feel completely good about this, Ella, I don't either but I do love you. I have always and will always love you, no matter what happens. When I come back will you marry me?'

'Yes.'

'It might be a very long time. I have the feeling we're being sent very far away. Promise me you'll wait for me.'

'I will.'

'No matter how long it takes?'

'No matter how long,' she promised.

Some people are given a whole lifetime to spend with the person they love. Some people are given a few months. The unluckiest people of all never meet that person or pass them by in the street, unknowing. Ella and Harry had one night and she was aware of that all the time.

When he had gone, when she had seen him to the station the following morning, she thought about Jack's funeral and how she would never be able to face such a thing again, and she spent the nights that followed trying to think how she would bear it if Harry were killed. But then if he had been sent to Africa or to India, if he died there, he would be buried there and she would never see him again and there would be no funeral here.

It seemed so stupid somehow. Durham Station was such a tiny normal kind of place with its unrivalled view down on the smoky chimneys, tiny rooftops and castle and cathedral, the city which she loved above all others but it would never again be cosy or ordinary. For her it remained the place where they said goodbye, their last embrace on the cold platform with a howling northern wind around their feet and even a few square snowflakes and he had laughed and said that it was typical of the northern weather.

By the time the train had gone around the corner out of sight the flakes had turned into a blizzard and the little grey town was covered in white, like one of those glass ornaments that you shook.

Experience of loss had taught her that there was no point in lingering. She went back to the café and got on with her work. There was nothing else to be done.

Twelve

It was a week later that her grandmother collapsed in the café, in full view of the customers. Ella was in the kitchen at the time but she heard Gloria cry out and she grabbed a cloth to wipe her hands – she had been taking vegetable pies from the oven – and she ran.

Her grandmother lay, still and grey-faced, on the floor.

'No, don't move her,' Ella shouted as willing hands would have helped, she wasn't sure what had happened but was sure that the best thing to do was wait for the experts.

She got down and talked to her grandma, even though the old woman was unconscious, and within an hour her grandma was lying in a hospital bed and Ella was sitting anxiously beside her while her elderly relative assured her that she was quite well and just wanted to go home.

Ella couldn't find anybody to tell her anything but eventually the doctor admitted that they thought her grandmother had had a slight stroke. They kept her in overnight and then allowed her to go home and Ella tried to stop her from doing too much.

'You are supposed to take things easy,' she told her, making her sit on the sofa upstairs beside the window.

'I'm bored and besides, there's a war on.'

'You fought your war last time. If anything happened to you whatever would I do? You're all I have.'

'What about Harry?' her grandmother said with bright eyes.

'He isn't here. Please, just be careful for a day or two.'

'I am an old woman, Ella, I have to die some time.'

'No, you don't,' Ella said, choking over the idea.

Her grandmother cuddled her. Ella loved the lavender scent of her.

'Please don't go anywhere, Grandma, I couldn't bear it,' she said.

'All right, my petal, I won't.'

Ella was cheered. She liked it when her grandmother called her 'my petal'.

Her grandma was right. How could anybody sit about when there was so much to be done? Keeping busy stopped her from worrying about Harry and the way that things were getting worse, and they were. There was now a very real threat of invasion and people were nervous.

Ella was starting to feel very tired. Her grandmother told her that she had been worrying too much and doing too much work.

'Everyone's tired,' Ella said, 'and much older women than me are working just as hard.'

Her grandmother urged her to sit down.

'You're not sleeping well,' she said.

'What a pair we are,' Ella said. 'I don't know how I find time to worry.'

'Of course you do. We all do.'

'What will we do if we have Germans here in the streets telling us what to do, taking everything?'

'We won't,' her grandmother said stoutly.

But Ella knew that it was what everybody was thinking and nobody was saying. She could not imagine the country ruled by an enemy.

'It's been a long time since William,' her grandmother said.

'Who?'

'The Conqueror. But we aren't ready for another invader.'

Ella, however, realized over the following weeks that she had her own personal invader and when the reality of the situation hit her she sat down and cried. All those months that she had been married to Jack and had often imagined what it would be like if she were to become pregnant, how excited and pleased they would be and how it would improve things between them.

Nothing had happened and at his funeral she remembered how awful it had felt that Jack had died and left no child.

He was an only son and she had even, despite the way that they had behaved, been able to feel sorry for his parents because they would never have grandchildren, and now she was pregnant with Harry's child after a single night. It was absurd, ridiculous, like God was taking pot shots at her. And Harry was hundreds, perhaps thousands, of miles away.

Her grandmother caught her crying in the empty café late at night. Ella tried to disguise the tears as perspiration because she was meant to be washing the floor.

'I thought you'd gone to bed.'

'I have not.' Her grandmother looked squarely at her. 'So you aren't just tired?'

Ella returned the look.

'No, I'm not. How did you guess?'

'You look different. Women in early pregnancy, they glow.'

'Are you ashamed of me?'

Her grandmother smiled.

'I could never be ashamed of you and I would love to be a great-grandmother. I think it's very exciting.'

'We are going to be married when he comes home.'

'It will be lovely.'

She did not even contemplate the fact that

he might not come home. She wrote to tell him but there was no letter back so she did not know whether Harry had any idea he was going to be a father.

She told Gloria and Winnie that everything would go on as usual and it did. The tiredness passed. The morning sickness did not. She was forever moving out of the kitchen to be sick.

'Lovely behaviour for a cook,' she scorned herself but dealing with food all day became such an ordeal that she was glad when she could go outside and get some air or retreat into the tiny office at the top of the house where she did the accounts and saw to all the ordering and paperwork.

Occasionally she even went up there on to her bed, and fell asleep for half an hour mid-afternoon when there was often a lull and would lie down, thinking of how wonderful it would be when the baby was born. Harry would come home to his child and they would be married.

She began to make plans for the baby and it altered her view of the war. Surely things could not be so bad when new life was being born? Best of all there was a letter from Harry. She recognized his handwriting and was inclined to open it straight away but she didn't. She carried it around in her apron pocket, patting it from time to time.

She gloated over the envelope all day and in the evening when it was late and she was alone in bed the anticipation got too much and she opened it. The pleasure in taking out the paper, in seeing his handwriting was wonderful. She read the letter very slowly, how pleased he was about the baby, how overjoyed. He said nothing about his life, nothing that gave anything away but he talked about the future, about them, about how he and Ella and the baby and Grandma would all live together and if she could bear to leave her beloved café they would buy a pretty house in town. His father was much better, he had heard, and his mother was coping.

He told her once again at the end how much he loved her. Ella kissed the letter, slept with it under her pillow, carried it around in the days that followed.

The pain, when it arrived, was quite sudden. She was alone in the kitchen. She dropped the knife with which she had been cutting bread and stood there, the sweat forming a layer, which sat at odds on her skin.

She clutched at the front of her body and waited for it to pass and then it was gone. When she moved Gloria was standing in the doorway, staring.

'Are you all right, Ella? Here, come and sit down.'

'It's gone,' Ella said, finally relaxing.

'Come and sit down anyway.'

Ella sat, grateful, waiting for the pain to return. It didn't.

'Is it busy out there?'

'Not at the moment. I'll make you some tea. Why don't you go upstairs and lie down for a while? We can manage.'

'I think I will. Thanks.'

Halfway up the stairs the pain came back so that Ella stopped, clung to the banister rail, cried out. Gloria went to get a young man from the café and much to Ella's dismay he carried her up the stairs and to her bed.

The pain got worse. Her grandma insisted on sending for the doctor. By then Ella already knew that it wouldn't make any difference. The pain was coming between her and her breath, between her and the world. It was beginning to fill every fibre of her existence and she could feel the warmth as she bled.

'Oh, Grandma,' she said, as her grandmother sat on the bed and held her hand, 'I'm losing our baby.'

Her grandmother tried to be reassuring but it was no good, Ella knew. She couldn't hear what was said, just her grandmother's reassuring tones. She didn't care about the baby or Harry or even herself. She would have given anything in the world for the pain to go away.

She was in hospital. Her grandmother was coming to visit her. Quite the wrong way round, Ella thought. What a depressing place it seemed with high walls, small windows, bare floors, the nurses flitting about like white flies, almost soundless, and then she slept and it was all she wanted to do, she was so very tired and everything in her life was so hard, everything now seemed impossible.

She didn't want to think any more. While asleep she thought she could hear sounds, it was afternoon sleep, not the deep sleep of the night, just the cosy unconsciousness of safety. Nothing could touch her, nothing could hurt her here.

She opened her eyes. Her grandmother was sitting by the bed as she was so often.

'You looked tired,' Ella said and her voice came out hoarse like a croak, as though it hadn't been used lately.

Her grandmother clasped her hand.

'How are you feeling?' she said.

'Rather low,' Ella confessed.

Her grandmother's kiss on her cheek was like rice paper, delicate, sweet and it was loving.

'They didn't even let me see the baby and I got brisk talk about how common it is to miscarry a first baby and how I would go on to have lots of other babies, as though it didn't matter,' Ella said, 'and I said to the nurse that if Harry was killed in this bloody war there wouldn't be any more bloody babies.'

Her grandmother smiled a little.

'Was the nurse shocked?'

'I think she was. Silly woman.'

'Brisk is the last thing you want when you're having a bad time,' her grandmother agreed.

'People don't think it is a bad time when so much is going wrong. People are being blown up by German bombs every night in some places, so a baby, especially an unborn baby, must seem like nothing.'

'It isn't nothing, it's a loss just like any other,' her grandma said. 'I tell you what, Ella, the sooner we get you out of this hell-hole the better.'

That made her smile for her grandmother must know that she was too weak to go far and the nurses and the doctor would fuss.

'How long must I stay here?' she had asked the doctor.

'Just until you feel a little better,' he had said. He was old, and he too looked tired. 'Just until we make sure you're well enough to be at home without our help.'

It was another two days before they let her go. To Ella it seemed so much longer. She went back to the café a different person, not pregnant any longer. The joy had gone. The dream of Harry's child was over and she had convinced herself by then that he would never come back. He would die as Jack had died and no good would ever come of anything any more.

She tried to keep her bad moods to herself and nobody said anything. It was as though the baby had not existed. The work went on and on and it was all that Ella cared for. She worked hard so that she would sleep and she took satisfaction in the people who flooded to her restaurant to talk and read and smoke and enjoy what little enjoyment there was left for people now.

They seemed determined to squeeze every moment. Late at night in the café she would play quiet music and more than one couple would dance close in the dim lights, in a world with everyone else shut out.

How she envied them. What wouldn't she have given for just half an hour in Harry's arms with the soft music in the background? The record player was old. It had been her parents'. It had a handle on one side and there were a couple of dozen records and there was always somebody wanting to hear something. Ella encouraged people to choose their favourites, to help themselves and she never grew tired of the tunes which her parents had loved. That music made her think of happy times so she did not mind how often she heard it.

Why did everything always go wrong at night? Ella wondered. And things going so wrong made the nights difficult to get through but then these days the nights were impossible for everyone. She tried to imagine the airmen, the sailors, the soldiers, people huddling in shelters, the women who had more difficult jobs than hers in munitions factories or in the forces. Her contribution seemed so small yet she knew that providing good cheap food for people was just as essential as anything else and the leftovers went to the pigs and the pigs provided food. The cycle went round and round and she was an essential part of it, her little restaurant inspired people, kept them cheerful. She had seen it over and over again.

She tried not to let things get her down. She told herself every day that many people had suffered as badly if not worse than she had and she got on with her work and maintained a bright front, but the nights when she was alone were difficult.

She wrote to Harry and told him about the miscarriage but in her mind she would not accept that there was no baby and she continued to make plans for his return, for the birth and had to stop herself short each time.

She knew that the nurses had been right,

she was young, that it was very common, that she would have other children, and tried to accept it and not to feel that the loss of her baby had left a great gaping hole in her mind somehow as well as her insides.

It was the bleakest winter that Ella had ever known. People were beginning to think the war would never be over. It was cold, dark and dreary and from half past three onwards the streets were deserted except on Saturdays and even then people did not go far. It was difficult to see, there had long been no petrol, and Ella thought of the population all huddling at home over their wirelesses and their sitting-room fires and she thought of Harry.

He did not reply to her letter. Was he too upset to contact her? It seemed unlikely, yet day after day she waited anxiously to hear from him and nothing happened. Where was he? Was he fighting in some jungle, suffering the heat and the cold and all kinds of other discomforts which she could only imagine; fighting and hoping for what?

One night when Ella had gone to bed early, exhausted, she woke suddenly in bed in her freezing bedroom and thought she had heard a thump. She got up and ran through the gloom into her grandmother's room and there by the dim glow of one light bulb she could see the still form of her grandmother lying slumped on the linoleum floor.

'Grandma? Grandma?' She went over and called and called but there was no response.

Ella panicked. She ran down the stairs and out into the dark street, shouting for help. The cobbled road was deserted. Then she could see the tall figure of a man walking up the bank, somebody young and energetic by the way he was striding out. She was so relieved that she didn't stop and think that she didn't know him, she didn't care. He was the only person about, she had no choice.

'Please help me,' she said. 'My grandmother has collapsed.'

He broke into a run when he saw and heard her. By the time he got to her Ella was incoherent in her distress, she just couldn't get the words out, but he followed her into the house and up the stairs and he got down beside the old lady and felt for her pulse and he paused there for a few moments, which seemed to Ella like a lifetime. Then he looked up reluctantly.

'I'm sorry. I think your grandmother is dead.'

There was nothing to feel any more. She was, she thought wryly, becoming an expert at funerals, and organized her grandmother's. Strangely she found it was comforting. The church was packed. All her grandmother's old friends came and she had not thought there were so many of them and many people who came regularly to the café came as well. They stopped her and spoke to her at the church and they came on to the do at the café afterwards. Ella had not wanted to make a big fuss and then she thought her grandmother would have wanted it, and deserved it, so she, Gloria and Winnie worked hard with the ingredients they could get to give her grandmother a proper northern send off; the old ladies telling her tales about her grandma and themselves and standing in groups by the window. They regarded it as a party, she thought, and what a lovely idea that was.

Once her grandmother's funeral was over, Ella felt completely numb. The work at the café took over for the next few days. Gloria and Winnie seemed to do most of it. Ella kept making mistakes. She dropped hot plates of food, she burned scones, she left the oven on by mistake, she kept forgetting to lock the doors and pull the blinds.

She did not sleep. She thought that she would never be tired again, that she would be able to go on and on. One day in the late afternoon when Gloria and Winnie were busy downstairs and she was sitting at the old roll-top desk trying to do her accounts, she could hear some sentimental war song wafting up the stairs, and she found she had put her hands over her face and the tears were slipping through her hands and beginning to run down her arms.

There was no sound, no sobbing, as though somebody else was crying, all she felt was the tickling sensation of the salt water slowly reaching past her wrists.

There was a small apologetic cough in the doorway.

She pretended nothing was happening with tears and dragged her hands along her skirt. He couldn't see her very well anyway, she reasoned, there was one tiny light on the desk by which she checked her figures. She couldn't see him properly. He was tall and slender and young and when she could see him better she thought he had beautiful green eyes and shiny pale golden hair and his eyes were full of concern.

'Can I help you?' she said, shocked and annoyed that he had seen her in such a state and that Gloria and Winnie had let a stranger into the upper part of the house.

'I'm David Black,' he said. 'I was here the other night when your grandmother died – I was walking up the hill, I'd been to see some friends–'

'Oh, yes,' Ella said, scraping back the old wooden chair and getting up. 'I didn't thank you.'

'You did, several times. I came to the funeral.'

'I didn't notice you. That was very kind.'

'I don't suppose you would remember me or anybody, you were so distressed.'

No, indeed, Ella thought, it was all just a miserable blur.

'You were so good,' Ella said.

'I just wanted to see how you were. I didn't mean to intrude.'

'Well,' she said, trying to lighten her voice, 'I think you can see how I am. I have the accounts to do and–'

'Would you like to go out for a little while–?'

'Oh, I don't think so, thank you.'

'My mother would be pleased if you would come to tea.'

'What a nice thing to say,' Ella responded before she could stop herself.

'Will you come?'

'I shouldn't leave. We're busy and...'

'They can manage without you for an hour, can't they?'

Put like that somehow Ella thought they probably could. He was very persuasive. Things which might have been offensive were softened by the tone in his voice. He had a very nice voice, no accent, just general northern dark somehow, very middle class, she thought, educated and sure of himself but sensitive and polite. It suddenly seemed ridiculous to refuse and Ella found herself hunting for her coat and going downstairs with him.

A large silver car stood outside.

'Is that yours?' she said.

'Yes, I've been away on business. Actually it's my father's. He doesn't drive it much any more. I don't think his eyes are good in the dark.'

'So you aren't in uniform and you drive a beautiful car. What does that make you, a government official?'

'Nothing so grand. I make castings for ships and sometimes there are meetings,' he said simply and opened the passenger side door for her. The seat was big and the car smelled beautifully of leather and she sank into the seat, grateful for the comfort.

She had come home. That was the feeling Ella had when she walked into the Blacks' sitting room. It had nothing to do with the house, Swan Island would always hold her heart, it was the people, his mother and father.

They both got up. Mrs Black was a solidly built woman, neat with white hair, wearing pearls and a flowered frock. She smiled as she kissed Ella's cheek and told her they had heard so much about her and that she had been with her friend to Ella's wonderful café several times. Mr Black shook her hand and urged her nearer the fire. He looked as she imagined his son would probably look in another thirty years, eyes like emeralds, white hair, smooth and sleek, brown skin as though he was outside a good deal. He was elegant too, well-dressed and his eyes twinkled.

Her first impression was of a very welcoming room and she noticed how they had made it so. There was a big log fire and to either side of it woodboxes with little leather tops so that they were seats. Small pools of light danced from lamps in the corners. There were books all down one wall and further over there was a grand piano.

Lying in front of the fire was a large black dog of indeterminate origin and there were big squashy chairs where half a dozen people could sprawl in comfort. Music was playing on the radiogram. Mrs Black made tea and they sat over the fire and ate scones with blackberry jam and Ella thought that she had not felt so comfortable or wanted since her father had died and she and her mother had left Swan Island.

When she left Mr and Mrs Black both said they hoped she would come back very soon and then David took her home.

He said, 'How about next Sunday?' and she thought it was a nice way to behave. There was nothing pushy about David, he didn't think they were going out, he was just being friendly or perhaps he knew that she needed a family, that she needed the comfort of other people and he cared enough about her to try to help.

'I would like that,' she said.

She spent her Sundays with them, it was no more than that until she became comfortable having David and his family around her and each of these days became precious until they fell into a pattern. She got used to the idea that she was part of their Sundays and they were of hers.

David's mother came to the café. Gloria called into the kitchen, 'Mrs Black's here.'

Ella looked up eagerly. 'You know her?'

'Course. She comes all the time.'

Ella wiped her hands and went through. David's mother was beaming at her and she was not alone. She had three other women with her.

'Ella, this is Phyllis, Betty and Sheila and they haven't been here before and I have told them that you have the best establishment in the area. Ladies, this is Ella who is immensely clever and runs the Silver Street Café,' and she beamed around and the women all beamed at Ella. It gave her a very warm feeling to see David's mother there with her friends, making the place lively and bright when there were so many downcast faces.

'I have told them you will play their favourite tunes.'

'I will,' Ella said, smiling.

After that David's mother came with her

friends and on her own and even sometimes brought Mr Black, who kissed her on the cheek and told her how wonderful she looked. Sometimes Mrs Black came by herself and even helped in the kitchen if Ella was short-handed or had too much to do and she brought other friends and would introduce them, telling them how clever Ella was, how bright and businesslike, just as though Ella was her daughter and she was proud of her. It made Ella feel as though Mrs Black was her mother and it gave her somewhere to go in her mind, she had people she could rely on at last.

Mr Black taught her to play chess. She had tried to refuse, but he had said, 'Do you play?' when she had been there one cold wet Sunday evening and Ella had shook her head. After she'd refused he had persuaded her she should learn. Sometimes they also played draughts in the evenings with bottle tops and an old board.

Very often after that, when the café shut in the evenings, David would come and collect her so she rarely spent time by herself and she had not realized how lonely she had become. Sometimes on Saturday nights she would stay with the Blacks and they would sit talking by the fire and it all seemed so normal, a real family as she had not known.

They all took the dog for long walks on Sunday afternoons and if his parents did not want to go if the weather wasn't good David would tuck her hand through his arm and they would walk through the rain or the cold wind around the riverbanks and she enjoyed the walks and coming back and his mother giving them tea by the fire, when they would toast bread and shut out the night.

She asked David about his work and he took her to the foundry, which his family owned, where they made castings for ships to keep the navy going. They worked six days a week. They had worked seven but they had got so tired, he explained, and were less productive that the men were better for a few hours off. She was very impressed with the place which stood behind huge tall iron gates and had the name Black's Steel-founders written on it in loopy letters.

There were great big buildings where the steel was poured into moulds to make castings. There were sheds and lots of machinery and a crane and the big Bessemer converter where the ingredients were melted down to make the steel. There were offices where David and his father and their secretary worked and the laboratory where the chemist determined the quality of the castings before they were transported to the various shipyards on the Wear at Sunderland and the Tyne at Newcastle.

Ella could tell by the enthusiasm in

David's voice how important the works was to them and she thought how good it was that he didn't have to go away to do his bit for the war. David would always be here.

Ella did not mention Harry Reid to David. She wanted to keep them in separate compartments of her life. David was just a friend, a good friend. The difference was that he was there, he was part of her immediate life. If she had any problems – and she very often did – he would help try to solve them. He did the books for her, gave her advice about the business when she asked for it. He was punctual, did what he said he would and was always available when she needed someone. Ella began to think that she could not imagine her life without the Black family.

Unlike Jack he did not ask her to marry him. Perhaps he thought it a foolish thing to do during a war when he was not going away so there was no hurry and they were both so busy with their different war work. Neither did he attempt to get her to go to bed with him as though he sensed that she would not have welcomed such ideas. He didn't touch her except to put a hand under her elbow when she got out of the car or take her hand if they crossed a stream and there were stepping stones. David had very good instincts; he seemed to know that she did not want intimacy.

It was only when Ella heard herself talking to Gloria and Winnie saying, 'David said' or 'David did', that she realized he had become an invaluable part of her life and so very quickly. In a way his parents took it for granted that they would be married. Mrs Black actually said to her one day at the beginning of 1945, 'Are you and David going to set a date now that the war is almost over?'

'I don't know.' Ella was glad they were busy in the kitchen at their house, gathering platefuls of sandwiches for tea and she didn't have to look at the other woman.

'I think you should,' was all Mrs Black said, before going in by the fire with the sandwiches where the two men were talking.

Ella's mind was in turmoil. She had not thought about marrying David but she was beginning to wonder whether he would ever attempt to kiss her. In fact she was worried about it, about the idea that he really didn't care that much about her and would announce that he didn't want to see her any more and she had come to dread that. She had spent nights lying awake worrying about Harry being away and David being here and how complicated the situation had become.

Over the past three years she had written again and again to Harry but heard nothing.

In between letters she had tried to put him from her mind, she was so afraid that he might have been injured, captured or killed though she had heard nothing. The Black family had become her only reality.

'Are you planning to keep the café on after the war, Ella?' David said about two weeks later when he was taking her home to Silver Street.

'What else would I do?'

'You could come and live with us.'

He didn't look at her while he said this. Ella faltered.

'Live with you?'

'Yes. Or was that not part of your plans?'

'I – I don't know,' Ella said.

'I tell you what,' David stopped the car outside the café, 'if you are very keen on the idea we could keep open the café until we have children but after we're married I would like us to have a little house of our own, somewhere for just you and me.'

'After we're... Why, David Black, how dare you assume things?' She spoke lightly but she didn't know what to say or what to think.

'I have to,' he said. 'It's not that I want to marry you but my parents will never forgive me if I don't.' He leaned over and kissed her. 'Will you marry me, Ella? I love you.'

She hesitated. David sat back in the driving seat.

'Oh, hell,' he said, 'I've got this wrong.'

'No, no, how could you have done, after all this time?'

'Is there somebody else?'

'Can I think about it?'

'Yes, of course.'

'Can I have a week?'

'You can have six months if that's what it takes,' he said and somehow that helped.

She got out of the car, went into the building, walked slowly up the stairs and went to bed and there she lay, looking at the ceiling. Harry seemed so very far off. He could even be dead, she had heard nothing for so long. He seemed unreal now. David was real and so was his family, and she didn't think she could ever give them up.

David didn't come to the café all that week and by the time Saturday night came, Ella started to panic. Then he turned up when she was closing.

'Are you coming over? My mother has made supper,' he asked.

Ella didn't know what to say.

'If you don't want to come that's all right too.'

'I do want to.'

'And if you'd rather go on as we were that's fine.'

She looked at him.

'You really want to marry me?'

'I really, really do.'

'David, I don't know. I don't know whether I care enough about you to marry you.'

He didn't look at her for a few seconds and then he said, 'That's all right. We can be friends.'

Ella said nothing, she had not expected such generosity. When she finally met his eyes he was smiling, just like his father did.

'I'm not going to go off in a huff, you know,' he said.

'Will you kiss me?'

'If you really want me to.'

'I do.'

He got hold of her very gently and kissed her and the kiss, Ella thought, was exactly right. And just when she was beginning to think that David's regard for her was as temperate as his speech he got hold of her and the second kiss was quite different from the first, and somehow in those few seconds Ella changed her mind about marrying him. She wanted to be with David and part of his family more than she wanted anything else in her life.

It was a simple wedding because Ella had no family and the Blacks were not the kind of people who would embarrass anybody. It was one of the things she liked best about them, how sensitive they were. Iris, David's sister, who had been a Queen Alexandra nurse and had worked abroad throughout the war, was back in time.

She was small with pale brown hair and the same green eyes as David. Ella asked her to be her bridesmaid because there was nobody else but although Iris agreed Ella was quite certain that her sister-in-law to be was not very happy at the idea of David's marriage, even though she said little. Ella was afraid that Iris didn't like her.

Mrs Black made Iris's dress. Ella wore her mother's wedding dress. Ella thought that she would feel closer to Iris but even when they were standing in David's mother's bedroom dressed in the pretty gowns Iris looked at her reflection in the long mirror with great dissatisfaction and when Ella said, 'You look lovely,' she merely shook her head and said nothing. 'I would like it if we could be friends,' Ella said. 'I don't have anyone of my own.'

Iris said bluntly, 'I've hardly seen David in six years and I feel as if you're stealing him from me. We were very close as children and nothing came between us, but I come back here and find you in the way. I'm sorry but that's how I feel about it.'

'Didn't you think he would marry?'

'I thought we would both marry but now...'

Ella didn't like to ask any more it seemed like an intrusion. It was difficult to feel anything positive towards Iris after that, so she just stayed friendly when they met.

The café had lost its appeal now that they were to be married and when she mentioned closing it David said that they would do whatever she wished.

'I've worked so hard there for so long, I think I would just like to have my own house and look after you and have a little bit more leisure time. Besides, the money will help us to buy a house of our own.'

When she said this to his parents in their sitting room the following Sunday they looked sheepishly at her and then his father said, 'I hope you don't think this is presumptuous but we've bought you a house.'

Ella was so excited that she squealed. They went to see it straight away and Ella thought it was the prettiest house she had ever seen. It was in the Bailey just across from the cathedral and had an upstairs Durham bay window and a lovely garden at the back, square Georgian-style windows, three storeys, four bedrooms, lovely fireplaces even in the bedrooms and a view beyond the city to the fields. Ella was determined that they should be happy there, not far from David's parents. She was starting a new life and it would be good.

Ella had not told David about Harry and it was only the week before the wedding, when she realized that she would have to sign the register as Ella Welsh, that she decided to tell him about Jack. Then she wished she had done so sooner.

It was Saturday night. They were decorating the sitting room and were just sitting on the floor in admiration of their finished work when David said, 'I've had enough of this, let's go out and have a drink.'

'There's something I should tell you,' she said, catching hold of his arm.

David pulled a face.

'That sounds ominous,' he said, smiling, 'don't tell me you're married already.'

Ella tried to smile at the joke and couldn't. David stared at her.

'I'm widowed,' she said. 'You must have realized I wasn't a virgin when we...'

She thought back to the first time they had gone to bed together. It was one of the advantages of having your own place because they would not have had such opportunities if she had lived with her parents as he did with his. She could not help comparing it with the night she spent with Harry at the little hotel near Framwellgate Bridge and the second night of her wedding with Jack. Was it good to have so much to compare things to and was it fair?

The funny part about it was that David always felt like a husband whereas none of the others ever had. She could trust him. He was not like Jack, drinking too much and going with other women and somehow she

had known that. He was used to responsibility, it sat easily on him. He was always
ready to cope with everything. If she had
become pregnant he would have married
her immediately, she knew without him
saying anything. And their bodies fitted. She
liked being in bed with him, she liked the
way that he made her feel. She did not,
however, like having to tell him about Jack.

'I was married. Welsh is my married
name.'

David didn't look at her.

'I knew,' he said roughly. 'I couldn't bear
to think of it, I wanted you to myself.'

'How did you find out?'

'I just remembered what had happened
and pieced it together. I remember the
newspapers and you being a local girl from
an important family and ... when we met I
knew it was you.'

'You didn't say anything.'

'It wasn't my business. The only thing was
that I was dismayed to find you'd loved
somebody before you loved me. I was
jealous of that and ashamed to think I could
be jealous of a lad who'd died so tragically
and I thought if you didn't want to talk
about it then we wouldn't, that it would be
something we would get to later.'

'None of us can help our past.' *I can never
tell him about Harry,* she thought.

She kissed him and David said, 'It's over

168

now. This is our new start,' and they got up off the floor and went to the pub to toast themselves in beer.

Rationing was still in place so their wedding was not a lavish affair except that David's father found some champagne he had been keeping and Ella was very aware that day how the Black family regarded her.

David's father was giving her away and he kissed her and told her she was the bonniest bride he had ever seen, and his mother came upstairs while she and Iris were getting ready for the ceremony and gave her a wide silver bracelet which she said had been her mother's and which she wanted Ella to have on her wedding day.

They had a small reception at the house and then David and Ella went to London for a few days. David did not like to leave his father in charge of the foundry, he was apt to forget things and he had been tired lately. David put it down to all the work they had done during the war. His father was worn out.

So they came back to their little house and there Ella did very ordinary things like hanging out the washing in the garden, tending to the flowerbeds, making meals for David because he came back at twelve for his dinner and half past five for his tea and she liked cooking now that she didn't have to bake every day for the café. He was very complimentary about the meals and told her how much he loved coming home to her.

'This is the happiest I have ever been,' he said.

Thirteen

Coming home was the hardest thing that Harry had ever done. It surprised him. It shouldn't have been hard, it should have been a relief. He wanted to feel excited when he saw Durham from the station but he wasn't. The wonderful view of the cathedral and the castle below did nothing for his mood. He was half inclined to get off there and run to the Silver Street Café but his instincts held him back.

He had long since thrown away the last letter he had received from Ella telling him that she had miscarried the baby. He had written after that but there was no reply. It was not surprising, he had moved around a good deal, to the point where he was always restless now, always ready to move on as befitted the life he had been leading for so long. His war had been fought in Burma, too far away to come home before the job

170

was finished and even once the war had ended there had been a great deal to do.

He got straight on to the next train, therefore, until he reached Sunderland. This part also he had been dreading. He got a taxi to take him home, back to the house on the headland between Sunderland and Seaham. It stood, looking out over the sea. It was a fine stone house and he should have loved it, only he didn't.

All he remembered of his early childhood was empty room after empty room because he was an only child. His father was almost always at work, his mother was always out during the day with friends or at charitable events and when his father came home in the evenings he took his wife out.

Their social life did not include their child which Harry supposed was perfectly normal at that time. His father was there on Saturday afternoons and went to football matches but Harry hated football and, although he had been asked to go, he didn't.

He read books, a thing his father deplored. He wasn't good at games, which his father had been and seemed to think mandatory. They had nothing in common when he was a child and then at seven Harry had gone to boarding school and any semblance of a relationship between them was gone. Harry couldn't help wishing that his father had seen him in the jungle, killing the enemy. I was brilliant at it, he thought, wincing.

He took the taxi home, hardly daring to breathe somehow. When he got there his mother came out of the house. She looked so much older but thin, elegant, her white hair swept up on to her head. She wore pearls at her throat and in her ears and a neat blue dress. She wasn't crying but the tears stood in her eyes and when he kissed her powdered cheek, she said, 'Welcome home, darling.'

His baggage was carried inside. There was a manservant to do that, someone he didn't recognize. Harry was embarrassed and helped. Nothing had changed. A fire burned in the hall because the weather was dull and the Labrador, Fern, though old and arthritic, got up and wagged her tail and made her way across the parquet flooring, her nails clipping against the wood as she walked. Harry got down to her and fondled her ears.

'Hello old girl,' he said. 'You remember me then?'

His mother said nothing more, but she led him into the library. Harry had been aware that his father had not been well for years but he was sitting on a chair with his feet up on a pouffe, a rug over him, a log fire burning in the big stone fireplace and his hair was white. His eyes were tired.

'You'll excuse me if I don't get up,' he said.

Harry had a desire to kiss him, hold him, but his father merely held out a hand. Harry shook it and smiled.

'High time you got back here, the works needs you,' his father said.

Harry knew there was no point in putting things off. It was obvious that his father could not run things any longer and he worried that the standards had slipped and he would find disarray on his first visit, but he remembered then that his father had high standards in everything.

'Yes, of course,' he said.

They did not talk about the war, in fact his father did not talk much about anything. He was tired and looked much older than he was, and sitting there over the fire with his parents that first evening it was like something unreal. Coming back from Burma to this was strange and he missed ... he didn't know what he missed but it seemed there was very little here for him.

For weeks and weeks after he got back Harry clung to the illusion that Ella was still at the café, that she had waited for him and he put off contacting her. Day after day he sat in his office – there was a great deal of work to do and he had so much to learn that he did not have much time to sit about thinking of his personal life. He was glad of that. He had not realized, or had not wanted to think, that his father might not get better but now he was convinced of it.

His father would never go to work again and he might as well get used to the idea. He had come back in the nick of time to prevent things from going downhill, his father had clung on just long enough and although the place was run by good competent men it lacked the genius touch which his father had had and it needed somebody with drive and ambition to see it through. He could do it, he knew that he could, and so he stayed there long hours, seven days a week until the day when he could stand it no more.

He thought he had battled against the idea of going and seeing Ella because he knew nothing good would come from it but once he reached this conclusion he was up and out of the office within an hour and he got Jim, who had been with him through the last five years and had come back to be his chauffeur, to drive him to Durham. He pushed from his mind all the memories, Jack, Agnes and the time after Jack had died when he had been torn between love and guilt.

By the time the car stopped outside the café in Silver Street the disillusionment was complete. The café was gone. He got slowly out of the car. It was a shop, nothing more on the ground floor with accommodation above it and no sign that it had ever been a café.

It was – of all the prosaic things it could be – a shoe shop. He went inside. He remembered the men in uniform sitting with their lovers on the stairs, the music and the smell of people smoking and the heavenly scent of newly baked scones with plum jam. The room inside had been halved, the back half no doubt was now a storeroom.

The assistant came towards him. 'Can I help you, sir?'

'This used to be a café. Have you any idea what happened to the people who used to run it? They were called Welsh.' She looked blankly at him.

'I've only been here six weeks,' she said.

'Is the manager in?'

She called into the back and a neatly suited middle-aged man came out to the front of the shop.

'This gentleman is looking for the people who used to own the café, Mr Harmer.'

'I'm looking for Ella Welsh. Do you know what became of her?' Harry said.

'Why, yes,' the man said, 'she's married. Has been for a little while, I believe.'

'Married?'

'That's right, sir.'

'Do you know who she married?'

'Mr Black, that owns the steelworks, well, his family does. David Black.'

Harry thanked him and stumbled outside. All his worst fears were realized, all his illusions were gone. I knew it, he thought. I knew that she would not have stopped writing to me without a good reason. I knew long ago that she had given up on me but I couldn't face it when things were so difficult and it was the reason I didn't come straight here, the reason I went home so that I would hopefully have something to cling to when I was certain that I had lost her. Whatever am I going to do now?

He got into the car, slammed the door and went back to Sunderland.

Fourteen

Men were always asking Rosemary to go for a drink with them, wanting to buy her meals and she watched the other girls, they were nothing but glorified waitresses she thought, accept their offers; lots of them had sex with men for money. She had never seriously considered it, no matter how bad things got.

She shared a room in a boarding house with another girl and they lived as frugally as they were obliged to do; no cigarettes, no alcohol, no pretty dresses.

One of the other girls Hilda, who was

nicer than the others, once said frankly to her, 'It doesn't matter what you wear, you still look better than everybody else. All the girls know it, that's why they dislike you so much.'

Rosemary hadn't thought until then that they did dislike her, but when she said so Hilda laughed.

'Look in the mirror some time,' she said.

Rosemary had tried not to. Her mother had told her that the devil made faces like hers in order to bring men down. Her mother was dead. Rosemary was glad of that sometimes.

She just went on taking drinks to the customers at the club, smiling and being polite, ignoring the hands that brushed against her body. And then there was the night when Harry came in. He was drunk. He fell in the door. Nobody noticed, otherwise he would have been put out.

He straightened up, gained a table in the corner and she knew what to do, he was so unostentatiously rich. Really rich men were, Rosemary had come to spot them. Not many of them came there. Flashy men were those who had made their money and wanted their pound of flesh so she was careful with them, and old money was just as bad in other ways, they were like boys, rude, thought of you like they thought of their servants, a person who was just there to be used.

Harry was not like either of these, Rosemary surmised. He was not what they called 'a champagne customer', so drunk that he would pay expensively for anything but he was judged to be such by the manager and she was sent across to offer him champagne, to pretend she assumed it was what he wanted and she was obliged to be willing to sit there with him and drink as much as possible so that he would soon order another bottle.

She walked into the shadows. In the background behind her jazz was playing, the singer was good, singing all the old sweet love songs about people losing one another. The saxophonist seemed lost in his music, she had noticed earlier, the piano player was always smiling, the double bass player was frowning, he had a hangover, he had told her earlier as they'd set up, and the drummer also seemed in his own world. The singer sang softly of stars and Rosemary went across to Harry.

'Can I get you champagne, sir?' she offered.

He lit a cigarette and looked at her as though he wasn't quite sure where he was and then harder at her and around the room.

'No, thanks,' he said clearly. 'Whisky would be all right but make sure it's something decent, none of that blended stuff.'

'I can sit with you if you order champagne.'

178

He looked at her again, his eyes screwed up against the lack of light.

'No, thanks,' he said.

'If you don't order champagne I have to go and sit with somebody else.'

He looked at her.

'All right then, but bring me the whisky.'

Rosemary nodded. He sat there in the corner for four nights and listened to the music and from time to time she would replenish his whisky and that was all. He didn't speak to anybody, he didn't ask for anything. And she sat there with him. Funnily enough it wasn't boring. She didn't mind that he didn't talk, she was so grateful that she didn't have to go and sit with other men, who made stupid remarks, indecent suggestions or at worst tried to get hold of her.

For two bottles of champagne she could sit with him as long as he was there. She didn't drink it. She sat with a half full glass and partway through the evening he bought another and they listened to the music and she was almost happy for the first time that she could remember.

They might have gone on like that for weeks except that one of the customers tried to get hold of her. She was coming back across the floor to Harry with the second bottle of champagne. The drunk customer kept her attention on himself in the crudest way, calling her sweetheart and telling her he would take her for a meal when the club closed. She didn't like to tell him there would be nothing open by then or that she would rather die than go anywhere with him.

He was drunk and it might not have meant anything but neither was it friendly, his hands all over her body. The bouncers were both outside, tackling another difficult customer. This man got hold of her by the waist and Rosemary never forgot the song the singer was singing as he tried to press his disgusting wet mouth on to her reluctant lips and she held her face averted. It was 'Cry Me a River'. He held her so that she couldn't get away without a great deal of fuss.

Harry emerged from the corner without speaking, hauled the man off her, dragged him to the door and hurled him outside, while everybody watched and the bouncers looked on in admiration. He did it so neatly, as though he had done it a thousand times before. The music didn't stop and though everybody watched it happened without breaking the atmosphere as the last words of the song died away.

He went back into his dark corner and sat down. He stayed until the end of the evening, until she finished work. She was dreading this. Perhaps he would think she owed him for what he had done. Sure enough he came to her.

'Would you like me to take you home?' he said.

'Thank you but I don't think so.' How many times had she said that to different men?

'It's quite safe. We wouldn't be alone.'

She didn't understand what he meant but she could not stay there, the evening was over, she was tired and the manager had told her that she could go. She collected her coat and they went outside where a large, chauffeur driven car was waiting.

'Is it a joke?' she said.

'No, it's Jim Tunstall. He doesn't like me to drive when I drink and since I always drink he insists on coming for me.'

The chauffeur got out and opened the door.

'I don't even know your name. I'm Harry.'

'Rosemary.'

'Jim, say hello to Rosemary.'

'Pleased to meet you, miss,' the chauffeur said. 'Would you like to get in?'

'We're taking Rosemary home, Jim. You'll have to direct him,' Harry said to her.

The car was enormous inside. It was also the most comfortable vehicle Rosemary had ever sat in. She directed them into the poorest part of the town.

'What are you doing in that place?' Harry

asked, staring out of the window.

'Working. What does it look as if I'm doing?'

'Can't you find something else?'

'Who are you, my dad?'

He looked at her.

'I'm nearly old enough to be your dad, aren't I?'

'Nothing of the sort,' she said, staring out of the other window. 'You needn't think you're getting nothing from me either,' she said.

'Anything.'

'What?'

'You mean "anything". It's a double negative otherwise.'

'Oh, shut up,' she said. 'Can I have a fag?'

He gave her a cigarette. She studied it.

'Russian,' he said.

'Ooh, aren't you posh then?'

He lit the cigarette with a silver lighter.

'You're too young to work in a place like that,' he said. 'How old are you, sixteen?'

'Mind your own business.'

'Where are you from?'

'Sunderland. I lived in London for a while though.'

'I could give you a job.'

She laughed.

'Yes, I can imagine.'

Having issued instructions as to how to get to the street where she lived, she sat back and waited for them not to take her but very shortly the car drew up right in front of her door. She didn't give the driver time to let her out. She got out very quickly and ran into the house, closing the door behind her and waiting for Harry to come knocking on the door, but nothing happened. She let go of her breath.

The following night when he came in she went over and waited for him to ask for whisky.

'That stuff you pretend is champagne, please, if you'll sit with me.'

'I can't tonight. I'm having a drink with somebody else. He was here first.'

'And who is that?'

'Him, there in the corner.'

As she spoke one of the other waitresses delivered champagne to that man and sat down. Harry looked at her. She gave in, relieved.

'All right,' she said.

She came back, sat down, and poured the champagne. She sipped at it slowly.

'Don't you like it?' he said.

'No, not much.'

'That's because it's rubbish. Good champagne smells like sick.'

'Charming.'

'No, it does.' He smiled for the first time. He was nice when he smiled, she thought. 'Tastes good though.'

'I don't like any drink.'

'You're better off without it.'

'Says you.'

'How old are you?'

'The champagne doesn't entitle you to ask questions.'

'What does it entitle me to?'

'Nothing very much and you're not taking me home again and you're not putting your hands on me.'

'I haven't asked.'

'You don't need to. You're not very likely to be the kind of bloke who doesn't want to, you have that look about you.'

'What sort of look?'

'Like I was blackberry and apple crumble with hot custard and you hadn't had a sweet in months.'

He laughed. She was rather pleased she had made him laugh, she thought he looked as though he didn't do sufficient of it.

'How old are you then?' she said.

'Thirty-two.'

'You look a lot older than that.'

'So would you if you'd spent the war in the jungle.'

'What were you doing there?'

'Killing people,' he said, pushing the last of his cigarette down in to the ash tray. 'This stuff's awful. Get me some whisky, will you?'

Rosemary got slowly to her feet. Men who had been soldiers never said things like that

184

about the war. It was only because he was drinking, she told herself.

'I'm seventeen,' she said when she got back with the whisky.

'You shouldn't even be here,' he said.

Later, when she went to the bar, one of the other girls, Freda, said, 'You know who he is, don't you?'

Was that supposed to mean something, Rosemary wondered.

'His dad's Philip Reid, owns the shipyard. If you could get him to look after you, you'd do all right there.'

Rosemary tossed her head at the information and didn't reply.

The whole thing got into a sort of pattern, she thought. Night after night he came to the place and they drank together in the corner. She drank champagne, though not much of it. The bottles lined up hardly touched on the table and he drank whisky and the manager got good stuff in for him now, single malt, and he smoked. She did well just to keep him company and it made her job so easy.

She could never remember what they talked about. She felt comfortable with him as she had felt comfortable with no one before. He didn't try to touch her, not even a brush of hands. At the end of the evening he would take her home, at least Jim would, and she would thank them and get out and they would not drive away until she had reached her door.

Hilda was intrigued, in fact all the girls were, and asked questions but Rosemary did not answer them. There was nothing to say. And then one night, it was a Saturday, he didn't come and she hadn't realized until then how much she relied on him to be there. She watched the corner all night until finally another man sat there and she was dismayed.

She hated that evening, it was the longest of her life, having to be nice to men who leered and slavered and made indecent suggestions and the boss pushing her to get them to order expensive drinks and have her sit with them. The conversation was boring, the men stared at her breasts, their breath stank, their clothes were greasy, their teeth looked decayed and foul. She had never wanted to leave the place so much.

It was not until it came to chucking out time that she went outside buttoning her coat against the cold, dreading how far the walk home was and found the big silver car sitting there just as usual and Jim saw her and got out and came around to her.

'His dad's poorly. He couldn't come but I'm here to take you home.'

'Thanks, Jim. Can I get in the front, I feel stupid sitting in the back by myself?'

'Course,' Jim said cheerfully.

They got in and Jim drove and she

thought how comfortably he negotiated the streets.

'How poorly is his dad?'

'Might not last the night, they reckon.'

'That's awful.'

'Aye. We hadn't been back home five minutes before his old man was taken bad.'

'Were you there with him?'

'I was. Did he not say?'

'He doesn't talk about it much unless he gets really drunk.'

'It isn't an easy thing to talk about. What about you?'

'I lost my dad in nineteen-forty, he was in the navy. My mam died in the Blitz. Didn't have nobody else but an auntie here in Sunderland where we came from first so I came all the way up here and then...'

'And then what?'

'We just didn't suit each other. She'd lived on her own for so long she couldn't tolerate nobody else in the house so I left.'

'You must've been really little then.'

'Yes,' she said, not wanting to think about it. 'My mam came from here and we lived here until we moved to London so I thought it would feel like home but it didn't and doesn't.'

Jim didn't say anything more until they reached her house.

'If you get stuck for anything me and him, we'll be there.' He handed her a card with a telephone number. 'Short of that I'll be outside at the end of the night and if you want anything you let us know.'

'Thanks, Jim.'

'Goodnight, miss,' he said and she got out. That was the moment Rosemary fell in love with Harry. Funny, she thought, he wasn't even there. She walked slowly up the stairs to the room she shared. Hilda had been washing her hair and was sitting over the tiny gas fire, drying it with a thin towel in her hands and a big candlewick dressing gown around her.

She sat down on the little bed and it creaked under her slight weight and the gas fire hissed. Hilda emerged from the towel.

'Summat up?' she said.

'Have you ever found anybody you really loved, Hilda?'

Hilda laughed.

'Like that, is it?'

'Do you think I shouldn't get involved?'

'You are involved, aren't you? He turns up every night. My advice – and this might sound awful – is to take what you can get.'

'What do you mean?'

Hilda looked directly at her.

'I mean sleep with him and get him to buy you things and get him to set you up in a nice house. You could do a lot worse.'

'I've never slept with anybody.'

'No, well... The point is that he isn't going

to wed you because he's who he is and you're who you are so don't go getting sentimental, but you could do very nicely out of it if you play your cards right.'

'I don't want to do that, Hilda.'

'No, I didn't think you did,' Hilda said, putting a brush through her hair in a no nonsense way that got it all gleaming. 'You're soft on him.'

'I am not.'

'Oh, yes, you are. When he finds out he'll sleep with you and then he'll dump you. That's what they do.'

She couldn't rest. The following evening Harry didn't come to the club again but Jim was waiting for her. He told her the funeral would be in three days' time and he told her the name of the church. Rosemary didn't know she was going to turn up at the church but she took the bus in good time and stood back across the road and watched the mourners arrive, the hearse, the coffin being unloaded and she could see Harry clearly with a tall, slender woman, her hand through his arm. There were lots of flowers and the rain poured down.

Rosemary stood outside the church and she could hear the strains of music and she thought of her parents dying and how much she had missed and missed them still even though she hadn't known her dad well and hadn't liked her mother particularly, they were still your family and you couldn't replace that and she was sorry for Harry and his mother.

That night he came to the club, halfway through the evening when she had all but given up on him. She had to stop herself from going over and putting her arms around him, he looked so thin and white and lost.

She went over, trying to sound casual, and said to him,

'Would you like some champagne, sir?'

'No.'

'Whisky?'

'Let's get out of here.'

'What?'

'Get your coat and let's go.'

'I can't leave.'

'I'll pay you.'

She stared at him and then she turned and walked away. He got up and came after her. She stopped and turned around.

'How much?'

'I didn't mean...'

'How much?'

'A hundred pounds.'

'You think that's all I'm worth?'

'Five hundred pounds.'

'For the night?'

'Yes.'

'No.'

'Ask the manager for the night off, tell him he can have your wages and I'll pay you five hundred pounds to spend the night with me.'

Rosemary looked clearly at him.

'I wouldn't do it for a king's ransom,' she said. 'And don't you ever ask me again.'

'I won't be coming back here.'

'Good,' she said.

She didn't think he would follow her into the back but he did. It was almost dark in there, one bare light bulb. None of the girls was in, they were all in the bar. There were clothes strewn everywhere and make-up and hairbrushes and a little mirror above an old dressing table which they all used, and two rickety chairs. It smelled of cheap scent from Woolworths and powder and faintly of the lavatories which were next to it.

'You can't come in here,' she objected, turning on him. 'I'll have you thrown out.'

'Please, Rosemary.'

'No. You can buy anybody with your sort of money. There are lots of girls who would do it.'

'I don't want lots of girls, I want you.'

'You know that saying "every man has his price"?'

'What of it?' he said wearily.

'Well, it isn't true. It never was true. The man was talking about a particular set of people and he said, "all those men have their price". I don't have a price and you had no right to assume that I do.'

There was silence.

'Would you do it for nothing?' he said.

'I might have, if you had asked me nicely.'

'I don't know how to ask anything nicely any more. You don't have any money and I don't know what to say. I buried my father this afternoon–'

'I was there.'

He looked up in surprise.

'Were you?'

'Yes, across the road. You should be with your mother.'

'She has lots of people with her. I wanted to be with you.'

'Only you left your manners at the church-yard,' she said.

'I'm sorry. It isn't what I meant to say.'

'What did you mean to say?'

'I meant to say it so much better. I meant to say that the price was irrelevant, as long as you left with me and never set foot in this place again. I just said that to get you out of here.'

'You don't know me very well if you think I would leave for such a reason.'

'I would have thought you would have wanted to leave for any reason.'

'It would have to be a very good one,' Rosemary said.

'And if I give you a good reason?'

'Go on then,' she scoffed.

'Will you marry me?'

Time passed. Rosemary could hear the pianist giving it everything he'd got out there. She just wished people listened to him, he deserved an audience who would. He was background noise, something to fill in the gaps while people drank and talked and thought about how they'd endure their lives when they left and went back to reality. 'You shouldn't ask that when your dad's just died,' she said, 'you'll regret it in the morning.'

'I won't.' He stood stock still for a few moments and then eased back and fished into his pocket. 'It was all planned you see, before my father was taken ill and had to go into hospital.'

He brought a little square black box from his pocket and flipped open the lid and inside was the biggest diamond that Rosemary had ever seen. Even in the dim light it shimmered brilliantly.

'So, why did you say all that?' she asked.

'Will you?'

She hesitated.

'You're not going to tell me it's all too sudden, are you?' he said, with a faint laugh.

Rosemary was still staring at the ring.

'Or that you'll have to think about it?' he prompted.

'Do you really want to marry me?' she said.

'I wouldn't be asking otherwise.'

Rosemary considered.

'Will you wait while I get my coat? I think we should get out of here.'

'That's what I was trying to say from the beginning,' he said.

They went to a hotel where they had real champagne. This was a first for Rosemary and he was right, it smelled of sick and tasted brilliant. How odd and how exciting. It was a very good hotel and here he organized a room for her but they stayed downstairs and had a meal and it was the best meal she could remember though what they ate was afterwards a mystery to her because she kept holding up her left hand, unable to get used to the idea of the diamond flashing there so unsubtly.

Over coffee in the lounge she felt obliged to say to him, 'We can't get married for at least a year because of your dad dying.'

'I want us to. We can do the ceremony discreetly unless you want a proper wedding.'

'I don't care,' she said, 'but will your mother mind?'

Harry had been putting off telling his mother he was planning on getting married. She was sitting alone in the drawing room when he approached her the following evening. It was a beautiful place, at least he had thought so when he was sent away from home to boarding school at seven. He had lain in bed in the long cold grey dormitory and longed night after night for the place where he belonged.

She sat there by the window, looking so small, so fragile and wearing dark grey. Somehow the grey looked worse than black had. She looked up when she heard him and she smiled.

'I keep waiting for your father to walk in, even though he hadn't walked in months. How foolish is that? Are you all right, Harry?'

'Yes, of course,' he said automatically.

'I don't think you are. I don't think you've been all right ever since you came home. It must be very hard coming back.'

He was surprised at her understanding. Her attention had been focused on his father before now.

'Would you have any objection to my getting married?' he said. 'I know Father has just died but...'

She looked surprised.

'I didn't know there was anyone,' she said.

'It isn't a great love story or anything, but I would like to have somebody to myself.'

'It's lonely being by yourself,' she said. 'Is it anybody we know?'

'No. She's just a girl, very young. She seems to like me and I thought ... I thought it might be nice.'

'Not a grand passion then?' his mother asked with a hint of sadness.

'Nothing like that.'

'You haven't got her into trouble, have you?' She said it lightly, not accusingly.

'She wouldn't dream of letting anyone that close. It's just a feeling that we'd be better together than apart. Would you mind, considering how things are?'

'Considering how things are I think it might be very nice if you got married. Why wait? You've had a dreadful war, you've gone through a great deal for your country and I'm very proud of you but I see no reason why you should go on being by yourself if you think you have any chance of happiness.'

Harry went over and kissed her and she put up a hand to his face in caress.

'She has no family,' he said, 'it would just be you, her, me ... and Jim, I think. She likes Jim.'

Harry took Rosemary to see his mother later that week. All the way there Rosemary sat on the edge of her seat and asked questions.

'It'll be all right,' he said for perhaps the twentieth time.

When they drove in at the huge gates Rosemary sat forward even further. It was not a long drive but the gardens were very big. The house was square and stone and when she got out she could smell and hear the sea.

He ushered her inside and there was a maid wearing a black-and-white uniform. Rosemary had been frightened before. Now she was terrified. In the biggest sitting room she had ever seen a very elegant woman whom she recognized from the funeral unfolded from a chair and got up, smiling and saying hello and offering her hand. Right from the beginning Rosemary knew that Harry's mother was only too aware that Rosemary was 'not one of us' and although she was polite there was a rigidity to her manner and Rosemary didn't like to speak, hearing her own thick accent in her head. She didn't want to make a mistake and she hardly dared eat her cake or lift her cup and saucer for fear she should get things wrong. And worst of all his mother questioned her about her family.

'Do your parents live here?'

'No. They're both dead. We used to live in Sunderland. In fact I think my dad probably worked for you. He was a carpenter.'

'Really?'

'He died in the war and we went to London to stay with relatives and my mam was killed.'

'You don't have anyone else?'

'Only my auntie and ... we didn't get on.'

'Would you like more tea?'

Rosemary drank the tea quickly and held out her cup for more but her hand shook and she thought she might spill it on the fancy rug in front of her. She blushed and stammered and couldn't think of anything to say.

'We'll have to live with my mother until we find somewhere we like,' Harry said as they left.

Rosemary's heart sank right down into her shoes.

'That'll be nice,' she said.

Fifteen

Ella and David's first child was conceived in the little bedroom overlooking the garden of their small house.

When Ella found she was pregnant she could not believe it. She remembered the symptoms and was afraid.

She did not tell David that she was pregnant, she was so very worried that she would miscarry again. Somehow she thought, if I keep it a secret, this time it will be all right.

She felt better than she had the last time right from the start. She had very little morning sickness; as she didn't have so much to do and was able to rest in the afternoons she thought it made a difference. Other people might call her lazy and she did feel guilty about lying down when everybody else was working but it was worth it.

She went to the doctor without saying anything to anyone and he told her that she seemed fine and that the baby would be born in about five months. Ella went back and could have danced all the way up the street.

She waited another month and by then she was beginning to put on weight and she had passed the dangerous time, the time she had lost her first child. She felt sad just thinking about it but knew that she must put the past behind her. She had a bright future ahead with David and they would have a child and everything would be perfect.

She waited for him coming home one particular Friday afternoon and then he was late and she was annoyed and when he finally did come back at almost seven o'clock full of apologies she waited. She waited all evening, she felt that if she told him about it, it would go wrong. She knew that it was stupid to believe such things but she couldn't help it.

Finally as they got into bed she said, 'Before you turn the lamp out, David, I've got something to tell you.'

'What's that?' David said, yawning.

'We're going to have a baby.'

He looked at her and said nothing. She waited.

'Are you sure?'

'I went to the doctor. In four months we're going to be parents.'

David hugged her, told her how pleased he was, said she must be careful not to do too much and that they must get somebody in to help with the baby as soon as it was born.

'I don't need any help,' she said. 'We have a small house, it doesn't justify anybody helping.'

'I think we should.'

'I don't want somebody else in my house,' Ella said.

'You'll probably change your mind as soon as the baby is born,' he said.

'I won't.'

He hesitated and then he said, 'You've known for a while, haven't you?'

'I didn't want to tell you.'

'You were worried?'

Ella didn't know what to say.

'I would have gone through that worry with you if you had told me, you know. You don't have to bottle things up, I'm here for you. I'm your husband.'

'I'll remember it next time.'

'You do that,' he said.

His parents were delighted about the baby; she and David went to see them on the Saturday afternoon. Iris was there. She congratulated them too but Ella thought that her sister-in-law envied her and was not surprised.

'You must move in here,' Mr Black said.

Everybody looked at him.

'It's the sensible thing to do. This house goes with the job and now you're having a child, I think we should move houses. You're doing so much more than I am, David, I'm sure this is a good idea.'

Mrs Black said she thought so too. Iris said nothing but her face darkened.

Ella protested. 'We don't need a bigger house. You are three adults. A baby doesn't take up much room.'

'To be honest,' David's mother said, 'we've had enough of living here. It's getting to be a worry.'

'I bought this place for my parents and they moved out when we were married and they were glad to do so,' David's father said. 'I couldn't think why at the time they would want to leave such a lovely place but I do now. You would be doing us a favour.'

'Iris wouldn't want to go,' Ella said.

'I don't care where I live,' Iris said, 'it's nothing to me.'

Then she got up and walked out.

'She'll get used to it,' her father said. 'Why don't you move in for Christmas and then we can all come to you for Christmas Day

and that'll make things much easier for us?'
He beamed.

'I'm worried about Iris,' Ella said to David that night.

'Oh, it's just her way.'

'David, we're putting her out of her home.'

They were in the sitting room. He looked uncomfortable and then admitted, 'I know, I feel bad about it too but the fact is that it's my parents' house and this is their decision. If my father was better it would be different but they've both looked so strained lately. I don't want them to have to do things they don't choose so Iris will have to put up with it, and before you suggest she lives with us, the answer is no.'

And they both laughed.

They duly moved but the night before David said to Ella, 'I know how much you miss the house where you were brought up.'

Ella was surprised. She hadn't thought he knew.

'You talk about it all the time,' David said.

'Do I? How very boring for you.'

'I know my parents' house is very nice and I love it because Iris and I were brought up there but if Swan Island ever comes up for sale we'll buy it.'

She kissed him.

'Oh, David, I'm so very happy with you,' she said.

'You've made me very happy,' he said,

'you're all I ever wanted.'

Their little boy, Clyde, was born in the February. Ella tactfully asked Iris if she would be godmother to him.

'Don't you want somebody else?' Iris said, picking him carefully out of his cot when she met him for the first time. 'I know nothing about babies and I'm sure I'm not going to be any good with them. I've done midwifery and it's much easier when you aren't personally involved.'

Ella thought that perhaps Iris envied them both the house and the baby. Iris put the baby down only seconds later and suggested she might go and make some tea, it would be something useful to do.

Ella realized from the beginning that David had been right, she did need help. Clyde was a very demanding baby, he didn't sleep and since David was there for all his meals and there was the shopping and cooking and housework she was soon very tired.

'Other women manage,' she said, trying not to burst into tears after one very difficult day when Clyde, now two months old, was troublesome and she was beside herself with exhaustion.

She wanted to accuse David of being no help but she couldn't. His father hadn't been well over the past few weeks and he wasn't at the foundry much. David was having a job managing everything just like she was so she couldn't ask him to do anything.

'I think I've found the perfect person to help,' David said.

'There isn't anybody.'

'What about the woman who used to look after you when you were a child?'

'What, you mean Flo? I don't even know where she is.'

'I do. I've just given her husband a job at the foundry and he told me that she was a maid at your house when you were little and was very fond of you.'

Ella couldn't think of anything better. Two days later Flo, now Mrs King, came to the house and Ella hadn't been able to do anything all morning, she was so excited. She wanted to gather Flo into her arms except that Flo wouldn't have liked that.

'My husband was a soldier all through the war,' she said, 'and we were living at Darlington, but we came back here when he got chance of a job. I didn't know you'd married Mr Black.' They sat at the kitchen table, Flo with the baby in her arms, while they had tea and cake. She ate half her cake and drank two sips of tea before she said, 'My Walter was never the same after he came back.'

'Wasn't he, Flo?'

'No. I think it was too much for him. He was like a stranger to me, like my husband had gone to war and died and another man came back pretending to be him.'

'Hasn't it got better?'

'No. I think it's got worse.' Flo wiped away a tear and then she finished her cake and her tea. Ella poured her another cup and offered her more cake. 'Maybe in time he'll be different. At the moment nothing I do is right. He's awful to live with. I shouldn't say that. He saw things I couldn't imagine, and wouldn't want to, and he won't talk about it. He's hardly said a word since he came home.'

'I'm sorry, Flo. If you've got so much to do perhaps you won't want to come here and help.'

Flo looked at her like she was daft or mad.

'Oh, yes, I do,' she said. 'You and the baby will be the saving of me.'

Sixteen

The telephone was ringing. Somehow David could hear it. He came to consciousness. The bedroom door was ajar. Yes, it was the telephone. He got swiftly out of bed just as Ella came round.

The cold night air hit him the moment he reached the landing. He ran down the stairs.

He got to it before it stopped, picked up the receiver and gave the number.

'David, it's Iris. Come over here. Father has been taken ill.' Then she put the phone down before he had time to speak again.

Ella was halfway down the stairs.

'What is it?' she said and David heard Clyde begin to cry from the top floor.

He didn't want to upset her. They had just found out she was pregnant with their second child and she had been unwell for weeks, but he had to tell her.

'It's my father. Iris sounds really worried and I'm going to have to go. Will you be all right here on your own?'

'Of course I will. You go to them.'

He ran upstairs and put on some warm clothes and then got into the car and drove the short distance through the sleeping city and up the cobbled street which led to the Bailey where the pretty house lay.

The doctor's car was outside the front door. David hammered on it, his heart sick and presently Iris came and answered it. She was in her nightclothes. David followed her upstairs just as the doctor came on to the landing.

'I'll have to use an ambulance,' he said.

Iris and her mother dressed, Lottie went in the ambulance and David took Iris to the hospital in his car. From there they spent what felt like a long time sitting outside in

206

the corridor while the night went on and on before they were allowed in to see their father. David thought his mother looked old for the first time. She had gone through so much with Iris away and she had looked after him and his father all the way through the war. Her only sister had been killed in the Blitz and he knew that she missed her. He went over and kissed her.

'They think he's had a series of small strokes before now. He never complained of anything other than tiredness,' she said.

'I know.' She had forgotten that he had been there various times when his father had been confused or fallen or felt dizzy and there had been other times at the foundry which he had not told her about when his father refused to see the doctor because, David thought, he had feared that the doctor would have told him he must give up work and stay at home. David knew it would have been the finish of him. Even before the war there had been bad turns, but his parents had ignored them and he had not thought it kind to do otherwise.

When it was daylight David left his mother and Iris at the hospital; his mother had said she wasn't going anywhere and Iris wouldn't leave without her so he went back to the house. He told Ella briefly what had happened and then he went to work though she tried to dissuade him. Anything was better than sitting around, he thought, and it would be what his father wanted anyway.

Work was easy by comparison, and he welcomed the distraction, but it was difficult to concentrate and long before teatime he was so tired that he wished he could give up and go home or that he had somebody he could trust to see to things when he was not there, but there was nobody. His father could not delegate and would never allow David to do so and this was now causing a problem. He had to be there all the time; there was nobody to take the weight of the business.

Iris and Lottie practically lived at the hospital over the next few days and then Mr Black was sent home but he did not make progress. They brought a bed downstairs into the back room. Ella offered to have him at their house because they had more space but Iris wouldn't have him moved again and she spent every hour with her father and sometimes sat up with him all night. David was grateful to his wife for offering and wished Iris would at least let them help, but she sat there, pale and grave over his bed, and it was a trial going to the house.

'Don't you think we should have a nurse in to help?' he suggested gently when she had gone without sleep for two days.

'I'm a nurse. Perhaps you hadn't noticed?' she said tersely.

'You need some sleep.'

'I went through six years of war, David, I think I can stand a few days of caring for my father.'

'It's a strain on Mother too,' he said.

'I know that.'

'You know it but you aren't prepared to do anything about it?'

Iris glared at him.

'This isn't your decision to make, David, and I haven't heard any offers from you or Ella to come over here and help.'

'Who's going to run the foundry? You?'

'You're being ridiculous.'

'I'm being ridiculous?' He stopped there. He knew from years of experience that there was no point in arguing with his sister. She loved an argument more than anything in the world and was prone to losing her temper and so he had learned not to do so. Iris did not seem to realize that part of becoming an adult was the ability to contain one's emotions or perhaps the war had made her this bitter person who took on every battle, who never ever gave in. Sometimes, he thought, it was better to do so. His mother would not thank him for what she would think of as him causing a row with Iris.

He went through to the sitting room.

'Maybe you would like to come and spend the day with us?' he suggested to his mother.

'I can't leave Iris.'

She didn't say, 'I can't leave your father.' It was Iris who was the problem. 'She feels as though she must take this on,' Lottie said.

'It's wearing you out.'

She came to him and took his hand and squeezed it.

'I'm fine,' she said.

Some weeks later his father had another stroke, this time very severe and it was a Sunday afternoon while he and Ella were both there. Iris held her father in her arms and begged of him not to die and it was very difficult for David to stand and watch while the tears poured down her face.

Ella took his mother from the room and he tried to talk to Iris.

'Let him go. It's his time.'

'I will never let him go and you have no right to expect it. He's my father and I love him.'

'Let me at least call the doctor.'

'He doesn't need a doctor, he just needs his family.'

'Think about Mother,' David said and she turned to him a face so white and so distraught that he wished he had not spoken, but he knew both then and afterwards that he had been right and he wished Iris had let their father die. He wanted to remember his father as he had been and not as he was now. It was difficult not to blame Iris for this but in a way he understood. He knew she had lost many friends during the war. She must feel as though she was losing everything and she must do everything she could in order to stop the last important people from leaving her.

The tears ran down her face and she stood there with her father's body in her arms like she had once done with a dog that was dying. David could not help remembering both incidents in the same way and he wished he did not. He sent for the doctor and when the man came back out from looking at his father he gazed around at Lottie, Ella and David. Iris had not come out of the room.

'The stroke was severe and I think he should be in hospital.'

'Then please do whatever you have to do,' David said.

The doctor nodded.

When he had gone to call an ambulance Iris came out, her face set and hard.

'You've allowed him to go into hospital, haven't you? Who do you think you are?' she said.

David didn't reply. The ambulance came. David couldn't look at Iris, he was so tired from fighting with her, hated it so much and he and Ella followed in their car.

He expected, even hoped, his father would die that night, it would have been so much better but he did not and after several days when he did not deteriorate further he was sent home to Iris's care.

Seventeen

Monday was always the heaviest day, yet Ella had learned to love it best. It was a fine windy August day, the end of the month and not as hot as it had been. In the back kitchen of the house Ella was putting the clothes through the washer. She was very pleased with how things were going. The washer was new and had an electric wringer and it was so much easier not having to do these things by hand. She loved how they went through by themselves and came out the other side, drip free, to be pushed into the basket.

From upstairs she could hear the sound of the vacuum, Flo was busy with the dusting and cleaning and she would have the windows open to the breeze, which ventured in from the river.

Clyde, Ella's older child, was with her, helping and the baby, Susan, was sleeping in her pram in the hall. The last lot of clothes filled the basket.

'Come on then,' she said to Clyde, 'let's go

out and you can help Mammy to put these on the line.'

She lifted up the heavy basket and walked through the big stone-flagged yard out into the back where the paddock lay beyond and there was the well which had once been needed for the horses and the old carriage houses which were used for the cars. There was the field where the local butcher kept his cattle and the neglected garden which belonged to the doctors who lived further along and the piece of ground where the cars backed out before they went along the top and out into the town.

Here she had her clothes lines, strung in a triangle and there were already a great many clothes dancing in the breeze, David's shirts in a line, lots of different coloured socks, the children's tiny clothes and the sheets pinned up so that they billowed. She put down the basket and Clyde solemnly handed the pegs to her. He was a tubby little boy with bright blue eyes and a broad forehead.

When the washing was all on the third line she looked at it with great satisfaction and went back into the house to put the kettle on to the Aga so that she and Flo could have their mid-morning coffee.

They sat at the kitchen table. Flo loved her morning coffee, mostly, Ella suspected because she put a tot of brandy into Flo's coffee. It helped her get through the rest of the morning.

After that Flo went upstairs to deal with the bathroom and Ella began putting on the vegetables for dinner. She had stewed beef overnight in the bottom oven and was making pastry. There would be little pies with beef tea, carrots, potatoes and cabbage for dinner at midday. David would be back at just after twelve. Flo went home for her dinner. Ella sat Clyde in his highchair, saw to the baby and before David arrived everything was ready. They ate in the kitchen because it was easier and she had not had time to arrange for them to eat in the dining room. She had always wanted to do such things but they would need more help and she didn't really want more people in her house. She was happy with the way that things were and she knew that David didn't care anyhow.

She watched him while he ate. She thought he was lovely. He had beautiful green eyes. She was mortified that neither of the children had inherited his eyes, they both had blue eyes like her.

'Did you decide about the dinner dance?' he asked.

'We can't go off like that and leave the children.'

'Why not? Flo would come and stay, you know she loves to and it would do us good to get away.'

'It isn't a dinner dance. It's a steel foun-
ders' and ship-builders' convention. You
make it sound so ... ordinary.'

'Not with us there,' he said, with a quiet
little smile.

'It's a very classy hotel in Scotland.'

'You could buy a new dress.'

'Bribery,' she accused him.

That afternoon when David went back to
work, Iris called. Ella gave her tea and they
sat down.

Flo had come back after her dinner and
was busy polishing the brasses in the
kitchen so Ella took Iris through into the
sitting room. She always felt mean doing it,
like Lady Muck, having Flo sit in the
kitchen with the brasses on newspaper on
the table and the two of them drinking tea,
all la-di-da in the sitting room.

It was daft but she feared that Flo might
be offended, but Flo just went on polishing
the brasses and it wasn't as though Ella
asked her to make the tea. She put a tot of
whisky in Flo's tea, just as she always did,
and Flo got on, humming to the lord to
abide with her while the posh lot drank tea
in the lounge.

'I need a new dress for the steelfounders'
convention,' Ella said as she handed Iris a
cup and saucer and offered her coffee cake
which she had made the day before.

Iris refused the cake, sipped her tea and

said, 'You are going then?'

'David wants to.' That wasn't quite true. She had decided since dinner time that she wanted to as well and when he talked of a new dress it wasn't just any old dress, she would need something long and spectacular. Iris was good with things like that.

'Will you come with me to find something to wear?'

'I suppose I could.'

'And could you ask Mrs Duncan to see to your parents for a few hours?'

David had approached Flo about the convention and Ella had known what the outcome would be. Flo had a soft spot for him, she always blushed slightly when he was there. Flo therefore did not know how to refuse and David had a way with women, his green eyes were always soft on them. It was a lot to ask anybody to take on, especially a woman who had no children, but Flo loved the children. She never said anything but Ella suspected that Flo would have wanted children of her own.

'Who is looking after the children when you go to Scotland?'

'Mrs King.'

'I could have done it,' Iris said.

'You have enough to do, I couldn't have asked it of you.' Ella's instincts shrieked when Iris offered to look after the children. Flo was good with them but Ella had the

216

feeling that Iris would be dreadful. She barely spoke to Clyde and was inclined to tell him to mind his manners. Ella thought Clyde was rather afraid of his strict and short-spoken aunt and when he saw her sometimes he hid behind Ella's skirts.

'Father is better, well enough to be left for an hour or two.'

He wasn't but the idea that he would not get better was obviously too much for Iris to bear.

'So you will come shopping with me. I need your opinion.'

Ella was also very aware that Iris had very little life, nothing but her parents, the church and the small social group of older family friends round which her existence allowed. Not for her a ball gown, a visit to the highlands; no excitement, no variety. But Iris could be generous and she was now.

'I would love to go. We'll have a proper day out and coffee in Bainbridges.'

Ella determined to buy Iris a meal. They had not had a day out together in a long time. She had recently learned to drive and was proud of her little A30, small and green, the first car which David had ever bought.

The Austin Shiline he took his parents out in on Sunday afternoons had belonged to his father. It was big and silver but the A30 was hers and she loved it.

Friday was the day they had chosen to go

to town. Lottie assured them that she could look after Mr Black for the few hours they were away, Mrs Duncan was just next door if there were any problems and David would call in at dinner time on his way home from the foundry just to make sure that his mother was coping. He would look in again later in the afternoon.

Ella drove carefully past the little villages, through Gateshead which was just south of the river and then into town, to park on the outskirts near the station and walk in towards the shops. She liked Newcastle. David had brought her here for her engagement and wedding rings and also before they were married to buy her a fox fur cape and a musquash coat. He had always been good to her.

There were many beautiful dresses to look at and she tried on several and was pleased to see that she could still look good even after two children. The one that they finally chose was aqua with sequins on the skirt, low cut across the top with thick raspberry velvet coloured straps and a square neck. It was very expensive and Ella almost didn't buy it, but Iris said it looked the best and she had to have it. It brought out the colour of her eyes and the gloss of her hair.

Ella felt guilty but found that she could not leave without it so they duly paid over a lot of the money David had given her and, remembering her reflection as she had turned and how Iris said she had never looked better in her life, Ella found herself carrying the dress home, along with new shoes, evening bag, underwear, stockings and a new almost blushingly decadent night-dress, Iris, in a fit of generosity, had told her was enough to give her any man's full attention.

Ella would have stayed and had a pot of tea and cake, but Iris was concerned about her parents and wanted to get back.

Ella was reluctant to go, she had enjoyed her quick jaunt.

The baby was crying when she arrived home and Clyde ran to her. Flo looked relieved to see her.

'They've both played up all afternoon,' she said.

David came back and reported that his parents were both fine and asked her if she'd bought a dress. She said yes but he wasn't to see it, it was a surprise.

As the days passed Ella began to want to go less and less. She had a kind of premon-ition about it, everything was going to go wrong and she felt like clinging to the house, finding she could not leave the children. It was beautiful here, the afternoons were warm and most of the flowers in the garden were in full bloom so it was a shame to go and leave it all.

She was half inclined to tell David that he should go by himself, that she suspected Clyde was coming down with something, except that Clyde was so obviously well and she had not even a snuffle from the baby as an excuse.

On the Thursday she went into town and had her hair done, not much because it naturally had a wave and fell to just above her shoulders but it needed a trim, and after that there was little to do but pack and issue last minute instructions to Flo, who took it all in with a mere pressing of lips as Ella told her for perhaps the tenth time where everything was and that if anything went wrong with the children she was to ring the hotel and was she sure that she had the number. Flo nodded, reassured her, then the packing was done and Ella and David were setting off on the Friday evening after he finished work.

They were to stay overnight at a hotel in Jedburgh. It was only a couple of hours drive away but she sensed that David wanted them to be by themselves, they got so little chance.

The early evening was fine and she had bought another new dress though not expensive, just to have something to wear for tonight. David put the cases into the boot, she kissed the children one last time and they were away.

For the first few miles she was convinced

something would go wrong but as the journey progressed she began to relax and enjoy the scenery as the car wound its way through Northumberland towards the border. They stopped there because the view was spectacular of the hills and once they were into Scotland she stopped worrying about everything. David had booked the hotel in advance and it was the fairy-tale kind with a lovely grey turret at one end, the kind of thing which Rapunzel, who had let down her hair, might have been keen to escape from but Ella wasn't eager to escape, she liked it right from the beginning.

They had a great big room with its own bathroom next door and a view of the River Jed and they bathed and changed and took a walk through the town and then went back for dinner. It was a candlelit dinner and they had wine and she smiled across the table at David and knew that they had been right to get away.

She wore the new nightdress, David said he loved it. She slept very well in the big bed and they had a huge breakfast and set off for the highlands. The weather was fine again. They stopped for lunch, David was making the most of the journey, Ella thought, they didn't rush there.

They went for a walk in the afternoon at a little village where they stopped. A tumbling stream fell below a humpbacked stone bridge and she thought she had never been happier. She was the luckiest woman in the world. She kissed David as they stood watching the water below and he smiled at her.

It was therefore late afternoon when they finally reached the hotel in the highlands and it was everything and more that Ella had imagined. It looked the nearest thing to a French chateau. It was so big and had such impressive grounds, all lawns and trees and various gardens that Ella was overawed and when they parked the car and walked inside she was struck dumb and had no idea what to say or do.

David was at home anywhere and spoke to the receptionist who stood behind the huge desk. They were escorted to their room on the first floor and it was even bigger and better than the room they had had the night before, all mahogany and brass with a huge bath. Their room looked out over a magnificent rose garden and the windows were open so the soft scent of other flowers wafted their way up towards her.

She was scared. She didn't want to go downstairs and meet lots of new people but she knew that the social side of this was the important bit and that she must, so she bathed and put on her make-up and then the new dress.

David looked wonderful in evening dress,

as all men did, she thought and he liked the new dress, she could tell, even though he didn't say much. His eyes went all soft and warm on her so that Ella thought in other circumstances David would have said he liked the dress so much that he wanted to take it off her and they would never have got downstairs to dinner, but this was too important to be missed so they made their way down the stairs.

It was easy. All she had to do was hang on to his arm and smile. The speeches after dinner were boring. David looked wrapt but then he always did about his work, he was almost fanatical about it. In the middle of the third speech Ella was so bored that she wanted to make an excuse and go to the ladies' room so when the speech finished and David assured her there was another to come she made an excuse and escaped from the room.

The open doors beyond her were too tempting and she walked out of them. The night air was warm on her bare shoulders and face. Then, as she admired the rose garden, somebody said her name softly behind her and when she turned around she almost fainted. There, behind her, tall, dark and wearing evening dress, was Harry Reid.

Eighteen

It was after one when David and Ella went upstairs and they were the first to leave but she wanted to go. It seemed to take ages to get ready for bed and nobody spoke. She stood on the balcony in her nightdress and there in the slight breeze from the loch she heard David say from behind her, 'Did you know Harry Reid was going to be there?'

'No.'

'I didn't know you knew him. They have one of the biggest shipyards on the Wear. His wife is years younger than he is. She must be in her early twenties, blonde girl, black dress, very good looking.'

'Yes, he was a ... a friend of Jack's, they joined the army together. She's stunning,' Ella said and had to breathe carefully to get the words out without falling over them.

'Yes, very beautiful.'

'And wearing a ... a dress so expensive she made everybody else's look cheap.'

Ella had thought that going on talking would make the words come out easier but it didn't. David said nothing more.

She could not however put Harry from her mind and long after David slept she stood on the balcony, smoking a cigarette, even though the wind was cold upon the water. She jumped when she heard David's voice behind her.

'How well did you know him?'

She turned around. David's eyes were so clear that she had difficulty in meeting them. He was not a fool and she was deceiving him. She didn't know what to say.

'I thought you'd gone to sleep,' she said.

'I did and ... this isn't something I want to talk about. On the other hand ... you didn't answer my question.'

'I did. I said that Jack knew him. You know him quite well though, don't you?' Ella said.

'Not really. We're in the same business.'

'Yes but there's more, I could hear it in your voice somehow.'

'When you went out of the ballroom he followed you.'

'I don't think he did, David, I think it was a coincidence.' It was the first time she had lied to her husband and she hoped very much that it would be the last.

'You came back in together.'

'We were talking in the garden. I hadn't seen him since the war.'

'War changes people, you know, Ella, and he spent a long time in Burma from what I heard, in the thick of it.'

'Yes, of course I know, we all do.' It made

her feel guilty just to be reminded of Harry's war.

'Is Harry Reid changed?'

'Very much so, I would say. What do you think of him?'

'Men don't judge one another like that, at least I don't think so and being here during the war was the easy option.'

'You didn't intend it to be, it worked out that way.'

David felt guilty about staying at home during the war. He often mentioned it as though there had been less value in what he was doing but she knew that it was his frustration at being stuck at home doing something which his father might have handled alone had things been different.

'Harry needn't have gone. He was a ship-builder.'

'He was very young and all his friends went. And I think he thought his father was capable of running the shipyard alone where-as your father wanted you there helping, didn't he?'

'Yes. His health has always been precari-ous, it would have been stupid and imprac-tical to leave him to cope.'

'Well then.'

'It was particularly horrible in the East,' David said.

'I expect it was horrible everywhere.'

'And this is an excuse for who he has

become?' David said.

'Maybe.' She looked at him. 'So what do you know of him?'

'That he isn't happily married–'

'Are you telling me he runs around?'

'He drinks to excess but then so do many men these days. I don't do so badly myself. I didn't know he was Jack's best friend–'

'They were schoolboys together. Was it Stowe? I can't remember now. Perhaps it was a good preparation for war.'

'I don't think anything is a good preparation for war,' David said. 'Does it matter to you that he isn't happy?'

'Why should it matter to me?' she said and felt her heart beat hard.

'His family is important, just like yours was,' David said. 'The same social level. I thought perhaps you had known one another when you were children.'

In some ways she liked to hear anything about her family on anybody's lips since there was nobody any more.

'Did your families know one another?' David said.

'No. I met him through Jack, that's all and he was very upset when Jack died because it wasn't an act of war it was just ... awful.'

David didn't say anything to that. They didn't talk about Jack much. Why was it, she thought, still so difficult to talk about him?

'He admires you. I could see it in his face.

He kept looking over at you during the dancing. I thought he was going to come and ask you to dance.'

'Are you jealous?'

'Yes.' There was something disarming about the rueful way that he said it and it made her laugh. 'He's a lot more successful than I am, he's a lot richer. He went to a top public school and he doesn't have Iris for a sister.'

She smiled in acknowledgement of his attempt at lightness, put the cigarette under the sole of her slipper and went to him.

'I'm all yours,' she said and she kissed him.

Their lovemaking had almost always been good, except after each child for several months she had not wanted to get close to him but that had passed. Perhaps because of the conflict or because of Harry, David was not happy until she was exhausted, sweaty and ready to sleep. That was men, she thought. They wanted to make everything theirs, even though, after two children, she would have thought David felt secure. He obviously didn't and she could not help but acknowledge that he was right in a way. There was some part of her which would always belong to Harry Reid and nothing could alter that.

Nineteen

Two days after the Scottish convention, Iris turned up at the house mid-afternoon as she was wont to do when her mother rested and her father slept.

They sat in the garden, it was a beautiful day, on the wrought iron bench outside the front porch and Ella told Iris about the hotel and the dinner. Iris didn't say much to that.

Ella said, 'Harry Reid was there.'

Iris would know of the Reids who had been for years top Sunderland shipyard owners.

Iris stared. 'Was he?'

'David didn't mention it?' Ella tried not to overreact.

'No.'

'He has a very glamorous wife. Blonde. Wearing a terribly expensive dress.'

'They're rich.' Iris always knew everything about everybody, especially rich and important people. Perhaps she envied them, perhaps we all do, Ella thought.

'Yes, I suppose they are.' Ella looked steadily down the garden.

'She's very young, I understand. What is

she like?'

'Absolutely stunning,' Ella said, pulling a face to lighten the mood.

Iris laughed shortly.

'He is very attractive.'

'Yes, I suppose.'

'No suppose about it,' Iris said. 'I've seen him recently.'

'Where?'

'It wasn't to speak to. I saw him on the street in Sunderland when I went to do some shopping. I didn't suppose he would remember me. We only met officially once, I think before the war and he was very young at the time.'

They went inside and then Iris hurried away down the street and Ella watched her, her thin back and her bowed head. What had she to look forward to? She had nothing in her life beyond the care of two old people in a little street beside the cathedral. No wonder she needed to live through other people.

Ella had been lucky. She had David and the children. She had a full life now. She would not look back, there was no point, there was nothing to be gained from it.

Ella knew that there was something wrong when David came home in the middle of the afternoon. It was a perfect autumn day, they were having what was known as an Indian summer, there had been almost a fortnight of good weather. She and Clyde had spent a lot of time damming a little beck outside the town, a small tributary which ran into the Wear.

It was peaceful there away from everything and you could not even see the little pit towns which surrounded the city and the scarred landscape with its pitheaps and pitheads, many of them abandoned though there were still working pits in the area and men coming home black with coal in the late afternoons.

She liked plodging about in the water and Clyde liked pointing to which rock he wanted moving next. They spent several afternoons soaking wet in the sunshine while Flo sat on the riverbank with the baby and it had been bliss.

They would wend their way slowly back up the winding road to the village. The hedges were thick with rosehips and at the bottom of their garden the fruit trees were heavy with plums beside the wall.

As the afternoon ended, Flo would go off to make Walter's tea and David would come back and the children, worn out from the heat and exertion, would go to bed early. Then she and David would sit with the French windows open, facing the garden, until the darkness and colder evening came down and even then sometimes they sat out there with thick sweaters on, thinking it might be a long winter and they must make the best of every day.

They would drink gin and tonic with plenty of ice and lemon or, if it was late and cooler, whisky and soda, they would smoke and talk of nothing in particular and it was heavenly, she thought. It was her favourite time of day.

That day, however, it had been overcast and threatening, so they had not gone to the beck and Flo was already chuntering that perhaps that was their lot for this year. Then, just before three, when she and Flo were arranging flowers which she had cut from the garden she looked up and David was standing in the doorway.

'Oh,' she said, 'you did give me a start.'

He said nothing, walked away through the gloom of the hall. She followed him into the little sitting room at the back. Clyde played there and toys were scattered on the floor. 'I haven't tidied up in here yet,' she said.

David turned away.

'My father died,' he said.

'Oh, David, no.'

'Iris ran into the office in such a state.'

'Is she all right?' What else was there to say? Iris had been keeping their father alive purely by will for months.

'The doctor came but he was already dead.'

'Shall we go? Flo won't mind staying with the children for a little while.'

'I don't want to go back just now,' he said, his voice shaking.

'Would you like me to go?'

'Iris screamed and shouted,' he said.

'And your mother?'

'My mother has been expecting it.'

Ella tried to take him into her arms, but he turned from her as though he couldn't bear to be touched. She wanted to run across the streets, past the shadow of the great cathedral, into the narrowness of the bailey and the pretty house there and comfort Iris but it would be disloyal to leave him, yet she needed something to do.

She put the kettle on even though the kitchen was so hot from the Aga and then the dark clouds gathered as they had been threatening to do all day and it began to rain, so heavily that it pounded off the roof and the window panes. She could see it bouncing off the flowerbeds in the borders at the side of the house from the kitchen window while she made the tea. Flo came in.

'The baby's asleep and Clyde's gone to his dad,' she said.

'Sit down and have some tea.'

Flo sat gratefully. Ella poured tea. She poured whisky into all of it and took David's through to where he was standing, Clyde clasped in his arms, by the French windows, gazing down across the gardens and houses at the far side of the river.

'Here,' she said, 'drink your tea.'

She took Clyde from him and insisted that David sat down.

'What will I do now?' he said.

Later, when he seemed a little less shocked and the children had gone to bed, she left him dozing in an armchair and went to see Iris. The house was most easily reached by following the path to the river and then up across Palace Green and beyond into North Bailey.

The house was pretty, all the houses in the street were, Ella thought. Theirs was the smallest. One of the neighbours, Mrs Duncan, opened the front door. Ella went into the sitting room where the old lady was and took hold of her hands and kissed her.

'It was for the best,' Lottie said. 'He'd had enough, more than enough. He should have died when he was first taken ill but Iris couldn't let him go. She's so very upset, Ella. Do go to her.'

Older people and their resignation. They faced things so much better than other people did. They had seen so much. She looked tired. Ella went through into the dining room where David's father lay in the bed where he had died. Iris was sitting there clasping his hand as though he were still alive or as though she could will him back to life.

'Do you know what David said? He told me to pull myself together.'

'It was probably just for something to say.'

'He could have said a lot of things which would have been of more comfort.'

'I expect he would have except that he is very upset too.'

'Is he?' Iris finally sat up and looked at her. 'He doesn't seem it.'

'People don't always show their feelings.' It was something David, like many men, she thought, found difficult. 'Is there anything I can do?'

'No, the vicar will be here shortly and Mr Gibbons, the undertaker, will deal with everything else. There's nothing more anybody can do,' Iris said and she turned away.

The funeral over, the solicitor came to the house. It was the big house, which had, as Iris pointed out, been their family house and it seemed appropriate that people should gather there from respect. When they had all gone the solicitor arrived and David, Iris and their mother went into the dining room.

Ella was not invited to the reading of the will, she had not expected to be. However, they were in there for so long that she left the little playroom and carried Clyde through into the dining room where David was to her surprise sitting alone.

'Has everybody gone?' she said. 'I didn't hear them. I thought your mother and Iris would stay for tea.'

'They thought best not. They were both tired and I don't think any of us is hungry.'

'What happened?'

He said nothing.

'Talk to me, David. Tell me.'

He looked at her for a few seconds, un-comprehending and she prompted him again.

'What?' she said.

'The works are left to me but there is nothing for Iris or my mother, just a few keepsakes–'

'No money?'

'A few weeks wages for the men and some owed which should come in soon. At least I hope.'

'How can there be no money?'

'My father started with very little and we've been struggling for years. He ... he loaned out a lot of money and he gave a lot of money to people who needed it or people he thought needed it and most of it was never given back.' David looked slightly ashamed of himself for saying this because his father had always been known as an open handed man. To call it a fault was unfair.

'I kept on hoping it would get better and

everything would be all right.'

What experience, Ella wondered, had told him such things.

'Then what are we to do?' she said.

'I have suggested to them that they should move in with us and I'll sell the house.'

Ella stared at him.

'You've done what?'

He looked levelly at her.

'The company was paying my parents a wage but it can't go on doing that obviously and as for Iris... I'm going to have to keep all of us,' he said shortly. 'It'll be cheaper if we're here together and the money raised from the house will cushion things for a while.'

'You might have consulted me.'

'I didn't see the point. They are my family and it's not as though there is a viable alternative.'

'I'm your wife. At the very least it would have been polite.'

'I'm sorry.'

He got up and walked out. Ella ran after him.

'How could you do that?' she said.

He turned around and then she wished she hadn't gone after him.

'I said I was sorry, all right?' They had never quarrelled, he had never shouted. 'My father is dead, for God's sake, why don't you leave me alone?'

Startled, Ella moved back and as she did so he strode off down the garden and she stood there shaking.

She felt mean about the whole thing but she did not want to let anybody into what she could see now had been a kind of paradise containing herself, David and the children, Flo coming during the week to help and the gardener, Mr Philips, quietly seeing to things outside. It was not that she disliked Iris or his mother – Lottie was a lovely person – she just didn't want them in her house permanently.

Iris came to see her later. She looked as though she had lost weight and she was tiny under normal circumstances.

'Are you eating anything?' Ella said.

'Did you hear what David said? That the works can no longer supply us with a wage. As though we were the poor dependents, as though my parents didn't run the place, own it. Does David have to be so unpleasant?'

'I'm sure he didn't mean it, Iris.' She tried to keep her voice level and not to defend David too readily. A row was the last thing they needed.

'Maybe in time we'll be able to look for something bigger.'

'We can't afford it.'

'I'd rather have a house of my own,' Iris said.

When Iris had gone Ella waited and waited for David to come back and then began to worry because he didn't. It was almost one o'clock in the morning when she heard the door. The children were asleep and she was in her nightwear. She came on to the landing and gazed down the stairs.

'David?'

'Yes.'

He paused in the hall and she went down to him.

'David, I'm sorry, I–'

'I don't want to discuss this any more,' he said and walked past her and went to bed.

That was when Ella became angry herself and almost went to sleep in the spare room but she made herself go into their bedroom. Nobody spoke and she didn't sleep.

She tried to talk to him again when he came in at midday, the next dinnertime, about the possibility of getting somebody in to look after his mother while Iris went out to work and how in that case they wouldn't need to move in.

All he said was, 'I come back here for some peace, Ella. Let it go, can't you?'

Ella said nothing and he smoked his dinner-time cigarette and went off back to work without a word but at tea time when she was getting Clyde up from his afternoon sleep – he wouldn't go to bed if he slept too long during the day – having successfully sorted out the baby, David put his head round the bedroom door and looked apologetically at her. She came out of the room with Clyde in her arms, closing the door behind her and smiled at him.

'Things are difficult,' he said, as they went downstairs. 'There are going to be huge death duties to pay, I've had the accountant at the works most of the day. I have no money.'

'How much will we need?'

'I don't know yet but a great deal more than I imagined.'

'Can we borrow it?'

'We shall have to get it from somewhere.'

They reached the sitting room. The garden was striking where Mr Philips had planted bedding earlier in the year, though his choice of colour wasn't exactly what Ella would have wanted.

There was lots of orange. He had a thing about marigolds which she detested but she didn't like to say anything because he considered the garden his territory. It was all getting a bit straggly now that autumn was setting in.

Further over the name of the house was spelled out in yellow. It was enough, Ella thought, to make anybody bilious. David didn't notice and it was not surprising. He said, sinking down into the nearest armchair, when Iris was visiting that evening,

'The bank refused to loan us any money.'

He must be worried, Ella reasoned, to talk like that in front of his sister.

'You could sell this house and move in with mother and me,' Iris said tartly.

He looked at her.

'Very funny,' he said.

'It's no worse than your idea of us moving in with you. I'm sure you could spare a few thousand for a little house for Mother and me.'

'What about the cottage?' David said.

Iris frowned.

'Are you talking about that hovel on the end of this building? You are joking, aren't you? Why don't you put us out on the street?'

'It was just a thought,' David said.

'You could get rid of Miss Grant. I could do her work. I'm sure you pay her a very good wage. I could rent a house for Mother and me with it.'

'What nonsense,' David said in brisk tones which Ella had rarely heard before and would have hesitated arguing with but Iris had no such qualms.

'It can't be that difficult.'

'You are a qualified nurse. Madeline Grant is my secretary and I know and trust her.'

'Does that mean you don't know or trust me?' Iris demanded.

'Must you two shout? I've just put the children to bed,' Ella implored them, desperate for a drink and a quiet sit down before the evening was over.

She hated the way they fought with one another and at such odd times. But then Iris did not like to leave her mother until Lottie was what she called 'settled down for the evening' so she would come up here at nine o'clock at night and do battle for something which she thought she was due.

Ella couldn't understand it any more than David could but Iris obviously saw herself running David's office and she had come to dread Iris's knocking on the door. Iris had even complained that she should have to knock in order to come into her brother's house, but the whole idea of Iris coming and going as she pleased was enough to make Ella shudder.

She wished David had used tact and found something that Iris could do but he was not tactful with his sister, just with everybody else.

'I need a job,' Iris said.

'Then for heaven's sake go out and find one and stop pestering me,' he said.

'I don't think you two fighting is going to be very helpful,' Ella said, knowing that if she did not intervene now they would end up shouting, or at least Iris would, banging the door and vowing not to come back and they could do without the complication, but they both subsided after she spoke.

'Is there nobody else who would give us the money?' Iris said.

'I can't think of anybody. Most of my business acquaintances are in the same boat or worse,' David said and he walked out of the sitting room.

Iris glared after him into the cold, dark night but David had gone to the bottom of the garden, climbed over the wall and was already out of sight of the house lights.

'You don't handle him properly,' Ella said.

'Why should I handle him?'

'I think it would get you further.'

'And is that what you do, handle him?' Iris said, ready to take up arms yet again.

'I certainly do,' Ella agreed. 'I am his wife and he is having a very hard time.'

'I don't know how you stand him,' Iris said, in exasperation. 'He's cold, he's unhelpful, unapproachable, as unlike Father as anybody could be.'

Ella understood completely. David's father had been a charming, warm person who had fed the area during times past when things were bad. David had a habit of walking out rather than fight just like he had done now. It was a good tactic, she thought. He could not justify losing his temper to his sister or his wife and there was nothing else to do but leave. He came back an hour later when Iris had gone and Ella had settled down with a book, a drink and the much wanted cigarette.

'Don't worry, she's not here,' she said, without looking up.

'You think I'm wrong then?'

'Good lord, no.' Ella put down the book and smiled at him. 'I think you'd murder one another within the week and Madeline is the perfect person to run the office.'

'Now you're humouring me,' he said.

'Call it self preservation,' Ella said and that made him smile.

David had become glad of Fridays because although he always went into the office on Saturday mornings it felt different and the end of the week had become such a relief. Sometimes he felt like he wanted to run away.

Madeline Grant put her head around the door of David's office, knocking at the same time since it was open, until he looked up from the papers he had been perusing.

She was a pretty woman, slight, with neat, short red hair and blue eyes, dressed in dark costumes and plain blouses, and was the only woman who worked at the foundry. He thought, with a touch of humour, that though most of the men were a little afraid of her, they all respected her.

She knew everything that went on in the

office and almost everything that went on in the works. She dealt with the telephone, shielded him from unwanted callers and visitors, was a touch typist, a good book keeper and her filing was perfect. She was just a few years older than he was and had been his father's secretary. He trusted her totally.

She said, 'Mr Reid is here to see you.'

'Reid?' David frowned. 'Harry Reid?'

'Yes. Can I send him in?'

'Yes.'

She nodded and went out. David got to his feet. Moments later Harry appeared, smiling. David didn't like the smile. In fact, he thought, on reflection I don't like anything about him at all.

Harry looked completely out of place among the dust, the piles of paper, the smudged walls, the carpetless floor and somehow he managed to make the small office feel even smaller and insignificant. He made David feel grubby but it wasn't an altogether bad feeling. David hoped he never wore an expensive suit like that to work, it would prove he was frightened to get his hands dirty and he had never been that.

'Good afternoon,' Harry said genially. 'You do remember me?'

'Yes, of course. Come in. Sit down. What can I do for you?'

Harry looked at the empty seat at the far

side of the desk as though it had dog muck on it, David thought, but he sat anyway. He appeared to sit back and consider things for a few moments or maybe he just liked the delay because you could do a lot with silence.

'It's more what I can do for you really.'

'Is it?' David did not feel good about this. In fact he thought he had never liked Harry Reid since the Scottish convention, since Harry had looked across the dance floor so admiringly at Ella even though he was with a woman young enough to be the daughter of many men present. David felt he had never got to the bottom of what had happened between Ella and Harry Reid.

'I hear you're having a bad time.'

'My father died.'

'Yes, I know. I'm sorry, I understand that, my father died a while ago and it's never easy but you were having a bad time before this happened to you, weren't you? The rumour has it that if you don't get some money from somewhere soon you're not going to last.'

David sat down again, sighing.

'The rumour isn't wrong,' he said. After all, what was the point in denying it? This was a small world and everybody knew everything about everybody. 'What's it to you?'

'I could lend you the money.'

Shocked now, David regarded him intently

but gained nothing with this attention. He tried to think hard.

'Why would you want to do that?' he asked cautiously.

'You could pay me interest.'

That wasn't answering the question.

'How much?' David asked.

Harry named a low figure, the kind of interest which a bank would have laughed at rather than given. David liked the figure but he didn't like Harry or the expression on his face which was smug.

'That's almost a favour,' David said.

'I'd be in a worse spot if the interest was such that you couldn't pay me back.'

'Why would you want to do me any favours?'

'For old times' sake,' Harry said.

David hesitated.

'Not my old times, obviously.'

'Jack Welsh was my best friend. I'd hate to see his widow in poor street.'

David had a terrible desire to knock him off his chair but acknowledged to himself that it was a stupid idea. He breathed carefully. It was hard for him to say that Ella wasn't Jack's widow any more yet of course in a sense and out of respect she was and always would be.

The implication from Harry was that he could not afford to look after her and although it was rude and offensive to David personally the point was that just at present there was sufficient truth in the idea so that it hurt. He hated even more that in order to stay in business he must take Harry's money and put up with his remarks. He said nothing. Harry got up.

'I'll arrange it straight away,' he said.

'Thanks,' was all David could manage.

He waited until Harry had gone out and closed the door before he fired a pen at it. He could not remember having been so angry. He wanted to dash home and question Ella about Harry Reid and since he did not feel he could do that he just sat there for close on half an hour before Madeline came in with some papers to sign and after that he made himself walk about the sandy floors of what was now his own business and be thankful that he would not have to close it down yet, put so many men out of work and endanger his entire future. He would not do it for a whim or for anything he might suspect Harry Reid of when there was no evidence for it.

It was the end of the week when things changed. Ella had got used to David's moods such as they were. He was never a noisy person, he spoke when he had something to say but quite suddenly it seemed to her he had nothing at all to say and she put it down to grief at first, that he was beginning to realize he would never see his father again and his father was the first person in David's life who had been so close to him who had died. It seemed strange that he of all people, who seemed so mature, so organized somehow, was the only man of his age she knew who had never lost anybody closer than his aunt in the war.

She put up with it for several days and then she said to him, over breakfast one morning, 'Is there anything I can do?'

He always went to the foundry for half past seven and came back at nine and she would make him bacon and eggs. Sometimes if his cousin, Jo, whose husband was a butcher, had been over from Consett, and had brought the wonderful black pudding she made, he would have that too or very often boiled eggs.

Clyde would hang around, having already eaten, and David would sit Clyde on his knee and give him the top off the boiled egg. It was all he ever wanted somehow. David was teaching Clyde the time with a little wooden clock Iris had bought him. But this week as though Clyde instinctively understood something was wrong he didn't come near.

David looked up.

'What do you mean?'

'You've hardly spoken in four days.'

He hesitated over the last of his bacon and

then put down his knife and fork.

'I've had to borrow the money that I needed.'

She sat down promptly in the chair next to his.

'Is that all?'

'Ella—'

'I thought it was... I thought it was something to do with you losing your father.'

'I lost my father months ago when he stopped understanding who I was or who anybody was, even himself,' David said. 'Harry Reid came to the foundry and offered to lend me the money.'

Ella stared at him. She tried not to but it was impossible.

'How did Harry find out?'

'You didn't go and ask him then?' He was looking at her hard.

She stared at him. What on earth had given David the idea that she and Harry were on such terms? Was this the result of the Scottish convention?

'Of course I didn't. I wouldn't do such a thing.'

'He was the only person who offered to help and without it we would have gone under so I took it. I didn't want to tell you,' David said.

'Why ever not?' Even her voice sounded false, she thought.

David's look was so straight that she

wished she had not started this discussion.

'Because I think he meant more to you than you've said.'

Ella couldn't breathe.

'That's not true.'

'Isn't it? Then why did he come to me and offer to lend me the money?'

'We were friends, that's all.'

'Some kind of friend who offers you money when the bank won't. And I had to take it. Without the loan we wouldn't be here in six months. I hate being grateful to him. I don't like him. I don't like anything about him'

Ella considered for a moment and then she said, 'You really do think I'm doing something wrong.'

He looked up, his face full of contrition. It had been the right thing to say but she hated the way that he hesitated.

'No.'

'I wouldn't. You do know that?'

He said nothing.

'David?' she prompted him.

'It's just that I don't see what he had to gain from it,' David said quickly as though he had been thinking about this for a long while.

'Are you paying him interest?'

'Yes, but–'

'Well, then,' she said and smiled. It took everything she had to give him that smile.

David sat still and said nothing. She got up, went to him, kissed him.

'I love you.'

'I know that. It's just that … I think he cares very deeply for you. Why else would he do it?'

'I was fond of him, that's all.'

'Are you sure?'

'Quite sure,' she said.

'Well, I don't think it's affection he feels for you and if there had been any other way round this problem I would have taken it.'

'There's nothing to worry about, David, really. Just be glad that somebody loaned us the money. Think what would have happened without it. He did it because of Jack, you know that. He was devastated when Jack died.'

'I just wish things had been different,' David said and he got up and went back to work.

Harry's office at the South Dock was nothing like Ella had thought it would be. She had imagined something all old wood and brass, with deftly carpeted stairways and middle-aged women with notepads, instead of which it was a gleaming new building, taller than most, all glass and aluminium shine and a reception and lifts just inside with a most efficient uniformed man to direct you.

Upstairs a young woman in a neat yellow

costume smiled and saw her in and there was nothing modest about his office either, it was huge, right at the top of the building with the most amazing view of the town behind the shipyard and the river in front of it.

'Your view is wonderful,' she said.

'It's the only yard which launches ships directly into the sea,' he said and she heard the pride in his voice. 'It means we get sand in everything and we're at the mercy of the weather such as other people aren't.'

His office had abstract colourful paintings, bare white walls, the floor was gleaming wood and there was a sofa and easy chairs at one end and the smell of freshly ground coffee wafted from a table where some intricate coffee machine was making comforting noises.

The secretary went out and shut the door.

'I doubted you could let an opportunity such as this pass us by,' he said.

'I don't know what you mean.'

'Yes, you do.'

She had forgotten how straightforward he could be and how disarming it was.

'David's paying you interest,' she pointed out.

'Yes, but he couldn't have got it at a low rate like that from any bank and besides he's too great a risk. Safer to let him go. Would you like some coffee?' He smiled and went over to the table by the window and began to pour the coffee into white cups.

'Why did you do it?'

'I just thought it would be nice for you if your husband didn't go bankrupt, that's all.'

Ella took a deep breath.

'How did you find out?'

'Everybody knows. This industry is a small world.'

'But why?'

'You know why.'

'You believed that I gave you up for David, therefore there is no reason for you to help us now, unless you have some motive which I can't work out.'

'Whatever would that be?'

'I don't know. I just don't want to be beholden to you, that's all,' she said.

He didn't say anything. Ella took a deep breath before she went on.

'I did write and tell you that I had changed my mind about us.' She couldn't look at him. She considered now that the letter had been one of the most shameful things she had ever done in her life.

'I got no letter. I worked it out eventually, of course.'

'Harry, I'm sorry. I really am so very sorry.'

'It doesn't matter now.'

'I am very grateful to you, that was what I came here to say.'

'You don't need to be.'

'It was over by the time I met David, you know.'

'What on earth do you mean?'

She couldn't think. She wished she hadn't said it but she knew that she had told herself that, willed herself to think it, possibly because it suited her purpose, because she could live with herself the better for thinking that they had had no future and at the time she convinced herself that they had not, that he would not come back.

'It will never be over,' he said, as though he was talking about the weather.

'It is. I did love you–'

'You loved me so much that the minute I left you went to bed with David Bloody Black.' The dark blue eyes so keen on her made her feel uncomfortable.

'I did nothing of the kind.'

'Hell, of course you did. I don't think you thought about me.'

She took the coffee cup and saucer from him and stood by the window and sipped at the hot liquid and she said, 'I don't want to dredge all this up again.'

'You were the one who came here,' he pointed out. 'If I hadn't intervened your husband would be considering whether the receivers were about to come in round about now.'

Ella put down the cup and saucer.

'I don't understand why you did it.'

'We could be friends–' Harry said.

She looked straight at him. 'I don't want to be friends with you. I don't think any of it would work, not after everything that happened between us. I want to forget the war and all that happened. It's over and I want it to stay that way. I am very grateful for what you did for David. He's a proud man and I want you to know that it was very good of you and that I will remember it but that's it. I love David.'

'You don't love him like you loved me.'

'How can you possibly know that?'

'You took him because he was there and put me from your mind.'

Ella didn't answer that.

'He doesn't know about us, does he?' Harry said.

'Please don't ruin everything,' she said.

'I would hardly lend him money if I was planning to do that,' he said.

'I have to go. Thank you. Goodbye.'

She tried to walk out and as she went past him he caught hold of her arm.

'That's the trouble, isn't it? He doesn't know about us and you're afraid that I'm going to tell him and because I've loaned money to him it tips the balance. You're afraid that I'll spoil your marriage, such as it is.'

Ella felt sick.

'And you think I'm going to blackmail you

into going to bed with me.' He let go of her. 'No wonder you didn't want anything more to do with me if you think that's the kind of person I am.'

'Of course I don't think that.'

'No? Ella, I love you. I shall love you all my life–'

'No!' She pulled free, almost crying. 'I don't want you to love me, don't you understand?' and when he didn't say anything more she walked out.

Twenty

Swan Island was for sale. Somehow Ella was astonished. She did not know why, just that it seemed all wrong somehow. She braked suddenly and the little green Austin skidded to a halt in the wet October day.

She sat there for a minute or two while other cars went around her. She barely noticed them. She tried to get used to the idea of the house being for sale, the board large and important looking on the side of the road. She sat there at the top of the steep hill before the road went down into Durham and looked across to where the wall cut off the view of the house. The grass was high and so were the trees, it must be very overgrown and the big iron gates were pad-locked.

She pulled the car over on to the side and got out and gazed at the space as though she had never seen it before and did not remember the way that the road curved from the gates towards the bridge, the buildings and the house itself. There was nothing to see, as though the architect had wanted to keep the whole thing a secret. She wished she could climb over the high gates, run up the drive and claim it for her own.

She could not contain herself any longer. She got back into the car and drove through the town, past the shops she had planned to visit and out the other side and into the foundry yard where the men who knew her smiled, the ones who didn't merely looked.

She walked up past the sandy road to the path which led to the office where, as always, Miss Grant was sitting just inside the door, ready there to fend off people if David was busy or absent. When Ella and David were first married she found that she had to adjust to Madeline Grant's presence in her husband's life.

The men, Ella felt, regarded Madeline as something of an oddity. She drove her little Morris Minor down the dale five days a week.

David's mother, suspicious of any woman who was single and worked in an office, had dismissed Madeline with a wave of her hand the only time Ella had mentioned her but she had come to acknowledge that Madeline was very important to David. She had his confidence and there was no point in anybody behaving in a jealous way.

Ella had not tried to make a friend of her, it would have been almost impossible since Madeline was a single woman and an employee but she had tried also not to take advantage of her position as David's wife and patronize Madeline. Madeline was kind to the children and Ella could forgive people a lot for that. She remembered them at Christmas and their birthdays.

'Miss Grant, good morning.'

Madeline looked up from her typewriter and smiled.

'Mrs Black, how are you? How are the children?'

'Fine.' She would normally have spent time over their exploits but she was impatient to see her husband.

'Is David about?'

'Mr Black is in the office.' Ella had a feeling that Madeline called David by his first name when there was nobody there, but she never did so in front of anyone else. 'There's nobody with him and he's not on the telephone. Do go in.'

'Thank you.'

Having been given permission Ella went

past the other desks, filing cabinets, piles of paper and into the relative darkness of the tiny corridor which held David's office and the door which led through to the laboratory where the chemist worked.

He was writing but stopped as she burst in.

'David, Swan Island is for sale.'

He didn't look up.

He said, 'Yes, I know,' in quiet, measured tones.

She was taken aback. It was as though all the excitement was knocked out of her.

'You knew?'

He looked up, green eyes cautious.

'You didn't tell me,' she accused him.

David put down his pen.

'There didn't seem to be much point in discussing it,' he said.

'But ... but…' She didn't like to say to him 'you promised', it made her sound like a child whining for a Christmas present and not a married woman with two small children, but he had told her that if the house ever came up for sale he would buy it for her.

'Things have changed,' he said, 'you know they have. We can't afford to buy the house. I'm sorry.'

It was all she could do not to burst into tears. Maybe, she thought afterwards, if she had behaved like a child, shouted, sworn, lost her temper, pleaded, things would have been better but she could not do that to David. She held back the tears.

'Why on earth will you never discuss anything with me? Do I behave like a child or you think that I might?'

'No, of course not, but I knew how disappointed you would be and I know that I said I would. I promised and now I can't keep that promise and it makes me feel ashamed of myself. I'm not the businessman I wish I was and even worse somehow it's an admission that my father wasn't either.'

'He cared about people, David, that's much more important.'

'I know. And it's selfish of us to want so much when so many other people have so little, but I feel it reflects badly on us as a family and that matters too. I … I can't be Harry Reid.'

Suddenly Ella wanted to run out of the office, to wish that she had not come here at all.

'Thank goodness for that,' she said lightly and with a forced smile. 'I would be lying if I said that I don't want the house but we already have so much. I'll get by without it. I have you and the children.'

She saw the relieved look in his eyes. He smiled.

'I wish I had told you now but I knew how much you wanted the house back.'

'How long have you known?'

'A fortnight.'

'And you didn't tell me?' Her lips felt like rubber. David would do anything to avoid confrontation, she thought, but then she knew that was not fair, he was busy, worried, had more important things on his mind than what would appear to other people to be a mindless whim, except that it was not, it had been somehow part of their marriage vows, one of the reasons she had married him, though nothing was said at the time. How cold, how calculating. She was ashamed.

He didn't say anything.

'I have a beautiful house,' she said. 'I have more than I deserve. Don't think any more about it. It doesn't matter at all.'

It was only when she had reversed away from the foundry that she let the tears flow, that she remembered her childhood, her father and mother by the fire. You could not go back.

She went home.

Flo said to her, 'The house is up for sale. Did you see?'

'Yes, I came past it this morning.'

She put the kettle on the Aga and didn't look at Flo. 'We have a lovely house here. I don't think I could move now.'

Flo caught her mood.

'No,' she said softly, 'who could leave the garden?'

Madeline put her head round the open door of David's office. It was early evening and she should have gone home long since. He said so.

'I saw somebody in the big workshop, or I heard something and then saw. It was Walter King.'

David put down his pen and looked at her.

'He doesn't take much, just light bulbs and things.'

'You know about it then?'

'His wife works for us and...'

'Several things have been taken over the past few weeks and one or two of the men are noticing. They don't like to say much because he's one of them but ... as long as you know.'

'We'll keep an eye on him, see what happens. Thanks, Maddy.'

When she had gone David lingered. He liked being here when everybody had finished work and he had the place to himself. He liked watching the sky darken, he liked his domain. The foundry meant more and more to him. He had not realized that having something so completely to himself would be so much more valuable than sharing it with his father.

That sounded awful, he thought, but maybe only when it was yours were you willing to make tremendous sacrifices for it and he had already sacrificed his self respect and the house that his wife had loved so much. It was a great deal to ask but he didn't care. He would go on sacrificing things for it and keep it safe for when Clyde was grown and then he would be ready to share it again.

He was sorry about Swan Island but it was only a house and he could not jeopardize the works for it. He had secretly gone and looked at it earlier that week and it needed a great deal of money spending on it. If he had been able to afford it he would have bought it because he knew that money invested in buildings was wisely spent but he could not borrow any more, not even to make Ella happy.

Keeping Flo's husband on when he was stealing was also a risk but a much smaller one and he would talk to him, let him know they were aware of what was happening and perhaps that would halt the pilfering which had been going on for some time.

He had an idea that Walter had suffered in the war, as so many men had, that somehow his life had been shattered and he could not cope with what he had come home to, so David was prepared to give him another chance and more time and see what became of it.

Iris came in to see Ella later during that long early evening time after Flo had gone and before David came home. She suspected him of putting off the homecoming. She was sitting by the fire with the children.

'Did you know that Swan Island was up for sale?' Iris said and Ella thought why did everybody ask her at once.

She wished she could express surprise but Iris would know it for subterfuge.

'Yes,' she said, weary of the subject.

'Are you going to buy it?'

She looked into the distance.

'David says we can't afford it.'

'But it was your home, your family lived there for many years.'

Ella wanted to hug Iris for her understanding except that Iris would have thought she had gone mental. Also she knew that Iris would have been pleased if they had bought the house, she was such a social climber.

Ella's father's family had been so well thought of at one time, so respected with an old name, something her father had lost. She had not realized until now that it was something she wanted to have back. Now it was gone, the name, the house, her parents.

But when she looked at Iris, her sister-in-law showed the same reaction as David, it was relief.

'For myself, I don't want you to move. Since Father bought this house I feel as though it's our home.'

'Don't worry, we're not going anywhere,' Ella said.

'Yes, but how will you feel when somebody else buys it?' Iris said.

Iris went and David came in. By the end of the evening Ella was exhausted from being so bright and unconcerned. She couldn't bear David's silence. She went off to the kitchen and made some tea.

She wished she could feel different. David loved this house and though rich people might think it modest, it probably meant as much to him even though it was a recently acquired place. His father had bought it when the family had begun to prosper.

Finally he followed her and there, as unromantically as possible, he said, 'Would you like a whisky and soda?' whereupon she managed enough grace to say that she would and even to smile and they sat over a big wood fire and listened to some music, but when she went to bed she could not help staring longingly from the window, out across the river towards the house that she had loved so much and wanted so badly.

David slept as though glad the crisis had passed so easily. He would move on now and they would probably never discuss it again. Somebody would buy Swan Island, fill it with children and be happy as she had once been before everything went wrong. She would never set foot in the house again

266

and she should be less stupid and forget about it.

As she turned from the window she could hear the sound of Susan crying in the little bedroom where she slept. Clyde had a room of his own but he was a very light sleeper so if Ella didn't go immediately and pick up the baby he would awaken and want his share of her attention, so she went swiftly across the hall.

The doors of the bedrooms were always open in case the children needed her during the night. Susan was not yet hot from crying, just a little restless and as Ella walked up and down with her she went back to sleep. Ella put her back down very gently, watched for a little while and then went back to bed. She must not forget, she told herself, as she settled down to rest, how very lucky she was.

Ella was unprepared for Rosemary Reid to visit the following Monday. She pulled up in a sleek, red MG. Her blonde hair was swept up and she wore a bright blue dress and black high heels.

'I didn't know your telephone number and I just wanted to come over and see you,' she said. 'I know we don't know each another but when we met at the Scottish convention and you just looked so nice and...'

Ella cursed the Scottish convention.

'I hope you don't mind,' Rosemary said.

Ella was rather taken aback. She had two lines of washing out the back and the iron set up in the kitchen. Usually she did the ironing on Tuesdays but there was such a lot of it she was determined to get through some of it today.

It had been a difficult day. Susan had cried most of the morning and Ella and Flo had alternated holding her. Finally worn out, she had gone to sleep. Ella had put her upstairs in the cool of the small back bedroom but Clyde began to cry too, so between Flo and herself they had done less than half of what they usually managed while trying to do twice as much. Visitors were the very last thing Ella wanted now.

Half dry clothes were folded in the kitchen in piles waiting for the iron. Nobody had attended to the tidying up. The beds were stripped and toys littered the downstairs rooms.

David had come home to minced beef, which was left over from the joint they had eaten the day before, and yesterday's vegetables and Ella could not move without one of the children crying so she balanced Susan on one arm and the washing basket on the other. Ella was annoyed when she heard the doorbell and she had never felt less attractive than when this cool, well dressed young woman walked in. Why did she have to come today? Why did she have to come at all? They could not possibly have anything in common and Rosemary was so young, she would know nothing of families.

Rosemary, however, proved to be an asset. She took Clyde so that Flo could do the ironing and though Flo said nothing Ella was pleased.

Rosemary said, 'I love taking the clothes in. I used to help me mam do it when I was little,' and disappeared with the big washing basket.

Susan had woken up and was crying again. Rosemary folded the clothes, chatted to Flo, they drank their tea standing up in the kitchen and then she and Clyde went off with Ella, the baby in her arms, to the back garden to gather plums from the trees near the wall because Ella had rashly promised to make crumble for tea.

'I hope you don't mind me coming here, Ella. Can I call you by your first name? I would very much like to make friends with you.' She gave Ella a piercing glance.

'I'm a lot older than you,' Ella couldn't help saying.

'Does it matter?' Rosemary looked frankly at her. 'You seemed so nice.'

'Have you been married long?'

'A few years, yes. I try to get on with his mam and I like her and I think she likes me but she's just...' Rosemary twisted her face because she didn't seem able to find the right words. 'I'm common, you see. She knows it and I know it–'

'You're nothing of the kind.'

'Aye, I am. I don't know what to say. She's ashamed when she tells people about me, I know she is because I don't know how to go on or what to say. And even though she's tried to learn me … tried to teach me, to show me … I'm not very quick at it and … We didn't marry because we were in love, we married because we were … this sounds awful, we were both lonely and Harry tried to help me and… It was never love, it was just … that the war had been so terrible.' She smiled. 'I know it was terrible for other people, I don't mean to sound self pitying.

'By the time I met Harry I was in a very bad way. He rescued me.' She laughed. 'He did his knight in shining armour bit. Who can resist it? He told me that you lost your husband. I'm so very sorry.'

'Yes, that was right at the beginning.'

'It must have been awful.' Then she said in quite a different tone, 'I want a house. We have been living with Harry's mother since we were married and it's not good like I said, even though she is very kind to me. We want a place of our own, somewhere away from his work because he's always there. Would you come with me to look at some houses? Harry is too busy, he says, and I don't want to go on my own.'

It was, Ella thought ruefully, exactly the opposite problem of the one she had but there was no harm in going with Rosemary. She liked her though she didn't want to. She thought it would be almost impossible not to like Rosemary who was so open, so direct and warm and Ella liked looking at houses. She didn't know Sunderland well but it would be fun.

'I would love to come with you,' she said.

'Would you?' Rosemary's face brightened. 'Oh, thank you, Ella. Can you leave the children?'

'If you tell me when you want to go Mrs King won't mind looking after them for a while and I'm sure I'm due a day off. Now why don't we have some more tea and some cake? I made it yesterday.'

'I'm hopeless at making cakes,' Rosemary said. And then greedily, 'What kind is it?'

'Orange.'

'Good. I love orange cake, it's my favourite.'

Flo left the ironing, Susan had at last gone to sleep again and they all sat around the big oak table in the dining room, eating huge pieces of orange cake. Rosemary insisted on Clyde sitting on her knee even though he put cake all over her dress.

The petty cash had gone missing. That morning David went in and Madeline turned

271

the cash box upside down.

'Did somebody break in?'

'Ted Smith saw Walter King getting through the window early this morning, so he says and I believe him. That window at the end is easy to pull open.'

'We should do something about that,' David said, angry with himself. He had been saying they should do something about it for months but he had had more important things to worry about and he was not aware that anybody knew about the window.

Walter King was not the most comfortable man in the world, David thought, as Walter mooched into his office that afternoon. He was tall and thin, with dark eyes which told you nothing and never looked straight at you.

'Mr King,' David said and hesitated but hesitation was no good here. 'Look, I'll come right to the point. There are things going missing.'

Walter stared and David realized this was not going to be easy, that Walter had no intention of making things any better.

'You were seen.'

'I never took owt.'

'I have witnesses who say you did.'

'Oh aye? And who's them like?' Walter looked straight at him then and David had to make himself look straight back. David couldn't say one of them had been Madeline. Goodness only knew what Walter was capable of and Madeline was vulnerable.

'People I can rely on.'

'Not like me then, eh?' Walter said with a touch of bitter humour.

'Look, Walter, I know you had a very bad time during the war–'

'You know nowt about it, you weren't there.'

'I know that you did and I'm prepared to help you when I can and if there is anything you need you only have to ask–'

'What would I want to ask the likes of you for?' Walter said.

'Are you short of anything?'

'Nowt you could do owt about,' Walter said.

'The point is, that if you do it again I'll get rid of you. Do you understand? And I want to see that money back here. I don't care how you do it but bring it back or I'll call the police.'

Walter turned out his pockets, threw the money on to the desk and then he walked out, cursing. David let go of his breath and sat back in his chair.

David was late back and didn't have much to say and Susan howled all the way through tea. Afterwards he went down to the green house and mooched about there. He didn't contribute much to their life at the house Ella couldn't help thinking.

David came from that class of men who knew absolutely nothing about gardens so she couldn't think what he was doing out there. His family had people to do everything for them but their work. Even she had her part to play. He wasn't much help with the children, but then he wasn't there most of the time.

She followed him when she had finally put the children to bed.

'It's cold.'

He said nothing.

'Did you have a bad day?'

'Somebody at work is stealing things from the foundry. I think I'm going to have to dismiss him,' David said.

'What kind of things?'

'Anything he can take without being noticed. It's happened half a dozen times. He takes things he can hide, sometimes valuable things. The last thing was the petty cash.'

'Why haven't you got rid of him before now?'

David gave her a look so straight that she began to wonder why she had asked.

'It's Flo's husband, Walter.'

'Oh, David, no. Are you sure?'

She knew it was a stupid question even as she said it.

'I have had him into the office and tried to talk to him about it. He gave back the money he had taken but I don't want it to be a police matter.'

'Flo is like one of the family. The children love her.'

'I'm not saying we should get rid of Flo–'

'But she'll leave when he does. How could she put her loyalty to us above her loyalty to him? She can't know. She would be horrified. Nobody is more honest than Flo.'

'I'm sure she doesn't,' he said.

'What is he like?'

'Very quiet.'

She smiled.

'What's funny about it?' he said.

'You're very quiet, David. For you to notice he must be silent.'

'He is. He doesn't even acknowledge me. I had to ask him personally twice to come to the office before he even showed up and then he just either shook his head or said nothing and finally he was … he was rude. What do you know about him?'

'Nothing much. I remember him vaguely from when I was a little girl but he was very young then too, just a boy. He doesn't come from around here.'

'Does Mrs King say anything?'

'She never mentions him. Can't you give him one last chance?'

'Yes but if it happens again I've told him

I'll dismiss him so I must.'

They went back into the sitting room and she talked about Rosemary's visit.

David said nothing.

'Does this mean you disapprove?'

'No, I'm sure she's very nice.'

'But?'

'I could never be friends with Harry Reid so don't go inviting them to tea or anything.'

'I don't intend it to be like that.'

Ella went back to the kitchen and began to tidy up. There was still lots of ironing to be done the next day and she was too tired to do much more. David came in.

'We could have more help you know,' he said.

'I thought we didn't have any money.'

'We could manage that.'

'Oh, I don't think so. Flo wouldn't like it.'

It was Friday when Rosemary picked her up in the little sports car.

'Are we going to look at several houses?' Ella enquired as she got in.

She was excited at the idea of having some time off away from the children and the house and Iris had promised to come for a couple of hours later. Ella wasn't sure Flo wanted Iris there as Iris had definite ideas about the help and a tendency to be condescending, but Flo would get very little done and no peace if she had the children all day so Ella had agreed to it.

'Just one house. I went to see it myself yesterday but you will be the first other person to see it. I want your opinion.'

Ella waited for Rosemary to turn the car up towards the Sunderland road but she didn't, she merely drove down Silver Street and over Framwellgate Bridge and then turned left into South Street.

'It isn't in Sunderland then?' she said.

'Oh, no. I don't want a house in Sunderland,' Rosemary said, pulling a face.

'How far is it?'

'Not far.'

It wasn't. Beyond the streets just a little way and then she turned the car into a narrow cobbled lane. Ella's heart did strange things such as it had rarely done before. Rosemary halted the car momentarily in the same place Ella had halted her own little car several days previously, but instead of seeing the For Sale sign and driving past she turned in at the temptingly open gates and began steering the car up the pot-holed drive.

Ella felt sick. A thousand childhood memories pushed at one another for space in her brain; her father driving, her mother sitting beside him, she hanging over the seat from the back, singing together.

And then a harder memory, sitting in the car beside her mother on the way back from her father's funeral, the day dark with rain. Coming up here with her, knowing that she must leave and go to live in Silver Street, that there was a possibility she would never see Swan Island again.

She wanted to shriek at Rosemary to stop but she couldn't. Rosemary's face was alive with pleasure and she obviously had no idea that this place had been Ella's dearly loved childhood home.

The drive seemed narrower and shorter than she remembered but the grass was high on either side and the walls were falling down. It hurt her to see the neglect.

She wanted to close her eyes when they reached the front of the house but she couldn't, and as they got there all the love she had ever felt for it exploded like a firework in her head. She remembered a hundred mornings there, the sound of her mother's voice in the front garden, her father when he kept bees in the orchard, the way that the wasps ate the plums, the tiny tumbling stream with the little wooden bridge and the honeysuckle which curved around it, the dovecotes at either side of the house, the big generous red bricks, the tiny round window on the landing which she could see clearly from as a tiny child.

The tears poured down her face, she couldn't stop them and as Rosemary stopped the car and turned to her the vivacity in

Rosemary's eyes dulled.

'Oh, Ella, whatever's the matter?'

'Nothing. Don't worry,' Ella said and she stumbled out of the car.

'But it is. Do you feel bad?'

The most awful thing about it was that Ella could not help but think that if she had married Harry she could have had this place for her own again. It's nonsense, she told herself strictly, you wouldn't have had your two gorgeous children, or David or anything which really matters. She wiped the treacherous tears away but Rosemary was pale with concern.

'Do you want to go home?' she asked.

Ella choked. 'Rosemary, this is my home, or it was.'

Rosemary said nothing more, she put Ella's hand through her arm and they walked along to the front of the house.

The grass was knee high on the sloping lawns and there were no longer doves which in the old days would come to meet you, tumbling in an air show before the car when you took the lane to the house. The flower-beds were tangled with weeds and in the orchard the plum trees were old and gnarled and many of the branches were broken off in the wind. She presumed from children climbing to take the fruit.

As they stood in the garden rain began to fall.

'I'm so terribly sorry, Ella,' Rosemary said, 'I had no idea. Do you think we should go?'

'I don't think anything of the kind. I'll get over it in a minute. I really want to see it now that I'm here. Do you have the key or do we have to wait for somebody to open it up?'

Rosemary produced the key and she opened the door and they stepped into the hall. It was light, it had been designed to be light from the window on the landing and it smelled just as it had always smelled, of wood smoke and furniture polish and flowers. How could it still smell like that after so many years?

There was no carpet and as they walked down the hall their footsteps echoed. The big reception rooms were empty and Ella went into the sitting room and regarded the white marble fireplace with affection. How many evenings had she sat there with her parents, playing with her toys? How many days with the summer rain pouring down the windows or sunshine flooding the place with warmth?

She and her father had built a snowman on the lawn every year. There had been a big Christmas tree here in the sitting room and they would have Christmas dinner in the dining room across the hall.

Nobody spoke. They went into the little

sewing room at the side of the house and the study which her father had used and another little room which had at one time been a playroom and further on the billiard room; all empty now. Then they moved to the kitchen which looked out over the yard and off this there were washhouses and pantries and a little room especially for the washing up and another for the dairy and another for hanging game and storing hams. There was a back staircase which led to the bedrooms where at one time the servants had slept.

They went up the main sweeping staircase to the bedrooms and bathrooms and she stood in the bedroom which had been her parents', looking out and trying not to think of everything that was past. She kept telling herself there was no point, you could not go back to anything, you had to keep on going forward.

Rosemary moved from room to room. Ella could hear her high heels on the bare floorboards and she lingered in each room so it was quite a while before she finally came back and joined Ella at the window.

After a long pause she asked, 'How long did you live here?'

'Until I was ten. My father died. We had no money and we had to sell up and go and live in Silver Street with my grandma. I think it was hard for my mother going back.

She thought she had come so far, only to lose everything.'

'What happened to your dad?'

'He died,' Ella said. 'Do you like the house?'

'I love it.'

'And Harry?'

'He doesn't care where we live as long as I'm happy. He's not bothered about seeing the place, he doesn't even know what it's called, but I don't want to buy it if it's going to make you cry.'

'Oh, good heavens, that's ridiculous. Of course you must buy it.'

Rosemary looked seriously at her.

'Yes, but I want us to be friends and I would hate it if you wouldn't come over here because you couldn't stand the memories of your dad dying and everything.'

'It was the happiest time of my life. Why should I not want to remember it?'

'Because you don't have it any more?'

'We lose everything in the end, if we live long enough,' Ella said, without looking at her. 'Besides, I have a beautiful house and David and the children. Why should I envy anyone else?'

Rosemary hesitated.

Ella stared at her.

'I do so much want us to be friends, Ella,' Rosemary said. 'I wouldn't do anything on purpose to hurt you.'

'We will be.'

'Do you promise?'

Ella took her hands.

'Don't worry so much about things.'

'But I do. How can you not when things have been so awful for you?'

'Because I'm determined to make the best of what I have and so will you.'

'Do you really think so, Ella?'

'I'm sure of it,' Ella said.

That night Ella dreamed about the house over and over again. She dreamed that she lived there with Harry and that he was going away. He went away and did not come back a hundred times before she awoke.

It was that night, the only night they had spent together. What she remembered in her dreams was the salt sweat of Harry's body, the taste of his mouth, the feel of his skin and the way that he had told her over and over again how much he loved her, that he would never love anyone else. Somehow now she hoped very much that that was not true.

If he didn't love Rosemary they had no hope of making their marriage work and therefore no chance of happiness and she wanted happiness for him so much. But in her memories was the little hotel in Silver Street down from the café next to the bridge, where they had lain with the curtains closed and the white sheets above and below them; where they had made love.

Somehow nothing had been as good before or since or had it just been the desperation of the times, the thinking he would be killed and they would never see one another again?

Twenty-One

The following day David came home while Flo was still there. He said nothing but he looked hard at Ella when she had followed him into the little study.

'I've had to dismiss Walter,' he said. 'I think we should tell Flo.'

Ella let go of her breath.

'How on earth can we do that?'

'We don't have any choice.' Without waiting he went back into the hall and said,

'Mrs King, are you there?'

Flo came in with the baby in her arms.

'Clyde has fallen asleep,' she said, 'at last but this little one she just won't go down.'

Ella took the baby from her.

'Mrs King, look, I've got something not very nice to tell you.' David was unusually tactful. 'Your husband has been taking things from the foundry. It's been going on for several months and I have given him

284

four or five opportunities to bring it back and to stop, but he's just ignored me. So I've had to dismiss him.

'I'm very sorry but there wasn't anything else I could do and I hate telling you, but I couldn't bear to think that you found out from somebody else. It wouldn't be fair to you. I know this isn't very fair and I have tried everything I could think of before this. I'm sorry.'

Flo went on looking at him for several moments as though he could magic things from the air, and then she said, 'Thieving? My Walter?'

'Yes, I'm afraid so.'

'And he doesn't have a job any more?'

'No. I couldn't keep him on, you see.'

'Right. Well, I think that I shall have to go home.'

'Yes, of course,' Ella said, wanting to say more but she felt as though she couldn't.

Flo put on her coat and left without another word. Ella watched her back. She seemed smaller, more weighed down. Ella had no idea what Flo's marriage was like. She didn't talk about it very much any more and Ella had thought it wise not to ask. She wished there was something she could do to help, say something, even hug Flo but she dared not. She could only wait to see what would happen.

Walter didn't come home. Flo waited and waited. In the end she toiled across the town and out the other side to the little pit village which lay just beyond the city and where Walter's sister, Bessie, lived. She had never married and had worked at the munitions factory at Aycliffe during the war. Her nose had now turned a dark pink colour which contrasted strangely with her white little face, and Flo could not help thinking of this when Bessie opened the door.

'What do you want?' she said.

'Is Walter here?'

'He's in bed.'

'Was he drunk?'

Bessie threw up her gaze to heaven.

'You know very well, Flo, that he's always drunk now. He hates that place he worked at.'

'He didn't have to thieve from it though. He never was like this. What will we do?'

'He's staying here with me. You go back to them. You seem to like them better than you like us,' Bessie said and she closed the door.

For the first day or two Ella managed to do all the housework and look after the children but when David was coming in for three meals a day and everything else on top she found it too much.

'We could find somebody else,' David said.

'I know that,' she said, sitting down exhausted. It was late at night, the children had finally gone to bed, and she had persuaded herself that she could do no more. 'I don't want to though. It wouldn't be the same.'

'Why don't you go and see Mrs King?'

'I don't like to. I feel bad enough about it all.'

'We could have somebody to help with the housework–'

'Let's just leave it, shall we? I can manage.'

'You're worn out.'

'I'll be fine.'

'You didn't tell me Harry Reid had bought Swan Island.'

'I didn't know he had,' she said.

'I thought you and Rosemary went looking at houses.'

'Yes, we looked at it.'

'You didn't tell me.'

'I didn't want to talk about it.'

'But you didn't know they'd bought it?'

She avoided his keen gaze.

'I knew Rosemary liked it.'

'And I know how much you wanted the place.'

'Yes, well. If I can't have it I'd as soon Rosemary and Harry have it as anybody else.'

'That bugger gets everything,' David said in such a low voice that she barely caught the words.

She excused herself and went to see to Susan who had, thankfully for once, begun to cry at exactly the right moment.

When she got back David was still sitting there and he was frowning.

'I don't care about the house, David.'

'Yes, you do. You didn't even tell me you'd been with her to see it. It must have been awful for you.'

'It was very difficult.'

'And you must have thought he'd buy it for her if she liked it. After all, he's got nothing else to do with all his sodding money!'

'Must you swear like that?'

'I've got more important things to worry about.'

'Why, what's the matter now?'

'I've got the union coming to talk over the next few weeks. There may be a strike.'

'What, local?'

'National.'

'Over wages?'

She thought he paid his men fairly. David might not bluster and shout but he had a determination to see things right which was more developed in him than in any man she knew.

'I owe a lot of money to Reid and I have a lot of money to come in,' he said, 'but the men can't go against their union. It's nothing to do with me personally and there's nothing I can do about it.

'If the men won't work and I can't turn out castings and the money doesn't come in I'll only last so long. We can hang on until the beginning of next year but I think the strike will be in the spring and things could be fairly bad by then, but I'm sorry about the house.'

Ella got up and went to him. That was characteristic too. Iris couldn't see it or didn't choose to but in among all the problems he had not forgotten her disappointment.

'I wanted you to have it so much.'

'I don't care.'

'Yes, you do and so do I.'

Ella got to the point after the next two days when she couldn't stand things any more without Flo, she missed her so much and the work defeated her so she decided to visit. It was quite a long way, she had not realized that Flo had to walk that far to work. It was away from the main part of the city.

The streets became poorer, dirtier and narrower until Ella stood in an unmade back lane where the yards had coalhouses and outside lavatories and she had to ask the way.

She was astonished, horrified to find that they lived in such poverty. Walter was a labourer, yes, but he made a decent wage and Flo was well paid because she had spent five days a week and sometimes more at Ella's house. There was such a contrast between the two that Ella was ashamed.

She went up the steep tiny yard. The door of the house was open. She knocked. There was movement from inside and then Flo appeared. She looked just as usual. Ella could have wept with the joy of seeing her and the guilt over everything else. All the polite words she had prepared were lost.

'I have missed you, Flo.' She stepped up into the house and hugged her.

Flo seemed taken aback.

'Why, Mrs Black,' she said.

Inside the downstairs was only one room but it was among the cleanest rooms that Ella had ever seen. There was a black leaded range gleaming in the light from an enormous fire and at both sides well burnished horse 'brasses. In the centre of the room was a table and two chairs.

Beneath the window stood a two-seater green sofa, off to the left was the pantry and across the room stood a tall and magnificent dresser. There was a sideboard against where the stairs went out of the room behind the door to the upper storey. Somehow it did not seem small or cramped.

Ella did not know what to say.

'You've got lovely horse brasses, Flo,' she said.

'I got all my mam's stuff after she died,' Flo said.

It occurred to Ella that Walter might be there and she looked about her before moving any further into the house but there was no sign of him. Flo urged her to come and sit down. The sofa, Ella thought, was the most uncomfortable chair she had ever sat in. There was no give to it and it seemed to go back too far so that her feet were almost off the floor, like a little girl.

The kettle was boiling. Flo made some tea and placed a big brown pot on the table which gave Ella an excuse to move on to a hard dining chair. There was a custard pie. Ella wanted to refuse, she was not sure she could swallow, but she sensed that Flo would be offended and she was glad when she tasted it. The pastry was light and the custard was just sufficiently set and had exactly the right amount of sugar in it.

Flo began to cry. It seemed to Ella that Flo was extremely out of practice, she made such a bad job of it. For a start she pretended she was not crying and ignored the tiny amount of water which ran unkindly into the creases on her face and when the tears got bigger she shook her head, stared into her tea and said, 'Walter's gone.'

'Gone?' Did Flo mean gone out or did she mean he had left her?

'He's gone to live with his sister.'

'What, for good?'

'He took everything,' Flo said. 'He won't come back and I don't want him to. I don't want anything to do with him ever again.'

'What do you mean everything?'

'All the money I earned, he gambled and drank it away.'

'I'm so sorry. I had no idea. I wish you'd told me.'

'I couldn't tell anybody. I was that ashamed,' Flo said.

'What are you going to do?'

Flo didn't answer that either.

'Would you consider coming back to work for us? I know it's awful and that Walter probably left because of it–'

'He'd threatened to leave lots of times,' Flo said.

'Might you come back then?'

Flo looked at her like the miracle had finally happened.

'Do you want me to?' she said.

'I cannot manage without you. Please come back.'

Flo hesitated.

'The children miss you and so do I.'

Flo agreed to come the following day.

When David arrived home that evening and she could see the relief on his face.

'Have I been awful to live with?' Ella said.

'Never,' he said and she threw Clyde's second favourite teddy bear across the sitting room at him. 'Why don't we suggest to her that she has the cottage? She won't want to stay where she is by herself and she'll be paying rent.'

'You don't think she would be lonely there?'

'I think she's probably more lonely now.'

'Well, we mustn't take her for granted.'

'Will you ask her?'

The cottage was on the end of the house and Ella assumed it had been where the coachman and then the chauffeur lived when people had been able to afford such help. The place was very neglected. She didn't blame Iris for refusing to live there. What a come down it would be from the lovely house in the Bailey, but it would be ideal for Flo if she agreed to it.

That morning when Flo turned up for work early Ella suggested to her that she might like to move in. They went to look. Clyde ran about excitedly. Ella tried to see the place through Flo's eyes but it wasn't necessary. Flo, normally a taciturn kind of person, stood in the middle of the sitting-room floor and her eyes filled with tears.

'It won't cost anything,' Ella said. 'There'll be no rent and David will foot the bills because it's considered part of the house, but I don't want to push you into it, Flo. The children would probably plague you though we would try not to take advantage, try to give you your privacy as best we can.'

Flo said nothing. She gazed out of the window at the front garden.

'And of course there's the vegetable garden which you can use. There's always too much.' She was in the habit of sending Flo home laden with whatever fruit and veg was in season. 'You could have your dinner with us in the middle of the day,' Ella said, 'and your tea too if you like.'

Flo went into the back which looked out over the yard. The sun was beginning to slant in there, spilling on to the big square flags. Then she went upstairs, Clyde followed precariously on his little fat legs, Flo holding on to his hand in case he stumbled.

Ella followed with Susan in her arms. There were two bedrooms and a bathroom. Flo stood in the bigger room upstairs and gazed at the view which took in the houses and even the fields which lay beyond the small city. She still had said nothing.

'Do you think you might be too lonely here?' Ella asked.

Flo turned and looked at her.

'When can I move in?' she said.

David sent two men and a van the following Saturday while Ella and the children spent the day in the cottage. She thought they were very little help. Clyde kept putting things back into boxes as she and Flo took them out. Susan sat contentedly on the floor and played with the newspapers which had held Flo's best white china with the pink roses and Ella moved things around when Flo asked.

After the first few days it was to Ella as if Flo had always been there, as though she was meant to be.

Rosemary called the following week and Ella had not the heart to tell her that she already knew about the house. Rosemary's face was a mixture of joy and trepidation.

'We've bought it,' she said, 'I wanted you to know and be pleased about it...'

'I am glad,' Ella said but she was grateful to David for telling her so that she had got used to the idea before she saw Rosemary because she didn't want to hurt her.

She took Rosemary in and gave her tea. It was one of those cold wet days when the darkness falls mid afternoon in the north. They sat over the fire and Rosemary helped Clyde to toast crumpets on a long toasting fork and they had butter and this year's plum jam, all seeping through the crumpets until there was a small puddle on the plate.

Rosemary was wearing what looked to Ella like a very expensive dress and she would have taken Clyde and his sticky fingers from her, but Rosemary said she didn't care and was happy with Clyde and the jam.

'We'll be in by Christmas, Harry is rushing things through so that we can be and he wants a party. You will come, won't you?'

Ella tried to make her children the excuse but Rosemary said, 'I want you there more than anybody because of how much the house means to you. I know you'll find it hard but if we're going to be friends and you and David and the bairns are going to visit often then you must come.'

Ella didn't like to say that David would have done a great many things before he felt inclined to spend an evening in Harry's company but she couldn't say so. She was therefore obliged to say that of course they would be delighted to come.

Twenty-Two

Ella had thought the only house she had any real affection for was Swan Island. She did not think much about the house in the bailey until it came to selling it. She called herself stupid and sentimental until she realized that her memories of the place were of her first days of marriage when she had enjoyed her house, when she had nothing more to worry about other than what to cook for dinner and whether the coalman was coming that day and if it would be fine enough to put the washing in the back garden.

The peace seemed doubly so living within a few yards of the great cathedral. It was the easiest time of her life. Sometimes she would walk by the river in the afternoons and admire its stillness and watch the ducks swimming around the edges or if it had rained hang over Framwellgate Bridge and be mesmerized by the brown rushing water and thank God for bringing her to this plateau in her life where she could rest and be easy and learn that the sweet monotony of day to day suited her.

She sighed as she looked around at the boxes, the packing that she was helping Iris to do. It did not look as though she would have any kind of peace from now on. Iris and David living in the same house was not an easy thought.

Iris, after her first protests, had been silent on the matter but Ella knew that she was very unhappy and Ella did not know how to improve that unhappiness. When Ella said to her that she could choose her bedroom and that she would have the little sewing room made into another sitting room to give them all a bit more space Iris erupted.

'Oh, don't bother,' she said. 'I don't want to be a lot of trouble. Any corner will do.'

'Iris–'

'David is incompetent. If he'd been any kind of a businessman at all things would never have come to this. How do you think it looks to other people that we have to move in with you?'

Iris was always very concerned about how things looked. It seemed strange to think that Iris and David had been brought up together because Ella didn't think David had any regard for what anybody thought about what he did, herself included most of the time. David was what people called 'a law unto himself' and it was something she admired or abhorred in him, depending on the circumstances at the time.

'I will help you with your mother,' she said. 'You'll have more free time.'

'You mean I'll be able to go out and get a job?'

'I thought that was what you wanted.'

'It isn't going to be easy. I gave up nursing to come back and look after my parents because somebody had to. You and David obviously weren't going to do it.'

Ella resisted the temptation to reply hotly but she could not help thinking that Iris dearly loved a fight, maybe it was the only exciting thing in her life any more.

'You and I will be able to go out more–'

'On the tiny allowance David is making for mother and me?' Iris cried. 'I never thought to become my brother's pensioner. I thought my father was going to provide for mother and me instead of giving everything to David.'

'There was nothing left to give.'

'No, and who's doing is that?'

'Oh, Iris, don't. We've all been through so much. Do let us try to get along.'

'Get along?' Iris's green eyes fired. 'Do you know why you married David? He's exactly the same as your father was, that's why.'

'You know nothing about my father–'

'Everybody knows that he was such a bad businessman that he lost everything. David's going to end up the same way, you mark my words,' and Iris stormed out of the sitting room where the winter sun was casting feeble attempts at sending light through the neat, square, small paned windows.

Ella was trembling with rage and could do nothing but stand still and remind herself how much Iris envied her, how Iris would never hold her own child to her, how she had no man to love her.

When Iris didn't come back Ella followed her down the steps into the kitchen. Iris was unloading pots and pans from the cupboards and putting them into cardboard boxes, banging them one on top of another making a lot of noise.

'We might as well get rid of these,' she said. 'We won't be needing them again.'

The invitation came from Rosemary and Harry just before Christmas. Ella could not decide what to do. She waited until David came in at dinner time and handed it to him wordlessly.

He studied it until he thought what to say while Ella put the meal on the table and then he sat down.

'Did you want to go?'

That, she thought, was tactful for David.

'Rosemary will be offended if we don't.'

'There will be lots of other people there? I don't want to have to spend the evening talking to Harry Reid.'

'Oh lots, I'm sure.'

'It's on Christmas Day. I wanted to be with the children then.'

'I'm sure you'll have had sufficient of them by eight o'clock and if it's anything like last year Clyde will be worn out and in bed.'

It was just before Christmas when Iris and Lottie moved in and Ella had a kind of family feeling about the whole thing. It would at least be nice for them all to be together in the house at Christmas.

Ella was reluctant to give up the little sewing room which she regarded as the only private room in the house. David, the children or Flo never came into this room and sometimes in the winter, when the children were in bed and David was listening to the wireless in the sitting room, she would sit by the fire there and read, make plans and enjoy the quietness.

She went into the garden where Mr Philips was digging over the vegetable patch and asked if he would mind helping and together they shifted the smaller things, her books, some cushions, the sewing machine, knitting patterns and papers, and when David came in at dinnertime he and Mr Philips moved the two easy chairs, the table and the little writing desk. David was reluctant to move anything.

'Won't you need all this?' he said.

'Your mother might like some privacy.'

'I can't think why she should. It'll be lonely if she feels obliged to sit in here.'

Ella didn't like to tell him that she thought it best to keep he and Iris apart, at least some of the time. And since they would probably disagree often it would be good if Iris had somewhere to retreat to other than her bedroom.

'The writing desk could go in front of the window in our room,' David said.

She found that she didn't want things like writing bureaus in their bedroom. They had enough of those in the office at his work and downstairs in the little study. When they were old they could have bookcases or writing tables in there, at present she wanted it to be a special place they had together and for nothing to intrude.

'No,' she insisted, 'I want it all in the attic and the furniture out of the blue bedroom and the red one because Iris and your mother want to bring their own.'

'I haven't time,' he said. 'I haven't had any dinner yet.'

'Then send two men from the foundry this afternoon.'

'We're busy.'

'David!' Ella was about to lose her temper. Luckily he noticed.

'All right,' he said.

'What time?'

'As soon as I get back to the office.'

'If you don't I shall come down–'

'I will, I will. Now can I have something to eat? I have people from Consett Ironworks coming over at half past one.'

Ella thanked Mr Philips and went back to the kitchen. She had made broth the day before, onions, carrots, pearl barley, split peas in a cloth so that it was now pease pudding and a piece of ham which had cooked in the broth.

It meant she had not needed to cook today which was just as well as moving the house around had taken time, but then it must be difficult for Iris and Lottie having to break up their house, giving so many of the things they cared about to the auction rooms to be sold.

There was so much extra work after Iris and her mother moved in and the balance of the house had altered somehow. In the past, after Flo had gone back to the cottage at teatime and there were no other adults in the house, she and David had been able to speak freely. This privacy was gone, the only place they could be certain of private conversation was their bedroom and by the time they got there she was too tired to talk about anything.

Also it somehow felt disloyal to say anything against his sister or his mother. After all, nothing could be done about it and it would make the atmosphere worse. She must not take sides.

David had been right. Neither his mother nor Iris was interested in the little sitting room and in the evenings when they were all in together they would sit by the fire in the living room. Not that it happened every evening. Iris was busy with various meetings at the church. Ella did not want to enquire too closely.

David would not go to church. The children had been christened at her insistence. Lottie was a big church goer and when she was younger ran the Mothers' Union, sang in the choir and always sat in the same pew. Iris dutifully went with her.

Iris said, 'You will be coming with us to

church on Christmas Day?'

It was breakfast, the Sunday before Christmas. Sunday was the only day they all had breakfast together and since there were now six of them and very often seven if Flo was there all formal meals had to be eaten in the dining room, there wasn't enough room in the kitchen.

It made more work, though Ella seemed the only person who noticed. Flo had merely shaken her head over the cooking, washing up, tidying up, washing and ironing but seemed offended when Ella talked about getting in extra help.

'You can't trust people, Mrs Black,' she said. 'We'll manage.'

Iris seemed under the mistaken impression that there was nothing for her to do and Ella could have accused her of taking advantage of the situation. She had not done the housework at the house in the bailey, there was a woman who came in to help twice a week. She had said she had enough to do looking after her parents. Now she contributed nothing at all.

Unfortunately Iris thought she could cook and was often in the way in the kitchen. She made soda bread, which David hated, rice pudding with a thick skin which both David and Clyde detested and she would often come back from town with ingredients when Ella had already planned and made meals, which was irritating.

David didn't even reply to Iris's question about church on Christmas Day as though it was nothing to do with him. Iris went on looking at him and the silence lengthened.

'Ella?' Iris prompted her.

Ella knew that David hated church due to the perhaps mistaken idea that in his younger life his mother had taken him to church twice every Sunday and wanted him to be a vicar.

'I have a dinner to make and the children to see to.'

'I'll do the vegetables and you can cook the turkey the night before.'

'I'd rather get up early and do it.'

'Then David and Clyde can come. Clyde is quite old enough to attend church without making a fuss.'

'He's not going,' David said, 'and neither am I,' and he got up and walked out before Iris could say any more.

'It's not very respectable behaviour,' Iris said, 'considering who David is. Whatever will people think when you don't go to church even at Christmas?'

Lottie usually didn't join in but now she said, 'His father did everything David does and was a local councillor and he still found time to go to church.'

Ella went on with what she was doing and said nothing.

On Christmas morning everyone did as they wanted and she thought it worked quite well. Clyde was busy playing with his new car, David looked after the baby, she and Flo sorted out the dinner and Iris and Lottie went to church.

While they were gone David handed her a small box with her Christmas present inside it. It was a pair of tiny diamond ear rings. She shrieked and hugged him.

'Thank you, David, they're beautiful,' she said. 'You shouldn't have bought me something so expensive when we're short of money but I'm so pleased you did.'

He kissed her and they laughed.

They had a pleasant enough meal. After dinner David and Lottie both fell asleep. Flo went back to the cottage to lie down for a couple of hours, Iris and Ella took the children out for a little while before the light went altogether. Ella was convinced that Clyde would sleep better if he had some fresh air but it began to rain before dark so they came back.

She was trying not to think about the evening and how difficult it would be, but somehow if you worried about it the whole thing seemed to matter less when it came to it.

She kept her mind blank as she and David drove up the long winding road but she could see the lights from the house well before they got to it and every window was bright. Lots of expensive cars were parked outside and several people in evening dress were walking in.

'Did Rosemary say it was evening dress?' David asked.

'No.'

'Well, then, we won't feel stupid.'

He parked the car and followed her inside. They were, she saw, underdressed. David's suit was dark so he looked fine but her cocktail dress was short and plain and she had no ornaments but the ear rings which David had bought her for Christmas.

Rosemary, wearing a long silver gown, came straight across. She was wearing sapphire ear rings, four small pieces making up a square, surrounded by silver. They were so exquisite Ella knew they were real.

'Oh, Ella, you look grand,' Rosemary said.

Ella was about to disclaim, knew how ridiculous it would sound and just smiled. And then she caught sight of herself in the big mirror and of David beside her. They were like a study in black and white.

'Thank you. I love your ear rings,' she said, when they moved a little apart from the men.

'Aren't they bonny? Harry bought them for me for Christmas.'

Ella accepted a drink and tried to appreciate how lovely the house looked. Rosemary and Harry had filled it with wonderful furniture, thick rugs, subtle lighting, mirrors all in the right places, bookcases filled with leather-bound volumes, and this in just a few days. Log fires burned in every room and there was laughter and talk and the popping of champagne corks. It had not been like this when she was little. People rarely came to the house. She couldn't think why not. It had been like a cocoon, the three of them together.

She did not know anyone at the party; she thought they must be Harry's business acquaintances. David knew and introduced her to various people but it was not the kind of party where you could relax among friends.

Eventually however Harry came to her, when David was talking to some other people in the group, and drew her aside to see the view from the big window in the drawing room. She thought it had not changed, still the same outlook, the way that the lawns ran down to the river and the trees.

'I didn't know this was your house until Rosemary told me. I mean I didn't know she'd chosen your house.' It was almost an apology.

'She's lovely.'

'Isn't she?' he said. 'How are you? How are the children? We never get to see them. You don't invite me to your house.'

'Don't we? I'm sorry.'

'Does David know about us yet? Have you told him? Is that it?'

'It's not about that.'

'What is it about?'

'He doesn't like you.'

Harry smiled at her frankness.

'Of course he doesn't like me. That's not the point.'

'You don't mind that David doesn't like you?'

'You don't understand anything about men, do you? I'm more successful than he is, a lot more, so that it's a completely different level. The only reason he was invited here tonight was because of you. And I knew his wife before he did, so he probably hates me.'

She looked quickly around her but nobody was near.

'You didn't … we didn't...'

'Oh yes we did. It was the most important thing that ever happened to me. I never loved anyone like that again. I think now that I never will. I thought I would. I thought you could move on and that everything would be all right but it isn't. I miss you. I miss the magic that you bring into the room with you.'

'What about Rosemary? You cared enough to marry her.'

'I had to marry somebody. You wouldn't have me. I loved you. I adored you. How could you do that to me?'

'Please don't talk so wildly. Somebody will hear.'

It wasn't true, his voice was soft and intimate and it was difficult to breathe under his intense gaze.

'Do you love him as much as you loved me?'

'It's – it's different.'

'How?'

She didn't answer.

'Do you love him as much as you loved Jack? He was your first love. People say you always love your first love best. Is that how it was with you?'

She trembled. She tried not to think about Jack. She dismissed him from her mind now. Harry took a couple of steps towards her and she was convinced that he was going to try and take her into his arms.

Luckily at that moment Rosemary arrived. Ella wanted to run away and hide but she was obliged to stay and talk.

Rosemary drew her across the room and she said, 'I want to show you around.'

'You have lots of guests.'

'I don't care.'

They went into the library and it had not changed and the relief was huge. It looked almost exactly as it had looked when she was a child. Rosemary closed the door.

'You knew Harry very well, didn't you?'

Ella wished to God she had stayed at home.

'He … is very fond of you. He doesn't talk about you so I know.' Rosemary smiled. 'Other women he talks about.'

'Other women?' Ella wished beyond anything that she had not said this. Rosemary gave a thin smile. 'Yes, other women. My marriage is full of them.'

Ella didn't have time to say anything before the door opened and David came in. She was so relieved to see him she could have kissed him. He was bored. She could tell he was. He wanted to go home. And she wanted to go home too, she wanted very much to leave this place where all the memories of her early life had been replaced by Harry and Rosemary's awful marriage. She took his arm.

'We should go. I promised Iris we wouldn't be late.'

Rosemary protested that the party had hardly begun but Ella was firm.

'It isn't fair to leave her with her mother and the children on Christmas night. We ought to get back.'

The goodbyes were said, they put on their coats, and once outside in the cold air David said, 'Thank God for that,' which was exactly what Ella felt and they got into the car and drove home.

She couldn't relax. Harry seemed to her

like a keg of gunpowder. She didn't want to go too close and she rather regretted now that she had made a friend of his wife.

'Did you enjoy that?' David said and she thought she heard a dry note in his voice.

'We don't have to do it again. I can see Rosemary without involving you.'

'You think that's possible?'

She didn't look at him but she could tell by his voice that he was relieved.

'I have several friends whose husbands you don't care for.'

'But this is slightly different, isn't it?' The question was soft and she silently cursed David for his perception. 'You were friends with Harry first.'

'He was there when Jack died,' she said. 'He came and told me.'

David didn't make any reply and she knew that he found talk of Jack difficult though he had tried to be generous. She remembered him once saying to her, 'I know it isn't a nice sentiment but I'm jealous of anybody you loved before me and of anybody who loved you.'

She had thought it a pretty remark at the time. Now she didn't.

'He cares about you,' David added.

'That kind of thing brings people close. It was the worst time of my life.'

'And you'd lost so many people you loved before that.'

'Yes, I did.'

'It makes me feel so stupid.'

'Why?'

'Because when my father died all I could think was how much longer I had him than you had had either of your parents and that you had lost Jack too. I had been so lucky.'

'But he was your father, David, and you loved him.'

They were at home by then, in the sitting room. She went over and took her husband into her arms. David tightened both arms around her and hid against her shoulder for a few seconds and she was glad that the moment was past.

Twenty-Three

Ella was pleased when Christmas was over and things got back to normal, though the weather was bitterly cold during January and February and being stuck indoors with the children, Lottie and sometimes Iris became difficult. Ella took to putting the fire on in the little sitting room first, in hope of persuading them to sit in there but nobody took the hint.

Lottie would stay by the Aga in the kitchen so that Ella had to go around her to achieve anything and with them all being there it took more time to make meals. Once the fire was on in the main sitting room Lottie would spend the afternoon asleep there.

Ella was inclined to suggest to David that they should put the fire on in her bedroom during the day but the idea of any of them having to haul buckets of coal up the stairs meant she took this no further. If anyone came in the afternoons she got into the habit of taking them into the small sitting room so she, the visitors and the children ended up in there, and if it was anybody interesting Iris would come through and very often Lottie when she awoke mid-afternoon. It was a ridiculous situation but there seemed little she could do about it.

One cold February day Rosemary arrived, Iris had gone to clean the church, Lottie was asleep and for once so were both the children so Ella was delighted to see her, made tea, offered coffee cake and they sat over the fire in the little room.

'I've got something very special to tell you,' Rosemary said.

'Oh, good, what is it'?'

'We're going to have a baby. After all this time.'

Ella hugged her and said how wonderful it was.

'Is Harry pleased?'

'I haven't told him yet. I've just come from

314

the doctor. He's never mentioned things like that to me, we haven't talked about it.'

'He's bound to be delighted.'

'Do you think? I'm worried but I want a baby so much. I didn't dare talk to him about it in case that was how he felt and I didn't get pregnant, but I've wanted to say to him that I do want bairns and I think he must, don't you?'

'Of course he will,' Ella said.

'It will help things,' Rosemary said.

Clyde shouted and woke up Susan so they went upstairs and collected the children and sat by the fire. Outside it began to snow and Ella thought it was a wonderful way to spend an afternoon; when the baby was born in the summer they could sit out in the garden and everything would be perfect.

Iris came in just after Rosemary left.

'I've got a job,' she said. 'I'm going to help the vicar.'

'Help him with what?'

'Secretarial. I'm going to run his office. It doesn't pay anything of course but it's good experience for me.'

Ella looked at her. She didn't like to say to her that there was her mother to look after, though to be fair Lottie wasn't difficult, there was all the extra work which Ella and Flo were doing between them without any help and she couldn't see that Iris's getting such a job would achieve anything.

As Iris was so pleased about it she said, 'Oh, that's wonderful.' It might be better if Iris decided to take a proper job and had some independence from them. She might even in time be able to move out. Ella felt uncharitable when this thought occurred to her.

When David came in Iris could not wait to tell him.

'I'm to go to night classes to learn typing.'

David said nothing except, 'The strike starts on Monday.'

Ella thought it would have been nice if he could have at least congratulated his sister but whether he was so worried that he couldn't think or he just didn't consider it of enough importance she didn't know.

'Rosemary is expecting a baby,' Ella said.

Neither of them said anything to that.

Ella couldn't see why David still had to go to work when nobody else was there. Madeline would continue coming into the office.

'Why don't you treat it like a holiday and spend time with me and the children if nothing is happening?' Ella said but he said that he couldn't.

She ventured into the foundry on the Monday afternoon and she had never seen it like that except the odd time on Sunday when she and David were first married and he would wander down to look at some paperwork and she was sufficiently interested to go with him.

A cold wind blew through the workplaces and there was a discomforting quiet. The telephones didn't ring in the office and Madeline sat there typing as though everything depended on it and giving a cheery smile when she obviously didn't feel like it.

'It's only a week,' Ella had said.

'Have you any idea how much work I can lose in a week, not just that which is planned?'

'But if everybody is on strike then it's the same all round, isn't it?' she said.

Strangely enough while they were there one of the men drifted in to the office and said, 'Sorry, Mr Black. I wish I was at work and so do all the others and that's the truth. The missus is fed up of me already.'

It brought a smile to their faces. One or two others came and mooched about even though they were not supposed to be near when the foundry wasn't working. David had unlocked the gates and a number of workers turned up, standing outside the office, kicking at the dust and talking in low voices about what a bad job it was. Ella thought how ridiculous that because the strike was national and the union had called it they had to obey when in such a small company there was no call for it.

Did they know how bad things were and that in a few months if things didn't get better the small foundry would have to close? If they didn't actually know it she thought they were instinctively aware of it or was it just boredom which sent them here when they could have been at the pub or reading the paper? David had said it was a bad time for the men to be on strike.

'What do you mean a bad time?' she had asked.

'Well, it's winter. There's nowhere for them to go. A strike in the summer is the best because it's like a holiday for them. They can sit outside and read their newspapers, work on their allotments, take their wives and children out. When the weather's bad like this they've nothing to do and nowhere to go so they hate it. Also...'

'Also what?'

'It isn't like a big company where the management doesn't know anybody. I went to school with a lot of these men.'

'I thought you went to public school?'

'I did later, but when I was little I went to school here. My parents thought it was a good idea and it was because now I know them all and they know me. They don't want to be on strike, they're losing pay. Their wives don't like it because there's no money. It doesn't benefit anybody and after it there will likely be a pay rise and although that's nice for them it doesn't help me.'

Ella walked home. She at least still had enough to do. The children hated the bad weather and it was sleeting. It went on like that all day and the children cried, Flo complained because there was wet washing everywhere, Lottie sat by the fire. Even the lunch was dull.

Only Iris was happy. She came back at teatime, wolfed down ham sandwiches and went off to her night class. Ella thought it was amusing that she could envy Iris anything, but she could get away and do new things.

She didn't mention her mother so presumably she thought it was all right to leave her there but then Lottie was easy, much easier than Iris, and had lately been playing games with Clyde, taking walks around the garden and she was looking forward to the spring.

She confided to Ella that it was lovely to live at the big house again so Ella thought it might be nice if Iris did move because although there was little outward friction between David and Iris they were never easy in one another's company.

On the second day of the strike David telephoned her from the office not long after he had gone there.

'We've been broken into. You couldn't come and help, could you?' he said.

Leaving rapid instructions with Flo, Ella

drove to the works. She parked in the foundry yard beside a police car and made her way to the office.

The big wooden door had broken panels, the wood was splintered. Inside it was such a mess that Ella was inclined to give up and cry. Filing cabinets were sideways on the floor, spilling their contents. Desk drawers had been pulled out. The floor was a sea of paper. Madeline's typewriter was also on the floor and paint had been emptied on to the desks, chairs, floor and windows.

Two policemen were there, looking dark and out of place and the older one said, 'Have you been able to ascertain whether anything has been taken, Mr Black?'

'As far as we know nothing but the petty cash,' David said, indicating the empty box beside him.

'We keep very little money on the premises,' Madeline said. 'There were only a few pounds. You wouldn't think anybody would do all this for such a small amount.'

The sergeant shook his head.

'I doubt the motive was money, madam. It looks more like somebody with a grudge either against the company or against Mr Black himself. I know the men are on strike. Somebody could think he has a grievance.'

They all looked at one another but nobody said anything. Was that because of Flo? Ella wondered.

'We employ sixty men,' David said, 'it's difficult to say.'

'Have you had trouble with anyone recently, sir?'

And then it all came out about Flo's husband. Ella felt awful. The police said they would talk to him but that they would be speaking to a number of people to see where they had been since early yesterday evening.

Ella couldn't very well leave Flo with the children, the housework, the shopping and the meals so she came back to make the dinner and for once she didn't need to prepare the ground. She had wondered whether to mention it to Flo but she felt guilty saying nothing. There was no need for her to worry.

'You're thinking that my Walter did it, aren't you?' Flo said.

'There's no evidence of it,' Ella said. 'The police will be going to see all of the men who work there and those who have recently left. Do you want to go and see him? I would come with you.'

'I don't know where he is,' Flo said. 'I went to his sister's last night to find him but she said he was long gone. She wasn't very friendly either. She's never liked me.'

'This isn't your fault, Flo,' Ella said.

'Isn't it? It's starting to feel as if it is,' Flo said, her voice wavering.

For once David brought Madeline home

with him at dinner time.

'I'm sorry,' he apologized in the gloom and privacy of the hall, 'that I didn't tell you, but I couldn't leave her sitting among all that and it would have been so awkward telephoning, it might have put her off.'

To make things worse the day was dark with rain. Ella lit the fire, hastily laid the table and put out steaming bowls of broth and great big chunks of bread. They sat down gratefully, Clyde dunking his bread into the broth so that it came back out orange, sopping, covered in pieces of leek, carrot and ham. Eventually, tired of dealing with it he broke all his bread into small pieces and stuffed it into the bowl and ate the whole lot.

Susan wouldn't eat, she hid her face against Ella and spent quite a lot of time sitting on David's lap so that Ella could eat her hot broth in peace and safety. They had chocolate cake and coffee to follow.

'I feel much better now, thank you so much,' Madeline announced when the chocolate cake was finished and they all smiled at one another.

It took the rest of the week to sort out most of the office. David could find nothing apart from the petty cash missing. They arranged to go out on the Friday evening, just the two of them, they had had such an awful week.

'I'll ring the County and see if they have a table,' David said.

'That would be nice,' Ella said.

She was cheered at the thought of it. She put on her favourite black cocktail dress, her pearls, put up her hair and the moment she stepped into high heels she was keen to go. David telephoned. He was at a meeting in Newcastle. He apologized, saying that he would be late and would she mind driving herself there and he would meet her, he hadn't time to come back to the house and change.

She didn't mind at all. As soon as she was ready she drove herself there but David was nowhere to be seen. The first person she saw was Harry, sitting in the lounge bar, smoking and drinking with a very pretty, slim, dark-haired young woman. When the young woman excused herself and left the room Ella went across.

'Good evening,' she said genially.

'Hello, Ella,' he said. He was rather drunk, she thought, it reminded her uncomfortably of Jack. His eyes were so bright, his smile so ready.

'Been here a while?' He nodded.

'Who's that?'

'What?'

'The woman you're with.'

He grinned.

'Keeping an eye on me, are you? Don't

worry, I'm being horribly good. That's my secretary and she has gone home.'

'How's Rosemary?'

'Fine. Can I buy you a drink?'

'No, thank you. I'm waiting for David. He's at a meeting in Newcastle. What are you doing?'

'Well, I'm drinking a martini and wondering whether–'

'No, I mean what are you doing? Shouldn't you be at home with your wife?'

Harry took a long drag at a Sobranie cigarette. She half wished he would offer her one, they were her favourite and he had used to buy the cocktail cigarettes for her in pretty colours. They reminded her of parties, dances, good times, being with him and it made her angry.

'You're not going to lecture me, are you?' he said, sitting back on his bar stool and considering her with care.

'Why did you marry Rosemary if this is how you're going to go on?'

'I needed rescuing.'

'From what?'

'From myself of course. What else? Christ, you're beautiful. Are you sure you won't have a drink? He's bound to be late if he's gone to a meeting.'

'Why are you here? Rosemary is pregnant, she needs you there with her.'

'I'm afraid.'

He was, she thought, more drunk than she had imagined.

'Of what?'

'Of going through all that again.' He looked down.

Ella took a seat beside him. The barman appeared.

'I'll have a martini please.'

'I'll have one as well, Frank.'

'You've had enough,' she said, though the barman had gone by then. 'It won't be like that, Harry.'

'Won't it?' He gazed at her. 'What will it be like then?'

'It'll be fine. Rosemary will go to the wonderfully expensive nursing home you've organized for her and she will have the baby and everything will be all right.'

He said nothing.

'You have to believe that,' she said.

'I daren't believe it.'

The martinis, thankfully, were not long in coming. Ella took a good swig out of her drink, swallowed it gratefully and then said, 'It wasn't your fault.'

'So it's my fault if something goes wrong now?'

'This is no good at all,' Ella said.

'Isn't it?' He stared into the drink which the barman had just put in front of him. 'I thought they made the best martinis in the area.'

Ella took another slug from her drink.

'It wasn't your fault I lost the child,' she said.

'Baby,' he said.

'What?'

'It was a baby. Can't you even bring yourself to say the word? You make it sound like it was nothing to do with us at all and it was my fault.'

'It wasn't and no, I can't bear the word. It was too hard a thing after – after what happened to Jack.'

'I wasn't there. If I had been there–'

'You couldn't be there. You were fighting the Japs. Even you can't be in two places at once.'

'We should have got married and it wouldn't have happened. You can't think how much I wanted that–'

'I'd just lost my husband–'

'You didn't lose him, Ella,' Harry said, sitting back in his chair. 'I hate that. It makes him sound like a letter or something. He died, for God's sake. First you write and tell me you've lost the baby and that sounds like you deposited it outside a shop and somebody ran off with it and then you write and tell me you don't want me any more.'

'I thought you didn't get the letter.'

'I didn't. I don't know which was worse really, the knowing or the not knowing, the hoping, telling myself that letters get lost, that you would never do such a thing, that you cared about me... What do you expect? A great deal, that's what you expect. Far too bloody much.

'I'll tell you what was lost, I lost you, I lost the woman I loved and my child and there was I ... there was I ... trying to make sure we had a future, thinking that I was fighting for something important, hoping and praying that I had a future to come back to. When in fact I didn't, did I? Have you any idea what it was like coming back after the war when you were married to somebody else? All those bloody years. And not just anybody else, somebody half as successful, a quarter as intelligent–'

'He is not,' Ella objected.

'Oh, stop lying to yourself. He runs a little tinpot company, he can't get it right, he owes money all over the place, he's got a strike on his hands. He was forced to borrow money from a man he doesn't like because he didn't have any option.'

'David is a very nice man, which is more than could ever be said of you,' Ella said hotly though in as discreet a voice as possible because at the far side of the room other people were sitting at tables, drinking and talking and she was aware that they were watching and trying to listen. She was angry with herself. She should never have come over. What would people think?

Harry considered his glass, which some-how was empty again.

'I used to be a nice man,' he said, 'when you were married to my best friend. I fell in love with you the night we met. You didn't even look at me. There was nobody for you but Jack. When he died I thought at last, in spite of how awful everything was, and in the worst possible way, I was going to have you to myself and then you write and tell me we're having a baby and then ... and then there was Burma, the jungle, the mos-quitos, the endless fighting, the men dying...'

The barman appeared.

'Same again, Mr Reid?' he asked.

'Yes, please,' Harry replied.

Nobody said anything while the barman was mixing the martinis, pouring out the measures of gin and vermouth, finding ice, shaking them in the bright shiny cocktail mixer. He poured them carefully into clean glasses and went away.

'Do you know what I think, Ella?'

'I'm not sure I want to know what you think.'

He regarded her steadily from eyes so blue they were almost black.

'You've spent the rest of your life making up for the people you lost, for Jack and for me and for the baby. You married David sodding Black for the guilt that you felt and you'll go on having his children until you somehow purge yourself of it. And how long do you think that will take before you come to me? How long before you forgive yourself for marrying the wrong man? How long before you admit to yourself that it's me you want?'

She smacked his face. She wished she hadn't. Everybody in the room was watching. The silence was enormous. Somebody put a glass down on the table nearby and the noise echoed.

'What's going on?' said a terse voice in her ear. It was David.

She didn't even look at him. She just glared at Harry.'

'Nothing, Harry's just being his usual objectionable, drunken self,' she said and swept off the stool and retreated into the ladies' room, the one place where neither man would follow her.

Harry didn't look up. David didn't say anything. Eventually Harry said, 'You want a martini?'

'What did you do?' David could hear his own voice, icily polite. He felt like knocking Harry off the bar stool and considering how drunk he was it wouldn't take much doing.

'I behaved like a bastard.'

Harry's voice was low. For some ridiculous reason David found himself smiling sympathetically even though he couldn't stand him.

'How?'

'I got drunk with my secretary while my pregnant wife was sitting at home by herself and your wife ... she didn't think much of it.'

'You're in love with her, aren't you?' David heard himself say and wondered how his mouth had got so out of control.

Harry frowned.

'My secretary?'

'No, you drunken clown. My wife.'

'Oh, hell.' Harry took another cigarette from the silver cigarette case which was on the bar, tapped it gently off the top as though he was contemplating the question, lit it from a small silver lighter and only then said casually, 'Why, yes, I thought you knew.'

'I suppose I did.' David didn't know what else to say and gazed around the bar, embarrassed.

'Are you sure you won't have a martini?' Harry urged him. When David didn't answer Harry called along the bar, 'Frank, more martinis.'

'No,' David said but it was too late.

Frank came over and began work with his cocktail shaker and in a way it was soothing, the sound of the gin and the crushed ice.

'Did you get a good deal with Ross?' Harry said.

Ross was a big Newcastle company and that afternoon David had secured a contract. David said nothing. Harry laughed.

'You don't have to tell me if you don't want to because you owe me money. I just thought that if you'd got the deal you might be able to pay me back the money you owe me. And wouldn't that be a shame.'

David accepted the cocktail glass from Frank and took a big swig. It made him feel better. It made him not think about the relationship between Ella and Harry in times past. He couldn't bear it.

'Did you get it?' Harry prompted him when David didn't say anything.

'Yes.'

'Good for you. There was a lot of competition. So now you won't owe me anything for much longer.'

'No, I won't,' David said and suddenly felt much better.

Harry drained his glass once again, and said, 'What a damned shame,' put the lighter and cigarette case into the inside pocket of his jacket, picked up the half smoked cigarette from the big glass ashtray in front of him, and got precariously to his feet. Everbody in the room watched him as he made his way very slowly to the door. David didn't watch. He drank the rest of his martini and when Frank came back he ordered another.

Ella was shaking, almost crying. She had made herself not think about the loss of the baby for so long and now it all came back, the pain, the horror, the way that she had had to be taken to hospital, the feeling of the life slipping away from her as so much else had, the bloody lump that was meant to be their baby, the feeling that she had somehow caused it, the certainty afterwards that nothing good would ever happen again, first Jack and then the baby and Harry wasn't even there, he wasn't there to take her into his arms and tell her that everything would be all right. And she had nobody to help and nobody wanted to know because they were not married.

And she knew in some way what his life was like then, how many men died, how prisoners were not taken, how the enemy would slit their throats, that you could be mown down running up a hill, that sometimes you didn't eat for days, that you could be wounded and scream for hours and hours and then die of thirst, that the Japs cut off their prisoners' heads, starved them, maltreated them in every possible way because it was not considered honourable to give up no matter what the circumstances. It was a tormented existence and she had left him to the hell of it.

Meeting David was like having the light come back on in the darkness for her, like a door opening. She had looked into his eyes and known she would get past all these things, and she would get past the war.

She had sacrificed Harry and their love for it. She had made him into this. He was not like this before, he was just another boy afraid to die, afraid to live, grieving over his best friend, falling in love with his best friend's girl. He had loved her then. He did not and never would love Rosemary.

Maybe he would never love anybody again, certainly not like that, with the innocence of belief in the future. He had thought everything was going to be all right, that it had to be and now ... now he was this clever, glib person for whom nothing was enough.

She began to cry. She wished she could stand there for an hour and cry it all out but God only knew what was happening in the bar and besides it was not fair to either of them that she should stay in here so she stopped the tears, powdered her face, reapplied her lipstick and went back across the thick carpet.

She could see as she walked in that David was alone by the bar. Harry had gone. Other people were still there. People loved a scene. Perhaps they were hoping for more. Not that he was giving them anything to look at and she thought that was what she loved best about him, he was so calm, so cool, just as though nothing had happened.

She went and sat down on the stool she had left and took a big swig out of her second drink.

'I'm sorry,' she said.

David concentrated on his drink. She cleared her throat.

'Are we going to eat? You did book a table?'

He looked at her, one of those who-do-you-think-you're-kidding looks that he was so good at.

'You still want to eat?' he said.

'No. No, I don't.'

'I'll cancel it then and we'll go home.'

She clutched at the sleeve of his jacket.

'No,' she said but softly, 'I don't want to, David.' Everything swam. She clutched at the edge of the bar.

He had got to his feet but he sat down again next to her.

'It's all right,' he said.

Ella began to cry and this time it was a serious job so David got up and helped her up and then he put an arm around her and shepherded her from the room, from the building, not into the car park but down to the riverside just beyond the hotel.

He put her musquash coat around her shoulders. It was a bitterly cold night. Her tears began to dry. He pulled her in against him and she hid in the lapel of his jacket.

'I'm fine now,' she announced. 'How did

the meeting go?'

'Why did you hit him?' Having comforted her he moved back and he was looking straight at her.

Ella had been hoping but not believing that David had not seen her slap Harry.

'He was there with another woman.'

'It's none of your business, Ella. Their marriage is between them.'

'He was so drunk.'

'I've never seen him sober.'

She remembered Harry sober. She remembered when she was married to Jack and they would go to the pub and play dominoes and she and Harry would drink cider like the children they almost were. And he was funny and kind and they were convinced they would live forever.

'Let's go home now,' she said.

Suddenly she wanted her children. They drove back and she ran into the house and for once both the children were asleep. She tiptoed into the baby's room and tried not to think what it would have been like had her first child not died. Susan was pink-cheeked, breathing so evenly. Her hair was curled like pennies and her tiny fist was clenched.

Clyde was lying with his favourite rabbit snuggled in against him. She watched him from a long time in the dim light.

When she got back downstairs David was

in the kitchen, searching the breadbin.

'What are you doing?' she said.

'I didn't have any lunch.'

'I could make you a bacon sandwich.'

'Could you? That would be nice.'

They sat and ate at the kitchen table because it was the warmest room in the house and she was actually hungry. They had big pots of coffee.

'Are you going to tell me what it was really about?' he asked.

Ella couldn't lie any further and she couldn't look at him.

'I can hear the baby crying,' she said.

It was true. Susan's half awakened sobs were almost screams by the time Ella reached her. It took a long time to calm her down and when she finally slept and Ella went into the bedroom David had gone to bed. He didn't stir when she got in beside him and neither did he move away when she huddled in against his back in the darkness.

Twenty-Four

Ella was not very surprised when Iris came back in the following afternoon and said, 'I hear you slapped Harry Reid's face in the lounge bar of the County last night.'

Oh God, Ella thought, everybody knows. She had been awake most of the night, regretting it.

'Rosemary is having his baby. He was there with another woman and ... isn't he going to try at least to be part of a family? I lost my temper.'

'She so obviously married him for his money. Why should she care what he does?' Iris said.

'That's a very interesting view.'

'Isn't it the reason most women marry, for money and position? I would.'

'Iris!'

Ella stared into Iris's clear green eyes, shocked.

'You're the only woman in the world who would have turned him down,' Iris said. 'I would have tried to change him of course,' Iris continued thoughtfully. 'That would have been fun.

'And he could have bought me a beautiful house and given me gorgeous children and I would have had fur coats and diamonds and an open-topped car and if he wanted to get drunk with little tramps now and then I don't think I would have cared. It's a lot better than what I have had, a life full of caring for old people.'

Ella had never heard his speak so freely and Iris's eyes were full of tears.

'You have no idea,' Iris said, 'all those ... all

those dreadful blessed nights alone.'

Ella didn't know what to say.

'You'll find somebody–'

'Oh, yes, of course I will. How many times have I heard that? I'm over the hill. Look at me now. Women like you and Rosemary, you have no idea what it's all about and if you want your prissy reputation intact you should stay away from her husband. If you end up in a hotel bedroom with him then my brother will never forgive you.'

Ella was glad she felt angry.

'I'm not going to do anything of the sort,' she said.

'When a woman slaps a man's face in a bar, Ella, she's three quarters of the way there–'

'I have never–'

'Oh yes you have. Don't lie. I went to war, I wasn't born yesterday. Do you think my war sweetheart Johnny and I were any different? You lay with Harry Reid, I daresay. I'm glad I had Johnny. But if David chooses to think you and Harry didn't have a raging affair that's his business. Do you know what I did after Johnny died? I wanted to sleep with anybody and everybody.'

'Iris–'

'Yes, I did. Wilkie who nursed with me, God bless her, she stopped me from making a complete fool of myself but each time I thought that I would fall in love again. I kept hoping that it would stop the hurt but it never did. Nobody ever stopped it, not even Tom Cruikshank and he's a dear. That's what you did. You used Harry Reid in an effort to get over Jack and now look at him.'

It was more or less what she had told herself, but Ella could not bear the truth on someone else's lips.

'Are you saying I'm to blame?'

'The war was to blame for the state we're all in. What I'm saying is please try not to hurt my brother. He may give the appearance of being like the steel he produces but he's been taking the responsibility around here since he was far too young to shoulder it. I care too much about him to let you mess his life up because you're stupid.'

'I resent that!' Ella cried.

'You can resent it all you like,' Iris said and she left, banging the outside door after her.

A week later on the Saturday morning, when David had gone to the office, a car pulled up outside the house and Harry got out. Ella could see by the way he hesitated and by his white face and bowed head that all was not well. He would not have come there without a good reason.

She went to the door.

'Is something the matter?'

'Rosemary is in hospital. She asked me if you would go.'

Ella hesitated.

'Harry–'

'Look, I'm sorry for what I said. I'd had too much to drink. This isn't for me, it's for her. Please.'

Ella ushered him into the sitting room which thankfully was empty.

'Is it the baby?'

'She started to bleed. They think she's going to be all right but she must have complete rest and they want to keep her in for a day or two just to make sure. She wanted to see you. Will you go?'

'Yes, of course.'

'I can drive you.'

'I can drive myself.'

'I'm going there anyway.'

'Wait here.'

She went off and found Iris upstairs.

'Can you look after the children for a couple of hours?' She explained about Rosemary.

'I was going to have my hair done.'

'Can't it wait?'

'Is Harry here?'

'Yes, he's downstairs.'

'Just call in at the hairdresser for me then and tell them that I can't come.'

'Thank you, Iris. I won't be long.'

Harry drove in silence to the hospital and she could not think of anything to say. When they got there he parked the car and sat still, hands clutching the steering wheel.

'I don't think I can do this,' he said.

'Of course you can.'

'I don't want to go inside.'

'There's no rush.'

'Yes, there is. She's all alone in there.'

'It's going to be all right.'

'How can you say that? You of all people.'

'This is not your fault, Harry.'

He looked wildly at her.

'Isn't it?'

'Will you stop blaming yourself for everything?'

He didn't answer. He opened the door, got out and then stood back against the exquisite creamy side of the car as if he had forgotten how to move. She got out too and went round to him, unsure what to do next but she knew what she had to say.

'It won't be like that again.'

'Is this how it was?' He looked wildly at her from wet dark eyes. 'Is this what happened?'

She didn't answer. She looked beyond him at the great mass of the hospital walls and then the noise of the city traffic. He moved as though he very much wanted to run away but knew he couldn't.

'Was it like this or...'

'Or what?'

He folded his arms and looked down.

'I've always thought...'

'What?'

'We should go in.'

'Not until you tell me.' He looked at her.

'That maybe ... that maybe you got rid of it.'

She stared at him, at the pain in his eyes.

'You thought I would do that?'

He didn't answer, he just stood there.

'Oh, Harry, whatever made you think so?' She didn't know whether to be angry at him or hurt for him.

'Because it was all wrong, everything that happened right from Jack being shot, everything was wrong.'

'What do you mean?'

He shook his head and she thought back to the days after Jack's funeral, those awful empty days when she got up every morning and cried for the person he had not been and for the way her first love affair had turned to ashes.

'You thought everything was always going to be like that again.'

'But it wasn't,' she said. 'It wasn't like that, Harry. You were there.'

'I wasn't though, was I, when it came down to it?' he said harshly. 'That was the trouble and I can't forgive myself and now it's happening all over again because I'm such a useless bastard.'

He walked away across the car park and

through the hospital doors.

Rosemary looked so tiny, lying in a room all by herself in a hospital bed. Harry went over and took her into his arms and hugged her and kissed her all over her face like she was a child, and then Ella kissed her and they sat down on either side of the bed.

'You'll get into bother sitting there. It's not allowed,' Rosemary said, half joking.

Harry pushed back the hair from her face.

'How do you feel?'

'I'm fine. I want to go home.'

'Not yet, not until they're sure everything's all right. You must lie still and be good.'

He seemed to be trying to diffuse the situation, Ella thought. Rosemary's eyes filled with tears as she looked at Ella and smiled.

'I'm bored stiff. Get me out of here.'

'You must rest,' Harry said, 'and you must get used to resting until the baby is born.'

'I will. I said I will but you have no idea what it's like being in here. Go and talk to the doctor.'

She persuaded him, he went and that was when she began to cry. Ella held her, cuddled her.

'I can't cry in front of him,' Rosemary wept. 'I want to give him this baby so much. It will make a big difference to our marriage, don't you see?'

'Don't upset yourself. We'll take you home as soon as we can and you will be all right.'

It was several more days before the hospital would allow Rosemary to go home and Harry persuaded Ella to go with him to collect her. Ella watched him carrying his wife from the car to the house as though she was a delicate, precious ornament. He came back and took the bag from Ella.

'You should have waited. I would have carried that.'

'I'm fine,' she said smiling, and she went into the sitting room where Rosemary was on the couch.

When he came back Rosemary said, 'Please go to work now, I know you have a lot to do. I'll get Jim to take Ella home in a little while.'

'Are you sure?'

'Quite sure,' and when he had gone and she had watched him from the room, Rosemary raised her eyes.

'He gets so worried,' she said. 'Stay and have something to eat with me.'

Ella stayed. They ate from trays by the big log fire and the day closed in.

'You don't mind being here?' Rosemary asked.

'Mind? Of course not. You're going to be fine now. Don't worry,' she said.

Twenty-Five

Ella could not think where she was when she came round, just that there was an awful noise from somewhere. Clyde was crying, Susan was screaming and that was what she registered first but there was other noise and after a moment or two she realized that her children had been woken by the sound of someone banging very hard on the outside door. David slept on.

She nudged him.

'David!'

He moaned in his sleep as though in protest.

'David! Someone is trying to knock the door down.'

He turned over, stilled to listen and when the noise went on he got out of bed, put on the lights and went downstairs. She went across the landing to collect firstly Susan and then Clyde and leading one child by the hand and the other in her arm she followed him downstairs just as David ushered two policemen into the hall.

The blast from the door was cold and she was only grateful when he shut it. The grandfather clock in the hall was striking three. The draughts made her shudder. David took them into the sitting room and she followed, grateful that they had shut the sitting-room door when they went to bed because it was still quite warm in there.

Both children had now subsided. Clyde let go of her hand and ran over to David who picked him up. Susan was crying very quietly into her shoulder.

They all sat down.

'Sorry to bring bad news,' the older policeman said, 'but there is a fire at the works, Mr Black. The offices. If you would be good enough to dress and come with us we would like you to see for yourself and give us as much information as you can, sir.'

David paled. All he said was, 'Yes, of course. Ella will you take Clyde while I put some clothes on?'

She did so. She would have offered to make tea for the policeman but she could not put the children down and she only hoped that Flo had not woken because, although Walter could not be found, it was generally assumed that he had broken into the offices when the strike was on and perhaps this had been his handywork.

Iris came downstairs and Ella explained so she went back upstairs to tell her mother.

'Go back to bed,' Ella advised, 'there's nothing we can do and you have to go to work tomorrow.'

David was down within minutes and they left. Ella had the task of getting the children back to sleep. She took them to bed with her and since it was cold and dark in the house and her bed was still warm they snuggled against her and were soon breathing quietly again. Ella couldn't rest.

When she was sure they would go on sleeping she put pillows against them so that neither would fall out of the big bed and then she trod downstairs. There was a hammering on the back door. She opened it to find Flo, swathed in a blanket.

Ella drew her swiftly inside.

'I heard the commotion and saw the polis. What is it? Is it something to do with my Walter?'

'We don't know anything yet.'

'But summat's happened?' Flo said.

Ella explained. Flo cried.

'Nobody knows anything. It might have nothing to do with Walter. Don't upset yourself.' She made tea and they sat gratefully by the Aga's warmth and sipped it.

Iris came down again.

'Mother went back to sleep but I can't rest. Is there any tea in the pot?'

Ella said there was and Iris poured herself a cup and she sat down with them.

'Isn't there anything we can do?' she said.

'It's my Walter, I know it is. Is it ever going

to end?' Flo said.

'You aren't responsible for him, Mrs King,' Iris said.

'I feel like I am.'

'Well, you shouldn't,' Iris said, 'nobody is responsible for anybody beyond themselves, how could we be?'

That seemed to comfort Flo and Ella was grateful for it.

David did not come home and in the end they all went back to bed but Ella did not sleep. She kept waiting for the sound of the door, but she finally fell into a doze and was awoken by a noise from downstairs. She fairly ran down into the hall and there David was; dirty, white-faced and narrow eyed from lack of sleep and maybe smoke.

'How bad is it?' she said.

'Everything in the office.'

'Oh, David, I'm so sorry.'

'It's worse than that. Walter was in there.'

'God, no.'

'He's dead, Ella. He must have banged his head or something.'

'How awful.' Ella started to cry from shock.

David hugged her. He smelled of the fire but Ella was grateful for his shoulder. It stopped her from crying. She huddled in against him.

Iris came slowly down the stairs.

'What's happened?' she said.

David told her.

'How simply dreadful,' she said. 'Poor Flo.'

As she spoke the outside door opened behind them and when Ella came out from David's embrace Flo was standing there, a pale grey figure in the early light.

'It was my Walter, wasn't it?' she asked simply and the way that she said it made Ella's heart give.

What must Waiter have been like for Flo to marry him? Had she been very young and had she looked over and known he was for her as she herself had looked across at Harry Reid the first time she saw him and thought he was the only person she would ever feel such affinity for? Or had it been like with Jack; mad and impulsive?

Her best memory of Jack was of running up Silver Street with him one night with the moonlight turning the cobbles to big white pearls and of him turning and pulling her into his arms and kissing her and of she thinking that she would never want any more.

Somewhere Walter and Flo had lost that. Maybe it had lasted only a few moments. Maybe Flo had not felt that at all and had married him because it was what women were meant to do but Ella didn't think so. The way that Flo identified him as hers was not just because they were a legal couple, Flo had lost Walter maybe a thousand times before now. There seemed to be no limit to such things but she would only lose him like this once.

All Ella said was, 'Flo–'

She didn't need to say any more than that.

'He's dead, isn't he?'

And David nodded.

The routine which was so well established kept them going and Ella reminded herself a dozen times a day of how good it was that Flo was there with them, that she was used to living alone in the cottage and both the children went back and forth between the two houses easily. There was nothing to make you feel better like children.

Very often in the evenings, when Flo was finished working and was sitting in front of the television in her sitting room, Ella would find the children there with her, Clyde with his short legs up and Susan in Flo's arms.

Walter's funeral was surprisingly well attended. Ella had not known that they had so many friends but they had lived in County Durham all their lives and had been married for years. The church was packed with the foundry men and their families and to Ella's pleased surprise Rosemary turned up.

Ella had organized food and drink back at the house and the vicar made an announcement that all were welcome. Iris had objected.

'Won't people think it strange? After all Walter burned down the foundry office. It will take months to put right. He stole from you, he–'

'It's for Flo,' Ella said. 'And besides...'

'And besides what?'

'And besides David insisted.'

He had and she was proud that he had. On the very day that he had to face the mess he was left with, the last thing he had said to her was, 'Ring the vicar, will you, Ella, and when he comes round to see Flo tell him we'll have the do here.'

Ella thought she had never been more proud of him. David was turning into his father.

Twenty-Six

That spring and summer David and Madeline tried to do what they could and the burned out offices were pulled down and the building began on new offices at the other side of the works. David didn't say so but Ella had the feeling he couldn't bear to replace them so chose a different site entirely. There were many problems. All the records were gone, all the orders, all evidence of what had been done over the past twenty years, all the important names and telephone numbers, the details of the men's wages.

During that time David began bringing Madeline home with him for dinner in the middle of the day. Ella didn't really want to cope with another person but since they had twice as much work to do and David said he could not afford to employ another person Ella put up with it. Madeline didn't eat much and she didn't say a great deal while they ate and Ella would have thought that with so much work, so many problems and all the disruption Madeline might be badly affected, but the opposite seemed to happen.

Madeline turned out to be the kind of person who was what Lottie called 'in her element' when there was a crisis. Madeline blossomed. She had always been skinny but Ella's good cooking meant that she put on a little weight and was better for it. She agreed with everything David said which Ella sometimes found amusing and sometimes not and if he was not there it was always 'Mr Black said' and 'Mr Black did'.

Iris took to calling her Echo. Most of the time Iris was at work at the vicarage but she was there at weekends and David and Madeline were working seven days a week trying to sort things out and sometimes Ella had to bite her lip if she happened to look over the table at Iris, and once in the kitchen when they were alone together they burst into giggles.

'If she says "Mr Black thought it was a good idea" once more I shall throw a potato at her,' Iris said. 'Be careful, you know what they say about men and their secretaries.'

That night Ella lay awake in bed and thought. Madeline was older than she was but having not been married and had children she didn't look older, at least not much. It was unfortunately, Ella thought, these things which put years on women.

Single women like Madeline and Iris didn't have as many lines and though they might have had problems in their lives they didn't have day to day problems as she did. David paid her generously. He didn't think it was generous as he thought Madeline justified her wage and Ella was sure she did. If his secretary had been a less competent person they would all have suffered but there were days when she envied Madeline's life, her freedom, her independence and the time she spent with David.

Ella said to him when they got up early the next morning, 'We never go anywhere or do anything any more.'

'I can't at present, I'm sorry.'

'Not even a day or two away? I could ask Flo to take the children. She wouldn't mind. Just you and me?'

'I'm sorry, Ella.'

She didn't like to go on at him about how dull her life was but they didn't even go to a dance or out for a meal any more. All she had was the housework, the children, Flo's company and the shopping.

She even felt bad leaving Flo with the children and Lottie when she went out because Lottie was apt to be forgetful and had to be kept an eye on and Susan was walking and couldn't be left for a second or she emptied the coal bucket, piece by black piece, on to the hearthrug, opened cupboards she wasn't suppose to get into or tried to escape, running down the lawn with Flo after her.

Iris was there less and less. Ella didn't like to question her and there was no reason why Iris should take any responsibility for anything in the house but she did live there. She too was blooming.

Ella was thinking that by now she could have taken a proper job, she could have afforded a little house for herself and her mother but she didn't offer and Ella could see a time when Iris would go off and buy or rent a house for herself and she would be left with Lottie and the children, so she didn't like to say anything.

One evening Ella asked whether she might like to go to the pictures.

'Sorry, I've got a class.'

'Are you still taking secretarial classes? I

thought you must know everything by now,' Ella said.

'There's lots to learn.'

The following evening Iris, resplendent in new dress, went out to the pictures with friends. Ella wanted to ask hotly why that was better than going out with her but she couldn't.

David would have his tea at half past five and go back to work and was never home before eight, and then he was too tired to make conversation and would fall asleep while Ella poured drinks and smoked a cigarette and it was all very frustrating. She told herself she must be patient, that it would not go on for ever but it was beginning to feel like it would.

Rosemary would come round in the afternoons and sit in the garden and that was the best time of day. The baby was due in August. At first she seemed well and excited but she was soon quite large and tired and they had long companionable sessions talking about their absent husbands.

'The doctor says I'm fine and have nothing to worry about,' Rosemary said, 'and that anxious mothers make anxious babies so I have to remain calm. I am getting horrible backache though.'

'We can go inside and you can have a comfy seat.'

'No, thanks, I'm fine here. I like the

garden,' Rosemary replied.

She lay on a rug on the lawn and slept for a little while and Ella watched her pale, drawn face and wondered whether she would not have been better on the sofa. It was a beautiful June day however and they didn't have so many of those that she wanted to waste it inside.

She couldn't sit still for long because the children quickly grew bored and restless and she had to provide entertainment of some type or ask Flo to take them and that seemed unfair since Flo always found something to do in the house even when Ella encouraged her to come outside and sit.

'I'm not used to it, Mrs Black, I can't sit still for long,' Flo said.

Ella wondered whether Flo would ever think she had paid her debt to them. She even thought sometimes it would have been better if Flo could have got away from here and the daily reminders of what Walter had done. In vain Ella assured her that it was not her fault and it had nothing to do with her.

One Friday evening in June, when Rosemary had reluctantly gone back to Swan House because Harry had promised he would be home early – 'he always promises but it rarely happens,' Rosemary said blithely – and Flo had gone to Bishop Auckland to stay with her sister for a couple of days and Iris was out, Ella felt she would go mad.

David did not come home. The children were both fractious, and when she had finally put them to bed and Lottie was asleep by the open French windows and it was almost nine o'clock she decided to go to the foundry just for the look out and see when David was if ever coming home.

She drove across. It was a lovely summer's evening. It had been hot earlier and now the temperature was perfect and it was going to be one of those nights when it got dark for only a few hours. The shadows were long when she parked the car in the mess which the builders were making outside the almost finished office.

Madeline's car was there but David's wasn't and although she looked around and even went up to the door and looked in at the windows there was no sign of anybody so in the end she had to give up and go home.

Lottie went to bed. She needed help getting there and Ella helped her just after ten and Lottie thanked her. Once she was in her nightdress and in bed Ella could safely leave her though the door had to be ajar, Lottie didn't like it shut any more these days. She went downstairs and waited.

David hadn't planned to take Madeline out

to dinner but once he had suggested it she seemed so pleased and he was glad he had done it. They never spent time together except at work, and he knew that was as it should be but it was pleasant sitting in the dining room of the hotel without the chaos of children, knowing there would be no interruptions. The dining room was perfect, white cloths, silver cutlery, crystal and he ordered wine and Madeline sipped it and he smiled across the table at her.

'This is nice,' he said.

'It does make a change,' she admitted.

The wine was very cold and tasted of sunshine and butter. It was a dark golden colour. They had chicken and grapes in a cream sauce and tiny new potatoes and a lemon pudding and it was so restful, so easy. David didn't want to go home. He had faced so many problems lately, he just wanted to let things slide for an hour or two. He didn't know what to say, they always talked of work and that seemed inappropriate and he realized then that he didn't know this woman very well, only amongst the papers, the work crises and the telephone calls.

'Do you go out much in the evenings?' he asked and then wished he hadn't because Madeline blushed and said that she didn't and he thought, no, there was no place for single women here or in other places where couples went. 'What do you do?'

'Oh ... I garden. My family were farmers originally, you know.'

'I didn't know that.'

'Our family farm was in Sweet Wells. It was ... it was beautiful.'

David could not help being impatient. What was it with women and houses?

'And ... I have family, sisters.'

There was music later, people danced and it seemed churlish not to ask her though he did not want her to think that he felt obliged to do her favours and so they danced. She was soft and light in his arms and if she didn't get much practice it didn't show. He could have stayed like that for hours, no-body needing anything, no problems, nothing happening until finally she said, 'I ought to go home.'

'I wish you wouldn't.'

'David–'

'I know. I know. I shouldn't involve you in my stupid life.'

'I'm already involved but–'

'Of course you must go.'

David closed his eyes against the person he was, thankful for her good sense.

'You're quite right. I'm sorry. I'm just tired.'

They drove back to the office and he saw Madeline to her car and there she turned and kissed him on the cheek and thanked him. David watched her drive away.

It was well after eleven when he got home. Ella was sitting in the garden and had had two large gin and tonics by then. He came over and kissed her.

'Had a good day?' she said.

'Sorry I'm late. There was a lot to do.'

'Really?'

'How was your day?'

'Just the usual. Rosemary came by. She looks tired.'

'She will be. You were the same. It's not long now, is it?'

'No, not long.' She pushed her half smoked cigarette into the glass ashtray on the little wrought iron table. 'Have you worked all evening?'

David looked at her.

'No, we gave up about nine and went for a drink.'

'Really? You took Madeline for a drink?'

'It's been a long week and it seemed a nice thing to do. You don't mind, do you?'

'No, no, of course not.'

He moved awkwardly in his chair. Mind you, Ella reasoned, they were very uncomfortable chairs, they dug into you.

'Where did you go?'

'The County.'

Just like that evening when she had seen Harry with his secretary, she thought. David was doing the same thing.

'I came by at about nine and you weren't there.'

'Oh, did you? Well, maybe it was sooner than that then.' David looked into the distance. 'It seems as though we've been trying to put things right for ever.'

'You have,' Ella said and she got up and walked into the house. They went to bed and when the lights were out and the night was silent he said softly, 'I'm sorry.'

Ella had had her back to him. She turned over and gazed at his face. All she could see was the pale outline.

'For what?'

'For taking Madeline out and not you.'

'You make it sound like a competition.'

'I just wanted... I just wanted to get away.'

'That was exactly how I felt,' she said and she turned the other way and went to sleep.

Twenty-Seven

Rosemary came to see Ella that week. She looked so unwell that Ella worried about her. She was pale. She had dark shadows under her eyes and she fell asleep beneath the shade of a tree on the lawn.

A week later one fine June evening the telephone rang and it was Harry.

'They've taken Rosemary in for complete rest,' he said. 'Could you go over and see her some time this week? I'm sure she would appreciate it.'

Ella went the very next day. Rosemary was alone in a big room. The isolation would have driven Ella mad but it was nothing to do with her so she didn't say anything. Rosemary seemed so pale and thin for somebody so pregnant. Ella hugged her.

'I hate it here,' Rosemary said. 'I want to go home but they won't let me. Please stay and tell me all the news.'

When Ella left Harry was hovering outside by his car.

'How does she seem to you?' he asked.

'Desperately tired.'

'The doctors have been worried for some time that the baby hasn't been growing properly.'

Ella made lots of reassuring noises. She couldn't bear to think that Rosemary might lose her baby. A child would be so good for their marriage. Things couldn't go wrong now.

When she got home Iris was there.

Ella didn't know what to say. She didn't want to talk to anybody but least of all she didn't want to talk to somebody unsympathetic like Iris. She stepped out of the French windows and into the garden. Iris followed.

'I'm so worried about Rosemary and Harry's baby. It means so much to them and everything is going wrong.'

There was a short silence and then Iris said starkly, 'Are you pregnant?'

Ella stared at her.

'Why, no. Whatever made you think so?'

'Your reaction to Rosemary's problem. You went white and clutched at your stomach.'

'It's just the idea of it, of losing a child.'

'Common with first babies but you've had two and you're careful and well looked after.'

Iris came to stand beside her on the lawn so that Ella was obliged to concentrate on the horizon so that she wouldn't lose control.

'It must be ... awful to lose a child.'

'I'm sure it is,' Iris said. 'I never got that far.'

The bitterness in her voice made Ella stop her own self-pitying.

'I'm sorry, I didn't mean to...'

'Rosemary has the best possible care,' Iris said.

There was nothing for Ella to do but agree.

That night she went to bed thinking of the child she and Harry might have had and she prayed for all their sakes that they wouldn't have to go through something so difficult again.

The following day when David came home she told him of her worries for Rosemary and Harry. He turned an exasperated look on her as she sat at the dining table, letting her meal grow cold. He was late and it was past its best.

'A miscarriage is not unusual,' he said.

Ella didn't say anything. She felt sick.

'How can you say that? It's a horrible thing to happen, it's one of the worst things that can happen to anybody,' and then she listened to her voice, she was almost shouting, like a childish outburst.

David hesitated and then he said, 'Tell me, what's really the matter?'

She couldn't find any words.

'It's been even worse since Harry bought Swan Island,' David said. 'Do you think that maybe if you had waited he would have come back and you would have married him and had your old home? Is that what this is about?'

'It's nothing of the kind,' she said quickly.

'You talk about them so much and how afraid you are about the baby and I don't understand. You haven't told me the truth. I wish that just for once you would be frank without my having to drag it out of you. Tell me what it is.'

Ella took a deep breath.

'All right then, I will.' The warning bells

were already clanging in Ella's head but she ignored them.

'Jack was ... after we were married he seemed to lose his taste for my company, especially in bed–'

'Ella–'

'You wanted to hear it. Let me say it, we've skirted around this for long enough. He was drunk every night. Very often he didn't come home. Other women came to the door asking for him. When he went off to Brancepeth to train I was relieved. I've never been as glad to see the back of anybody. It was all a horrible mistake, I should never have married him. And then he died and I felt so guilty.'

'Had you wished him dead?'

'No, of course I hadn't. It isn't as simple as that. Harry came with the officer to tell me that another boy had shot and killed Jack. It was just an accident. Victor had a wife and child. He couldn't bear what he had done and he hanged himself. It was so truly awful, all of it. I don't know what I would have done if it hadn't been for Harry. He helped me to make the funeral arrangements.

'Jack's parents seemed to blame me for what happened. They didn't even come to the funeral. Can you imagine that, when it's your own child? Harry and I spent a lot of time together. I was in a very bad state. He was in love with me, had been for quite a while and I...'

David looked down and pressed his lips together.

'You were in love with him?' he said finally.

'I think he had always loved me and if I was honest with myself I had loved him since the moment I met him. We slept together. We were going to be married but he was being posted abroad and we didn't like to tempt fate. When he ... when he had gone I discovered that I was pregnant.'

She wished that she could have stopped before she got that far but it was too late. David was staring at her and his face was dark with dismay.

'I wrote and told him.'

'You told me you were nothing but friends,' David said.

'I was convinced he would be killed.'

David was silent, and Ella couldn't think of anything to say now. She wished the last five minutes unlived and the last few things unsaid.

'And then I lost the baby.'

Ella badly wanted to cry. She couldn't control her breath.

'You lost his child and then you gave him up.'

Put like that it sounded so awful but it had been awful for her too, she wanted to say this but she couldn't. It seemed that somebody must take the blame.

David sat for a few moments before he said, 'And then I turned up, good old dependable David. It was my lifestyle you liked, the security of my family that you wanted, wasn't it?'

'I'd never had that. I wanted a family of my own so much.'

'And then Harry came back and when he did you saw all the other things which had meant so much to you, most of all that he could have given you Swan Island and you couldn't bear it. There's something desperate about your need for that wretched house. Maybe you only wanted Harry because he had enough money to deliver the place for you.'

'That isn't true,' she said, stung by the idea. 'I loved Harry more than I've ever loved anyone in my life.' She put her hand over her mouth but it was too late.

There was silence. David stayed at the table for a while, letting it go on and on and then finally he said, 'Yes, I know. I think I've always known,' and he got up and walked out.

Ella would have given almost anything not to have said the last thing she said but it was, she thought, rather like losing your virginity, once you'd done it you couldn't get it back. They did not speak again that evening and she went to bed early and left David downstairs. She struggled through the following day with the work and the children but he did not come home.

Iris found her crying when she came back from the vicar's.

'Now what has David done?' she said.

'Nothing. It's what I've done.'

'It's about Harry then.'

Ella looked respectfully at her.

'Oh, Iris, I wish it wasn't.'

'I did warn you. What did you do?'

'Nothing, it was what I said,' and she told her.

Iris sighed and was much more sympathetic than Ella expected her to be.

'You married David, you had his children, what more does he want?'

'Things have been very difficult at work.'

'Things are always difficult at work. What did he think he was getting himself into? He could still come home. He could still contribute something towards family life.' Iris pulled a face. 'Men think they're so flaming important. Don't cry, it isn't worth it and if you haven't done anything then he has very little to complain about.'

'How would you feel if you were told by your marriage partner that they had loved somebody else more than you?'

'If I had as much as David has I don't think I'd care as much as you think he does.'

'If he sleeps with Madeline I shall kill them

both,' Ella said, trying to smile through her tears.

Iris laughed.

'Do you think she would call him "Mr Black" in bed?'

'It isn't funny.'

'She would.'

Iris looked long at her.

'Did you really love Harry Reid so much?'

'Iris, I adored him.'

'Then why didn't you wait for him?'

'Because I kept on remembering how the last post had been played over Jack's grave. David was here, nobody was trying to kill him, nobody was trying to take him away from me and also, I wanted to prove to myself that I could have a healthy child.'

'You lost Harry's child? I guessed when you were so upset about Rosemary. Please don't cry, Ella, nothing has happened yet.'

'I can't forget that child, what it might have been, who it might have looked like. I felt such a failure, first Jack, then the baby and finally Harry. I don't want things like that to happen again and now David doesn't want me.'

'Don't be ridiculous. He's potty about you,' Iris said.

Iris went to bed and then the front door went and Ella got up. It was late and David rarely came in that way.

'David?' she said nervously as she opened

the door.

'No, it's me.'

A figure appeared in the doorway but it wasn't David, it was Harry.

'The baby died,' he said.

She stood there for seconds staring at him in the gloom.

'Oh, Harry, no.'

She took him into her arms to stop the worst of both their nightmares from possibly being true.

He huddled there like a hurt child, finally saying in hoarse tones, 'I don't think I can bear this again.'

Ella couldn't think of a single thing to say which would help.

'It had been dead inside her for some time, they said. I knew it was going to happen. I think I knew right from the beginning and so did she and now I don't know what to do, I don't know what to say to her.'

There was a moment's pause and then David appeared behind him.

Ella slowly let go. David walked straight past them and into the house. From where she stood she heard the slamming of a door.

Twenty-Eight

Ella went to visit Rosemary the following morning, and she was quite unwell.

It seemed as though she was beginning to get the flu; she was cold, headachey, she couldn't eat anything. She hadn't eaten much for weeks and her face and arms were thin and white above the bedclothes. Ella sat with her but things got worse and when she became hotter the nurse came and the doctor and Ella came out and sat in the corridor.

Shortly afterwards Harry arrived.

'They telephoned me,' he said, 'she has a high fever.'

Ella and Harry sat in the corridor for hours as nurses and doctors went to and fro. They barely spoke. It didn't even seem like a long time. Worrying about Rosemary absorbed the time so quickly. Ella was aware that she should have been at home but somehow she couldn't leave him there alone and she comforted herself that there were sufficient people at home to cope. The day wore on, evening came, and then darkness.

In the depths of the night Harry said, 'She only married me for my money.'

'That's not true, she cares about you.'

'And I married her because she was so young and pretty and so lost.'

'Nothing's going to happen to her,' Ella said steadily.

'That's right and when this is over I am going to take her away from here and try to be a decent husband to her, the one she deserves.'

It was early morning, just after sunrise when the doctor came into the corridor and told them that Rosemary was feeling better.

They ventured into the room and she was sleeping. Ella watched her young tired face on the pillow and felt such relief as she had not known in years.

'You go,' Harry said.

When she didn't move he looked at her and his eyes were bright with unshed tears.

It seemed wrong that she should be there when David and the children were at home but she felt cut in half, betraying David by being at the hospital and Harry by leaving.

'Go,' he said again and she got up. It took everything she had to get to her feet, all the energy she had to walk out and leave him there. She did not look back. She felt as though she was betraying him again. She thought of the letter she had written to him when she gave him up for David and she was ashamed of herself. How could she have done such a thing?

She and David had nothing left to say to one another and that night, without a single word, he went and slept in the spare room. They had not been apart for a night since they had been married and Ella didn't know how to sleep without him. She lay hour after hour listening to a clock striking the quarter, the half hour, three quarters and then the hour, on and on.

The following morning she went straight to the hospital and was allowed in to see Rosemary. A thin white face gazed at her above the blankets. Ella sat down on the bed.

'They've told me I won't have any more children,' Rosemary said.

'I'm so sorry.'

'However will I hold on to my husband now?' Rosemary said and the tears trickled down her thin cheeks. 'I love him, you see. I love him so very much but he has always wanted you.'

Ella shook her head.

'Yes, he has. The moment I saw you together I knew it was the truth. If you choose now, Ella, you can have Harry and Swan Island, everything you ever wanted.'

Ella sat for a few moments and the sunshine poured in the narrow hospital window and for the first time since before the war, when they had gone to Scotland and she had fallen in love with Harry, she realized that what she wanted was to go home to David and her wonderful little boy and her baby and her life, all the stupid things, like the washing hanging out the back on a Monday, and Flo sitting over the Aga while she drank her coffee and Iris and Lottie and the foundry and all the special complications of her life. They needed her, she was part of them. She was lucky.

'I have no intention of doing anything of the kind,' she said, 'and you mustn't think such awful things. You and Harry belong together and he'll look after you.'

Later, when Rosemary slept, Ella telephoned Harry at his office and was told by his secretary that he was not there, he had stayed at home so she drove across to Swan Island.

She went in by the back automatically. The door stood open and there were voices from the kitchen. She sneaked down the hall, beyond two small reception rooms and then into the main hall where the staircase rose, covered in sunlight. The house was silent at the front. She opened the drawing-room door. She could not help then thinking what it would have been like if they had been married and lived here together and been a family.

'Harry?'

She didn't see him at first, he was standing

in the shadows, hidden by the sunlight which poured in past him from the long Georgian windows but he moved and said her name and she went over and put her arms around him. She wasn't sure whether she did it for her or for him.

Ella held him tight, all her hopes dashed, all her ideas that somewhere along the line they might, the four of them together, reach civilized behaviour.

'I went to the hospital to see Rosemary and she told me you can't have any more children. I'm so sorry,' she said.

He stood for a few moments and then moved back and Ella let go of him.

'You obviously haven't slept. You look so tired.' His face was pinched, narrow, drawn.

'I will later.' He smiled. 'You don't look so good either. Would you like some coffee?'

'I would love some.'

They went out on to the terrace. Ella had always loved the view there better than any other in the world, the small, square fields, the hedges around them like flounces, the Wear running silver in the bottom, the way that the hills rose up on the other side.

The coffee was brought by a smiling girl from the kitchen and when they were alone and he had let Ella drink in the view as well as half a cup of coffee, Harry said, 'Have you made it up with David?'

Ella put down her saucer.

'I don't know what to say to him.'

'Your instincts were good when you married him. You found a man who could provide a home and give you children and that was what you really wanted. And you'll be glad when you're middle-aged and your children are grown and with a bit of luck you'll have grandchildren and David and the pretty house where you live. It might even mean more to you than this place in time. Don't waste your time on what might have been, Ella, enjoy what you have.'

'What will you do?'

'Sell up and move. I never really cared for the shipyard or any other part of the business and I don't love this house as you do. It was all Rosemary's idea that we should live here. I think she thought it would make things better. When Rosemary is well I'm going to take her away somewhere warm for a few months and try to behave like the man I should be and not the bastard that I am. Would you like some more coffee?'

'I should get back. When will you leave?'

'As soon as she can travel.'

'Go to her and tell her.'

'Ella–'

'It would never have worked. You know very well it wouldn't have. It was a youthful thing, passion. Try to be kind to her. She loves you very much and if you don't take better care of her it will be destroyed.'

'I've had my warning. I thought she was going to die.'

'She's not going to do anything of the sort but you must look after her.'

'I will.'

They got up and went out the front way. The lawns were neat and the garden was full of flowers in the colours that she liked best, pinks and blues and whites.

She and Harry walked around to the back where Ella's car was parked and there he took her into his arms and kissed her as he had kissed her when they had lain together in bed and she had planned their future, the future which would never be.

And then he let her go. They didn't say goodbye. Nobody said anything.

Twenty-Nine

She wanted to see David but she didn't want to go to the office and be confronted by Madeline. None of this was Madeline's fault but neither was it anything to do with her so Ella waited until teatime. The afternoon dragged.

David did not come home at five, nor at six and finally Ella ran out of patience and she got into her little car and drove to the works so quickly that she thought afterwards she must surely have been a liability to other drivers and to pedestrians. Luckily, she noticed, Madeline's little car was missing. Good, Ella thought, she has gone home.

She made her way into the office. It was deserted. She went through to David's office and that was empty too. For one horrible moment she thought he had gone off with Madeline and then she saw him coming out of one of the big shops, he looked tired, it was the way that he walked and it was, she knew, a lot more than that.

He sensed rather than saw her and stopped. He was so grubby, his face was all streaked and his hat was covered in dust and she felt a rush of love for his stubborn endurance. He looked as Clyde would look when he got older.

'David...' she said and then ran out of words.

He brushed past her and went into the office. She followed him inside. It still smelled of plaster drying out. It was so bright with big windows, modern and full of evening light.

'It looks all right, doesn't it?' he said.

'Fine. Will you come home now?'

'I don't think I want to,' he said. 'How's Rosemary?'

'She pulled through. They think she's

going to be all right.'

'You went to him then?'

'Yes, I did.'

David didn't look at her.

'Ella, if you want a divorce–'

'I don't want anything of the kind,' she said hotly.

He turned his green gaze on her.

'You'll always love him best and I have the feeling that their relationship won't stand the loss of a child.'

'Like mine and his didn't you mean? It was different, David, it was war time and everything was awful.'

'I don't think our marriage will stand much more strain,' he said softly.

'There isn't going to be any more. Please come home with me. They are leaving, Harry told me. They're going to change their lives completely.'

'Even so.'

'It's over,' she said. 'For the first time now I feel as if it's completely over.'

'Are you sure?'

'Yes.'

'What about me? I'm going to have to put up with being second best.'

'You're not second best. It was something else entirely. We have two wonderful chil-dren and the rest of our lives to be together and I want that, I truly want it. Harry and me – it was a young person's thing, but you and me that's for life and it's the best thing I ever did. I wanted to have your children so much and ... if you like there's no reason why we shouldn't go ahead and have more. We really could, David.'

He didn't say anything for a few moments.

'I managed to pay back what I owed Harry.'

'That was a good idea,' she said.

'The work is starting to go well, just for once. I hardly dare say it. We are making money at last.'

'Let's go home and see the children.'

He didn't move.

'Ella, we could buy Swan Island, we could get a mortgage...'

He stopped there because Ella was shaking her head.

'No,' she said.

'But you wanted it and I promised–'

'No,' she said again. 'We aren't going to go back to anything, not even the things I wanted. Swan Island was the house of my childhood, the place of my dreams. I'm a woman now and I'm your wife and we're going to go forward and we're going to live in the house where your parents were happy and we're going to carry on the tradition as families should.'

David collected his dusty jacket and wiped his brow so that it was even dirtier than before. Then he and Ella walked out of the office together and he locked the door.

They walked down the slight bank of steps to their cars. Ella kissed David.

'I could murder a g and t,' she said.

'What a good idea.'

'We could sit in the garden. It is a beautiful view.'

'I like the view right here,' David said, looking into her eyes and he kissed her.

I will always think of Swan Island, Ella thought, but I will never ever regret it any more. I've finally managed to leave it. I've moved on.

When they got back to the house Flo and the children were playing on the lawn. It was a perfect summer evening and Clyde saw them first and ran to her and then Susan staggered across the grass and Ella swept the little girl up into her arms.

The sun was sinking in the sky and the flowers smelled wonderful.

'How about a drink, Flo?' she said.

'A drop of gin would go down a treat,' Flo said and they walked back up the garden and into the house.

The publishers hope that this book has given you enjoyable reading. Large Print Books are especially designed to be as easy to see and hold as possible. If you wish a complete list of our books please ask at your local library or write directly to:

Magna Large Print Books
Magna House, Long Preston,
Skipton, North Yorkshire.
BD23 4ND

This Large Print Book, for people
who cannot read normal print,
is published under the auspices of

THE ULVERSCROFT FOUNDATION